THE TRIBUTE BRIDE

Published by Acorn Digital Press Ltd, 2014.

ISBN 978-1-909122-63-5

www.acorndigitalpress.com

For my brother David

ACKNOWLEDGEMENTS

Many thanks to Leila Dewij of Acorn for her meticulous final editing and also to Sue Keates and Joan Johnston for their very thoughtful and encouraging editorial help along the way.

A novel set at the turn of the seventh century – in the two Anglian kingdoms of Deira and Bernicia that eventually became Northumbria

THE TRIBUTE BRIDE

Theresa Tomlinson

www.acorndigitalpress.com

CONTENTS

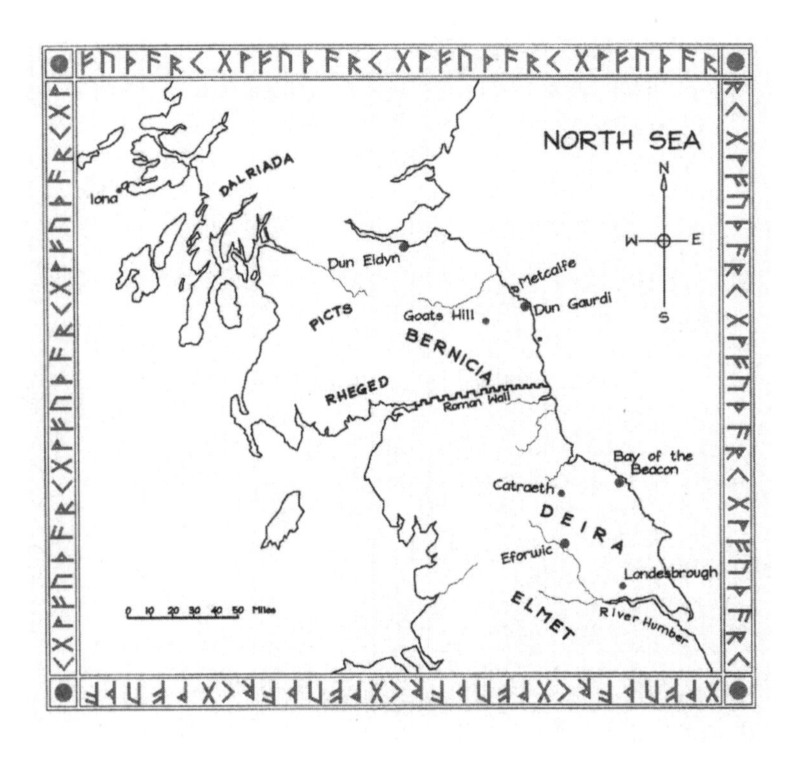
NORTH SEA
N
W
E
S
Iona
DALRIADA
Dun Eldyn
Metcalfe
Dun Gaurdi
Goats Hill
PICTS
BERNICIA
RHEGED
Roman Wall
Bay of the Beacon
Catraeth
DEIRA
Eforwic
Londesbrough
ELMET
River Humber
0 10 20 30 40 50 Miles

CHARACTER LIST

IN THE KINGDOM OF DEIRA

Aelle – the ageing King of Deira
Edwin – the king's son and heir
Acha – the king's daughter
Godric – the chief thane
Megan – nurse to the royal children
Coifi – son of the high priest of Woden in Deira and eventual high priest.
Lilla – Edwin's bodyguard
Emma – Acha's waiting woman

IN THE KINGDOM OF BERNICIA

Athelfrid – King of Bernicia
Bebba – Athelfrid's wife
Theobald – Athelfrid's brother
Hering son of Hussa – Athelfrid's banished cousin; a claimant to the throne of Bernicia
Bron – reeve at the fortress of Dun Guardi
Edith – the reeve's wife and Bebba's waiting woman
Duncan – a slave taken in battle, originally from the Goddodin, now in charge of horse breeding in Bernicia
Ulric – Athelfrid's closest hearth-companion

FROM DALRIADA

Donal Brecc – a hostage, grandson of the King of Dalriada
Brother Finn – Donal Brecc's tutor, a Christian monk from Iona

MODERN PLACE NAMES

Catraeth – Catterick
Eforwic – York
Goats' Hill – Yeavering
Dun Guardi/Bebbanburgh – Bamburgh
Pockleton – Pocklington
Danum – Doncaster
Bay of the Beacon – Whitby
Dun Eidyn – Edinburgh

HISTORICAL NOTE

At the time of this story the North East of Britain was split into two kingdoms – Bernicia to the North, which stretched roughly from the River Tees, to beyond what is now the Scottish Borders – and Deira to the South, from the River Humber to the Tees.

"I make this song for myself, deeply sorrowing,
Through my own life's journey I am able to tell
All the hardships I've suffered since I grew up,
But new or old, never worse than now –
I suffer the torment of my exile."

From: The Wife's Lament
Anonymous Anglo-Saxon verse

CHAPTER 1

DARK WATER

The timbered hall at Eforwic was ripe with the smells of wood smoke, humanity, stale cooking and damp fur. The hunting dogs and house cats growled and hissed at each other as they jostled for warmth around the hearth. It had rained steadily for two days and even the beasts refused to put their noses outside. The ageing King Aelle grumbled at everyone around him, though he had, by right, the warmest spot, which was close to the centre of the long fire-pit that ran down the middle of the main living space. Wet weather made his bones ache, so movement grew painful and difficult. A bard strummed softly on his harp, while Godric, the king's closest companion and chief thane interrupted from time to time to tell a new riddle, in an effort to cheer the company.

Edwin, the king's thirteen-year-old and only surviving son, born late from a second marriage, huddled with his companions at the end of the hearth; they quarrelled loudly over a game of merrills. The priest of Woden crouched in the corner to cast runes, but from the way he shook his head, it seemed the answers brought little hope of relief. As the king grew irritated by the noise, Lilla, the prince's bodyguard, reached out to touch the prince's shoulder. He glanced sharply in the king's direction. "Your father grows weary of our argument!" he warned.

Acha reached out to ruffle her brother's hair, as she walked past with a mug of warm mead. "Listen to Lilla," she advised.

Edwin dropped one of his gaming pieces and sighed, grinning up at her. "I'd give anything for a ride out in the sun," he said.

Coifi, the high priest's son, glanced up at her too with warm affection. "Wouldn't we all?" he agreed.

Acha herself loved nothing better than to ride out with a few companions over the gently rolling hills that surrounded the ancient town, but it was not to be. She moved on towards the cushioned chair where her father lolled, restless and uncomfortable.

"Father, this may take the sting from your aching joints," she said soothingly as she offered him the mug of mead. "Megan has laced the mead with nettle juice and flaxseed, as well as honey."

"Nothing takes the sting away," the king answered testily, but he took the mug and began to drink.

It had been a long, hard winter, and by now they should be moving on to the king's summer hall at Londesbrough – just as soon as the rain ceased. There, amongst the fertile hills and gently sloping valleys, Acha would be able to ride out every day with Edwin and his companions, who were her friends too, especially Coifi and Lilla. Here in their winter quarters at Eforwic, it was much more difficult to escape the onerous housekeeping duties that fell to a motherless king's daughter. The hall, that Aelle had built as a young warrior, tucked into a corner of the Roman walls of Eforwic, was now in need of repair. The timbers were damp and the thatch leaked, but the heavy tributes demanded by the Bernician overlord stretched resources, so that the plan to rebuild was repeatedly postponed. However uncomfortable the accommodation, the king still insisted that they must follow the ancient tradition of the Romans and the famous King Peredur and spend the winter months in the ancient capital of Deira. Since his second wife and oldest son had both died, Aelle had grown gloomy and impatient with everyone. He'd arrived long ago in these lands as a ferocious young warrior, with his followers from over the sea. He'd taken by force the vast stretch of land between the Humber and the River Tees; the ancient kingdom, named Deira – the land of the oak trees.

Aelle had slaughtered the inhabitants into submission; then pacified them a little by marrying Deidra, one of their British princesses; he'd made her his queen. It seemed that he'd loved her too, for after Deidra died giving birth to Prince Aelric, her husband spent years mourning her. Eventually Aelle took a second wife, Betha, from a family that claimed descent from Roman Emperors. Betha became the mother of Acha and Edwin before she died too.

Prince Aelric had been Deira's great hope for the future, a brave and handsome young warrior, ready to rule in his father's place – but he'd been killed at the battle for Catraeth, when the ancient British kingdoms made their last and desperate stand, in an attempt to drive the invading Angles back into the sea.

When Aelric died, the heart went out of Aelle. Now his bones ached, his bowels gave him gripe, and he constantly snapped at his children and companions; it seemed that nothing pleased him.

The rain continued through the afternoon and evening; and Acha was relieved when the last of her father's hearth-companions settled to sleep on the wide benches that edged the great hall. They soon began to snore, well fed, sleepy with ale, wrapped in furs, with willing companions, or warm stones in their beds. At last she could go to her own private chamber with her women.

Later that night Acha woke from a restless sleep to find her candle flickering. Her sleeping space stank not of dogs or cats, but of the quayside. Feeling weary, she tried to ignore the smell, but when she attempted to pull up the wolfskin coverlet, it slipped heavily away, leaving her hand cold and damp where she'd touched wet fur. She sat up, realising that she could not settle to sleep; the stench that filled her chamber was foul.

Light snores rose from the foot of her bed, where her old nurse Megan slept on a pallet alongside her young maid, Emma.

"Megan?" Acha called, but there was no reply, only a louder snore.

With a growing sense of alarm, she became aware of a distant booming sound, and as she listened the noise increased. The wooden door to her chamber creaked back and forth as though buffeted by strong wind.

"Emma!" she shouted. "Are *you* awake?"

Megan snored on, but Emma groaned. "What… what?" she murmured.

"Wake up! Listen! What can you hear?"

"It's just the wind, Princess… go back to sleep!"

"Wake up you fool! My bed-skins are soaked!"

Emma sat up at last and Acha could see her face, pale and bleary, in the flickering candlelight, her eyes still heavy with sleep.

"What's that sound?" Acha asked. "Wake up and help me!"

Emma struggled to rouse herself, but at last her eyes flew open and her expression was alert and tense. "I don't know what *that* is! I never heard 'owt like that before."

"Get up and look outside," Acha ordered.

Reluctantly, Emma swung her legs down from the truckle bed, only to shriek with shock, for her bare feet splashed ankle-deep into cold water. "Flooded!" she cried. "We're flooded!"

Acha cursed. She braced herself for the shock of icy water as she got up. "You get the candle!" she said. "I'll wake Megan!"

Pausing only to pull on her boots, she paddled towards her nurse who, being hard of hearing, still slept. It would not be the first time that the Ouse had burst its bank and flooded the land around the river, but Aelle's timber hall was built well back from the water, and they'd never heard that terrifying sound before.

Emma snatched up the candle in its wooden holder and held the flickering flame up high. "This light won't last much longer," she warned. "We'll be in darkness soon."

"Megan. Megan, wake up quick!" Acha shouted. "We're in trouble – you must wake up!" She shook the old woman's shoulder hard.

"Freya, save us!" Megan cried, as she woke with a jolt.

The roar grew louder, followed by a wave of screams. The alarming sounds appeared to issue from the main hall and were soon followed by angry shouts.

"Spring tide…" Acha said, as she hauled her nurse out of her bed. "The river's burst its banks. Freya, save us! This is more than the usual seeping flood; we must get out of here fast!"

Megan struggled to her feet and tried to make sense of what had happened, but they heard more screams as the door started to groan and shake. They stared aghast as it battered back and forth and then a steady ripping sound followed a tremendous crack. The door crashed down into the room, narrowly missing Emma, who dropped the candle and howled, engulfed by darkness and a sudden powerful wave of water that rushed into the chamber. The water filled the small space fast and brought even fouler smells with it. Acha struggled to grab at her floundering maid. She hauled her upright – and then a sudden eerie silence followed. All that could be heard was Emma coughing and spitting and Megan's teeth chattering with cold and shock. To Acha, the quiet was more terrifying than the noise had been.

"You go!" Acha told her maid. "Get out of here! I'll bring Megan."

Emma struggled and coughed as she waded through the darkness towards the dark hole where the door should have been. Acha turned to grab her nurse's bony shoulders and, supporting the old woman's slight weight, she determinedly steered her towards the space where Emma had vanished.

"I've got you!" she whispered, in an effort to reassure herself as well as the old one.

Megan gave a small grunt. "I know you've got me – don't you worry. I've been through worse than this my lass."

A flicker of light appeared and then they heard the sound of splashing. A deep familiar voice called – "Princess! Princess!"

"Coifi... we're here!" Acha answered.

Coifi – son of the high-priest of Woden – had been her closest friend since early childhood. Now, to her great relief, he waded through the ragged gap where the door had been, carrying a blazing torch high above his head. Lilla, followed close behind.

"Thank goodness you are here!" she whispered, as the flames threw shadowy light around them. It illuminated a scene of devastation; her chamber was all but destroyed.

"Your father has left with Edwin," Coifi told her hurriedly. "We're to follow as soon as we can get you out of here; horses will be brought for us. We passed Emma on the way; she's making for the entrance. Will you take Megan?" Coifi nodded to Lilla, indicating the old woman.

"Blessed Freya," Megan muttered. "I'm too old for this… Lilla, you cannot carry me!"

"I can," Lilla told her firmly. He lifted her bodily from the water and turned, despite her protests, to head for the passageway.

Coifi held the torch higher and glared red-eyed at Acha. "Hurry!" he shouted fiercely. "You need your mother's jewels – quick! This hall is falling… we're likely to lose everything in it."

The full danger of the situation came to her and, with shaking hands, she reached up to lift down an ornate wooden box from a high shelf.

"Give it to me… tuck it under my arm," he told her.

"But can you manage with the torch?"

"Of course," he said, and he turned to follow Lilla. "Come quickly! We must leave *now*!"

Acha still hesitated.

"What is it?" he asked impatiently.

"My girdle," she said. "I can't go without it."

He shook his head frantically, but she began fishing about beneath the water, where the bottom of her bed should have been.

"No time!" Then he gave a horrified cry as Acha held her breath and ducked down into the filthy water, but to his relief she reappeared almost immediately, to shake gleaming wetness from her face and hair. The strong leather girdle with its clinking tools attached was there in her hands. She coughed, spluttered, and grinned at him.

"Come," he begged, frantic to grab hold of her, impeded by the torch and the box that he now carried.

She went obediently to him and snatched hold of the damp cloak that still trailed from his shoulders. "I'm coming," she said. "Lead on."

They waded through the passageway into the main hall, to find moonlight creeping through an ever-widening hole in the roof. The hall was waist-deep in dark, stinking water that grew quietly deeper all the time. Some of the huge upright posts that held the roof had begun to lean together and pull the upper beams down on top of them. Patches of wet thatch fell with a soft plopping sound, while benches and broken planks swung dangerously back and forth.

Soaked clothing, broken pots, smashed looms and dead cats and dogs floated everywhere.

"Sweet Freya!" Acha gasped. "Life will be lost."

"Life is already lost," Coifi told her. "And ours will be too if we don't hurry."

In the flickering light, Acha saw the plump white outline of a hand beneath the surface of the water. A blue veil drifted up beside the hand.

"It's Mab – the cook," she cried. "We cannot…"

"She is beyond help now," Coifi growled, his voice unusually harsh and angry.

Acha gritted her teeth; she forced herself to look away from the drifting hand and waded resolutely onwards, pushing her way through the floating debris.

At last they found themselves standing in the ruins of the entrance porch, where the proud totem of a painted oak tree that proclaimed the honour and importance of the king lay, half covered in water, across the fallen timbers that had held the fine carved pediment.

The sheltered corner in the Roman walls behind the hall had been chosen to provide protection, but now those walls formed a basin that had caught this unexpected floodwater as it rushed in from either side and threw it back with such great power that it dragged down the very beams that supported the thatched roof.

Splintered planks still fell around them, and frantic neighing announced the presence of waiting horses. The frightened beasts bucked and whickered, up to their hocks in swirling water. Lilla was mounted on his stallion, with Megan pillion behind him. He struggled to keep the beast steady, while at the same time he held Acha's dappled mare on a leading rein. Emma grappled with a lively roan.

Coifi purposely dropped the torch into the water, where it spluttered and went out, so that he now had one arm free to help Acha mount. She reached for her horse's reins.

"Coifi, your black gelding is lost!" Lilla shouted. "We must make shift with what we have."

"You go," Coifi said, as he reached up to pass the box to Acha.

"Here – take your precious goods. I'll follow when I can."

"Do you think I'd leave *you*?" Acha turned on him furiously. "I'd rather ditch the jewels, than go without you! Climb up here behind me! This mare can carry two!"

She leant down from the saddle and hauled on his arm. With difficulty, he struggled up onto the horse's back behind her, the heavy jewel box still clutched to his side.

"We head for Meldun!" Lilla shouted as he urged his stallion towards the city's north-eastern gate. "We stop for nothing and no one!"

"Not Londesbrough?" Acha asked. "I thought..."

"Flooded there!" Coifi gasped behind her. "The river..."

Acha understood – all hopes of summer rides had vanished over night.

Their progress through such deep water was of necessity slow and steady. The smaller buildings that had surrounded the king's great hall had now collapsed into ruins, leaving torn clothing, doors, trestles and chairs floating everywhere. Only the sturdiest walls and pillars stood solid amongst the devastation. The ancient Roman meeting place, still used for important feasts, stood deep in water, a wave of bones and stinking offal carried inside it from the butchers' stalls close by. The air was filled with the cries of the drowning. Old and young, beast and fowl, struggled for life in the moonlight; half-naked, people scrambled and grabbed at anything that might keep them alive. Those who lived in the smallest hovels built of wattle and daub had little chance of survival.

"We cannot just leave them," Acha cried.

"*You* can't help them," Coifi hissed in her ear. "We must get out of here!"

Her chest tight with guilt and anger, she guided her mare through the ghastly wreckage of the once great trading town. Her father was the king – but how could they ride away and leave their people to drown? To her it felt deeply dishonourable, but nevertheless she shook the reins, gritted her teeth and headed northwards away from them.

They headed north-east and left the town through the old Roman gateway where they found the water shallower. Bitterly cold and soaked to the skin, they rode on, everything about them stinking. At last they could move faster and keep ahead of the rising river. Acha felt Coifi shivering against her back, one of his arms wrapped round her waist while the other still clutched her jewel box. Holding the reins in one hand, she pressed his cold wet fingers. "I knew you'd come for me," she said, leaning back against him. "How could you think I'd ride away and leave you there?"

They headed north through the rough woodland of Stockton Forest, sheltered a little by the trees, as wolves howled in the distance. Black night closed in around them, so that they were forced to trust solely to their steeds' good sense and night vision. At last they emerged onto a wide, flat, fertile plain, just as the gold and pink streaks of dawn began to lighten the sky. They galloped onwards, scattering flocks of rooks and crows. The faster pace warmed both beasts and riders, and only as they came to the hamlet of Sand Hutton, did they slow down to a steady canter.

The villagers hurried from their hovels at the sound of hooves and Lilla dismounted, to discover that Aelle had warned them that his daughter would follow.

"Oh my poor Princess, come inside our hall!" the headman's wife was all concern. "We've a good fire going and a pot of mutton stew. Poor fare for a princess, but it will at least warm you through."

Acha dismounted grateful for their kindness.

They huddled together in tight-lipped silence, unable to speak of what they'd seen. Nobody complained, for much more dreadful images filled their minds.

The headman who rented the farmland from one of Aelle's thanes offered what help he could. His wife served up a warm, herb-scented stew, and provided them with some decent dry clothing and a hearth to sit beside. Acha cared nought that she found herself dressed like a farmer's daughter, in a rough linen kirtle and short woollen cloak. Clean, warm, washing water was brought for them to use, but still the dank smell of the river hung about their hair and bodies.

"It must have been terrible," the headman said, expecting them to enlighten him.

A difficult silence followed and it was almost a relief when a rider galloped into the village from the north.

"Flood-water rising… flood-water rising," he called. "The Derwent has breached its banks!"

Lilla got to his feet, as the villagers hurried outside. "We must ride on," he said firmly.

They left the hall to reclaim their horses, as the inhabitants began to drag wattle hurdles and sacks of sand from inside their barns.

Acha opened her mouth to protest again, but Lilla forestalled her.

"No," he warned. "I'll take you bound and helpless if you won't come willingly."

Acha said no more, for she understood well enough. It would be worse than death for Lilla, should he fail in this mission. The punishment would be nothing compared to the loss of honour. Reluctantly she remounted her mare, hauled Coifi up behind her, and turned the beast's head northwards once again.

They crossed the wide, spreading plain known as the 'the bread basket,' – it was the envy of many kingdoms for its wealth of grain. The rich soil, flat lands and gently rolling hills should be full of golden wheat and barley when harvest month came. It was this fertile land that had inspired the young Aelle to settle here.

"There's more true gold in those fields, than can be found on any battle field," he was often known to boast.

But as they rode on they discovered fields of young crops ankle deep in muddy water, bad enough to rot the stems and ruin the produce.

"This must bring trouble," Acha said, low-voiced, to Coifi. "Athelfrid of Bernicia has demanded a heavy tribute of grain from my father this year. We must pay, for his continued protection."

Coifi shook his head. "Let us not worry about Athelfrid just yet," he said. "We must see you safely to your father first."

"But what will happen if Deira cannot produce the tribute he demands?"

Coifi squeezed her waist. "Just ride for Meldun," he replied.

They splashed through deeper water still as they approached the town, for the great lake that lay to the west of the settlement had flooded. And as King Aelle's Meldun hall came into view, they saw that things were little better here than they had been in Eforwic. The courtyard was filled with mud so that horses, dogs and men were mired to their thighs, but at least their homes were not, as yet, destroyed.

Acha found her father in his great hall huddled in front of a smoking fire of damp logs, while Coifi's father crouched beside him on the floor casting the runes. Edwin sat and shivered by the fire. The boy looked pale and fearful, though his face showed relief when his sister strode in.

"We are here!" she announced. "Safe – thanks to Lilla and Coifi."

Godric, her father's chief thane, smiled warmly, but Aelle looked up and frowned. "You look like a filthy field-girl," he said.

"But I'm alive," she replied blithely. Then with a quick flare of anger she added – "*We* are alive, when many in Eforwic are not."

Her father turned quickly back to watch the casting of runes, not interested in further conversation with his daughter, though Acha continued with determined cheerfulness, refusing to be cowed by his bad temper.

"I shall wash myself and find some better clothes."

Aelle grunted as she turned to go and Edwin got up to follow his sister from the hall. "You stay here, boy," the king growled.

Edwin looked crestfallen but he turned back obediently, just as the priest looked up from his divinations. "Not the answer we want," he said, shaking his head. "The runes tell us that the rain will continue for seven more days… the gods are angry… they make us suffer."

"Then we'll ride on to Esa's Wold," Aelle declared.

CHAPTER 2

CATRAETH

Esa was a loyal thane who held a wide stretch of rich, fertile farmland one day's journey to the north west of Meldun. They set out early, looking forward to an overnight stay in a comfortable hall, for Aelle demanded lavish hospitality from his supporters.

"What's going to happen now, when it comes to harvest time?" Edwin asked anxiously, as he rode at his sister's side.

Though she was only two years older than him, Acha had protected Edwin in every way she could, since early childhood, and she hated to see such a worried expression on his face. He'd voiced the question that hovered on everyone's lips and occupied her own mind a great deal.

"Perhaps there will still be enough grain to pay Athelfrid," she said soothingly. "Let's not worry before we need to. Father's lands are wide and surely the rain cannot have ruined all the crops."

Athelfrid of Bernicia had led an Anglian army of both Bernician and Deiran warriors at the battle for Catraeth, and though Aelle's own son had died in the fighting, the Angles had won the day. They'd also won the acknowledged right to stay on the lands they'd claimed.

His leadership and battle skills brought Athelfrid the kingship of Bernicia, for – buoyed up with confidence after the battle – he'd forced his cousin Hering to flee in fear of his life, rather than compete with the victor for the throne. In recent years Athelfrid had built himself a fortress on the northern bank of the River Swale at Catraeth. Aelle had tactfully raised a smaller hall on the southern bank, to mark the boundary of their lands.

Though the two kingdoms were now allies, it was an uneasy partnership, for Athelfrid went from strength to strength as each year passed, while Aelle grew old and frail with no young battle leader to support him, Edwin being far too young and inexperienced to take command. It was acknowledged that a king must rule by might – and by battle. The sad truth was that Deira's fiercest young warriors had died at Catraeth.

Acha often wished she'd been born a boy, for she believed she'd have relished leading an army into battle. Though she was skilled at both spinning and weaving, the gentle chatter of thane's daughters often bored her – making her prefer the company of Edwin and his companions. A gallop over the rolling hills to the east of Eforwic, with Lilla and Coifi brought more joy to her, than anything else.

Such thoughts made her mind jump ahead. "We can ride to the hunt at Esa's Wold," she told Edwin.

He nodded, cheered a little at the thought.

But sadly, when they arrived at the substantial settlement, they discovered that things were little better there. The heavy rainfall had destroyed much of the crops and the thatch on the hall was leaking. Esa made them welcome as ever, but it was clear that he could not feed so many people for very long. Aelle's temper was short and everyone was tired and tense. They rested for three days and then, much to the thane's private relief, they moved on to cross the Cod Beck at Thirsk, and head up the old Roman Road that they called Dere Street. Here they discovered somewhat better conditions – small farmsteads with fields of barley and growing wheat – and after two more days of travelling, reached the town of Catraeth. Suddenly everyone was smiling, cheered by the sight of Aelle's sturdy, northernmost hall.

"Here's hope for the harvest yet," Acha pointed out to her brother. "I shall go to the sacred circle and make sacrifice to Freya. I'll pray that she send us more sun and just enough gentle rain."

They found the king's hall, and the surrounding smaller halls, sturdy and dry. Servants and slaves had gone ahead to announce the king's arrival and a glowing fire welcomed them to the hearth, along with the smell of roast venison and boar. The meal they ate that night, though modest by their standards, felt like a feast and Lilla took up his lute to sing a song of praise in honour of Freya and the fertile valley of the Swale.

Exhausted, Aelle and his court settled to stay in Catraeth through the summer months. They licked their wounds and lived modestly on the hunting that the surrounding hillsides afforded. Acha rode out to the mysterious circular temple, built long ago in honour of an ancient, mother goddess. Now cared for by a group of Freya's priestesses, she presented small gifts of fruit and flowers, and pleaded that the land should grow fertile.

When harvest time came, almost everyone went out into the fields to gather and glean, but no feasts followed, for they knew that these meagre stocks of grain would quickly be consumed if the court stayed at Catraeth for much longer. Messengers were dispatched to the farmsteads that lay to the south east, in the valley of the Tees, to discover whether a better harvest had been garnered elsewhere. When the men rode out to hunt, Acha rode with them.

Late in Harvest-month, riders came south from Bernicia, to demand the promised tribute of grain. Aelle spoke to them privately in the great hall and they rode away empty-handed, their faces grim. Acha was summoned to her father's presence soon after they'd gone and she went willingly enough, hoping that she could find a way to soothe the humiliation that he must feel at being forced to renege on the payment of tribute.

"I'm so sorry, father," she began. "But Athelfrid must see that we cannot give what we don't have..."

Her father looked up sharply and, for once, he smiled at her, but his eyes held little warmth and her initial joy vanished quickly, leaving shivers of doubt that prickled up and down her spine. It was rare that he really noticed her and she wasn't left wondering why this particular expression chilled her for long.

He narrowed his eyes. "Athelfrid will not get the better of me," he said. "Prepare yourself to travel north, girl. I'm going to offer *you* to him as a secondary wife – a consort, in place of the grain. And from what I hear, he won't refuse."

Acha stared at him, astounded.

"Close your mouth," her father said. "You look like a fish – no man wants a wife who looks like a fish."

"But… but he already has a wife," she managed to say. "Queen Bebba."

Aelle shrugged dismissively. "A great king may have as many wives and consorts as he wishes," he said.

"But… Bebba may not *want* him to take another wife."

"Women's wishes matter little. Athelfrid has no son! And you shall give him one."

She stared at him aghast, shocked into stunned silence.

"Go to your women," he said. "And start preparing to leave at once."

Later that evening, Acha and Edwin crept out of the hall together and headed towards the old Roman Tower that had been built as a look-out post across the Swale. Acha's mind was numb and her knees were shaking as she climbed the still sturdy steps to the top of the tower. She'd always known that she would have to make a politically expedient marriage, but she'd hoped it might be to an important thane from Deira at least – marriage to Athelfrid meant exile from her home – from the land she loved.

Edwin, too, had been astounded to discover what his father proposed.

"He has no right to send you to that brute," he growled, as he followed in her wake. "Even his own men don't trust Athelfrid – they call him The Trickster! Did you know that?"

Acha nodded; her expression blank. "But I have no choice," she said faintly.

"His cousin Hering was forced to flee Bernicia," Edwin continued. "Because he discovered that Athelfrid planned to kill him. He is ruthless in pursuit of power and he may treat you… cruelly!"

His voice shook.

The brother and sister stood side by side looking towards the strong new wooden palisade that rose on the north bank of the river, marking the beginning of Athelfrid's land. It was going to be hard on them both to be parted.

"Father's gone mad," Edwin insisted. "He needs you here with us now more than ever. How will he manage without you? Who will carry the mead-horn to his thanes? Who will order the feasts?"

Acha replied with a touch of desperate humour. "There will *be* no mead-feasts, if the Bernicians make war on us," she said. "And there's plenty of lasses willing to carry the drink-horn round, and they'll all be trying to catch *your* eye, once I have gone."

"I want no maidens giving me the glad eye; I want my sister at my side."

Acha sighed and sadly stroked his hair away from his face. "And I don't *want* to leave you, but I have seen sixteen summers and that is quite old enough to be a bride, so I must go to Athelfrid and pray that he accept *me* in place of the grain he wanted."

"I should gather an army and fight the Bernicians, instead of sending *you* to them," Edwin said.

"You can't fight anyone until your warrior training is completed," she told him, sharply. "Athelfrid's army is second to none. No… if I go to him as a peaceweaver bride, honour may be satisfied for a while. When you are older there'll be time enough for you to fight."

"But how could I fight Athelfrid, if you were his wife?"

Acha sighed. It was hard enough to accept it herself without having to explain it to her brother, but she did not want him to fret at her loss, and so she searched for patience. "Kinship," she whispered. "Kinship is the whole purpose of a peaceweaver bride; you and Athelfrid would become kin by my marriage, so that he should in all honour keep peace with Deira."

Edwin still shook his head. "And they send you to him as a secondary wife… it is dishonourable. If you are to go to him, at least you should be his queen."

Acha shrugged. "But he already has a queen and Bebba is sister to the King of the Picts. Freya's priestesses claim there's no dishonour in my going as a secondary wife, if the kingdom is at stake… and it is."

"I… I will miss you," he admitted.

"But you'll have Lilla and Coifi at your side and I will miss you all," she said firmly.

They stood in silence for a while. Then Edwin spoke again,

reluctantly. "Coifi loves you," he said in a whisper. "*He'd* marry you if he could."

"I know," Acha said softly. "And I love him too, but Coifi will become Woden's high-priest in his father's place and I could never marry Coifi, even if I stayed here. Princes and princesses must marry for the sake of the kingdom… you know that. *You* will have to marry the princess father chooses for you, whether you love her or not."

There was quietness between them for a while again and Acha slipped her arm about Edwin's shoulders. "Let us swear an oath up here in sight of the two kingdoms," she said. "An oath that will keep us bound together in our hearts and in spirit, even though we're far apart – and the fates bring hardship to us."

"I swear it," Edwin agreed at once, his gaunt cheeks pale.

"Words are not enough," Acha insisted. "We must *do* something to seal our oath."

"Do you mean to seal it in blood?"

"Not blood." She took her meat knife from the leather sheath that swung from her girdle, beside her thread-box, and brandished it. "I shall cut a lock of your hair and plait it with mine as a symbol of loyalty and allegiance. Turn around!"

Edwin reluctantly turned to allow her to cut a long wheat coloured lock from the back of his head, then he watched as she sliced a shining, slightly darker tress from one of her own glossy braids. She deftly worked the two shades together and held up a neat plait.

"There – this braid mingles the strands of our hair as a token of our sworn oath. Hold it out," she ordered.

Edwin held the braid at either end, while Acha found a length of costly, purple silk in her thread-box.

"Not your silk – that is your treasure, from beyond the whale roads!"

She hesitated for a moment, but then spoke decisively. "It should be the best I have, to make the oath more solemn." She cut the silk into four pieces and tied each shortened length around the plait; then solemnly took hold of one end and spoke in a strong clear voice. "I Acha, Princess of Deira, daughter of Aelle, do swear to you my brother Edwin, that I will be your loyal friend till death. By Freya's midnight cats, I swear it. Now *you* make your oath!"

Edwin swallowed hard, his mouth dry. "I…" he faltered, his voice croaking. "I cannot remember it."

His sister sighed. "*You* must swear by Woden. I Edwin, Prince of Deira," she prompted.

He swallowed hard and tried again. "I Edwin, Prince of Deira, son of Aelle, do swear to be your friend."

"Loyal friend," she corrected.

"Loyal friend," he repeated. His voice grew steady and deep with feeling as he added, "by Woden's dark ravens I swear it."

Acha sliced firmly down between the two central ties, but the braid was stronger than she'd guessed and, when she sawed through, the knife skidded to the side and sliced the tip of her thumb, as the braid split in two.

She gasped, startled rather than hurt, and sucked her thumb, as half of the braid dropped to the ground.

"You drew blood, when you said you wouldn't," Edwin protested.

"I didn't mean to," she said defensively. She stooped to pick up the fallen part of the token. "Now… you must keep your half with you, to preserve our oath – always."

"I will do it," Edwin agreed. "But what does the drawing of blood mean? It must surely be a bad omen."

Acha sucked her thumb. "I don't know," she admitted. Privately she doubted that much worse could happen to her than was already happening.

Reluctantly they turned to climb down from the tower. As they wandered back into the courtyard they found a group of men gathering with axes and hammers. Curious, Edwin went to watch them, forgetting his sister for the moment. Acha went on towards the hall, sorry that the brief moment of closeness between them was gone. Although, Edwin would soon be a man and not need his sister to fight his battles for him, she thought that leaving him would perhaps be the greatest wrench of all.

As she stepped into the thatched entrance porch, a dark figure emerged from the shadows, where there were rough benches kept for servants, far away from the busy hearth. It was Coifi, his eyes red-rimmed and his cheeks pale. She knew that news of her father's order had reached him.

"Please..." he murmured, his voice husky with distress.

She took his arm and pulled him with her into a more private area, behind a high backed bench that provided a depository for weapons as the men came into the hall.

"He cannot send you to that man," he whispered. "Athelfrid is utterly merciless – the most ruthless warrior in all the northern lands. I cannot bear to think of you with him."

She reached out to take both his hands in hers, as her stomach twisted into a tight knot of sadness. Shaking her head, she struggled to find words to express her sorrow at leaving him. "But... that's why I have to do it," she managed to say at last. "Deira hasn't the strength to fight against him. He may reject me, but..."

"But... he may treat you brutally Coifi spoke with quiet anger. "And though I know you could never be mine, I... "

It had never been spoken of before, the impossibility of their love; they'd simply enjoyed the close friendship that had been allowed as they grew up together. Now as she looked at him, his eyes dark with concern, his lips twisted in anguish at the thought of losing her, a reckless impulse to rebel flooded through her.

"Kiss me," she said, surprising even herself.

He hesitated, then leant forward and kissed her tenderly on the forehead.

"No, kiss me properly," she insisted. "Kiss me as a husband kisses his wife."

For a moment he looked afraid. Though they'd ridden, fought, joked, sung and laughed together, Acha had always kept to the strict code of conduct expected of a king's daughter. Now she reached up to touch his cheek and suddenly his lips were pressed to hers, and his arms moved to clasp her tightly. A sense of warmth and sweetness flooded her body, and she was desperate to stay there forever with his lips on hers and his arms around her, free to love like any woman of the fields with the man of her choice.

The sound of a low cough made them turn. Edwin was watching

them, a startled expression on his face. Awkwardly, they pulled away from each other.

"If father were to see..." Edwin warned, "If he were to see... or even hear."

Neither Acha nor Coifi could find the words to reply.

Suddenly Edwin seemed to change his mind. "But it is so cruel!" he said. "I will stand guard for you, but you must hurry!"

As good as his word, he turned his back on them and moved a few paces away to give them some semblance of privacy. But the moment had passed and the enormity of the damage that could be done by such reckless action bore down on Acha. If her father heard the slightest rumour of impropriety, he'd have Coifi killed – son of Woden's priest or not.

She looked at him and smiled, though her eyes were suddenly tearful. "I'll remember that kiss, always," she whispered.

Coifi tried to answer, but no words would come. She brushed his cheek again, then turned and walked determinedly away, touching her brother's arm as she passed him. "Thank you," she whispered. "You will make an honourable king one day. Look after him, for me."

Edwin turned back to see that Coifi had slumped into the darkest corner. While he went to him, Acha paused to dash tears from her eyes, took a deep breath, smoothed her hair and gown, and then marched resolutely back to her chamber.

When she got there, she found Megan and Emma cutting and stitching frantically. She stood quietly watching them for a while, trying to muster the courage to face again what must be done.

"What now?" she asked at last.

"That man," Megan said, in a tone that dripped with disapproval. "Your father has had this gown and cloak stored away in a chest in the queen's old chamber all these years." She held up a strip of beautiful but fading embroidered braid. "This is trimming from your mother's wedding dress and we are to make it all fit you. Any other father would insist on a new gown, but no, we're to make you presentable with this – and all to please The Trickster! And he's had the queen's old litter brought out of the back barn!"

Acha shook her head, puzzled. "What does he want with the litter?"

"You are to ride in it," Emma said. "Haven't you seen the men in the courtyard? They're going to mend and paint it."

Acha went to the open shutter and looked down at them. It was true. Edwin and Coifi had emerged from the hall and stood quietly together watching the carpenters and slaves as they set about the work. Godric oversaw it all.

"No," she murmured, horrified at the thought of the slow, jolting, confined means of transport.

"Well, the old man says you must," Megan said irreverently. "Godric is to escort you to the palace at Goats' Hill, where Athelfrid collects his tribute."

Acha sighed, and took some comfort in knowing that Godric would be with her on her journey; she trusted him more than any of her father's other thanes. Then a frightening thought struck her. "*You* two will come with me... won't you?" she asked, looking at her nurse and maid.

Emma nodded frantically. "We'd never leave you," she said reproachfully, her needle flying fast through the fabric.

Megan too looked appalled at the thought; she put down the shears and stood up straight, hands on hips. "Do you think I'd hand my lamb over to a wolf and not go with her?" she said. "We are both coming with you, like it or not."

"I'm glad of that," Acha said. "But don't call him a wolf... it doesn't help!"

Emma finished the frayed hem she'd been stitching, bit the thread, and held up the dress.

"Take off that tunic and try this on," Megan said. "You are slimmer than your mother ever was and that's a blessing. We can cut out the old worn seams where the linen faded... then tighten it here and here."

Wearily Acha undressed to her shift and allowed them to drop the gown over her head. She turned this way and that for them. When they were satisfied at last, she dressed and returned to the hall to find her father with a tight bud of rebellion in her breast. She was giving up so much for the sake of this kingdom; she would not let him have it all his own way.

"Father!" she began without preamble. "I will go to Athelfrid as you wish, and I'll do my best to present myself as a willing peaceweaver bride. But I *won't* ride in that litter."

Aelle looked up at the intrusion angrily. "You'll do as I say, or I'll have you whipped."

She swallowed back tears of rage. Despite his unfeeling nature, he *was* her father and she'd tried all her life to win his affection. Now, despite everything, she found she didn't want to part from him with angry words passing between them. So she tried again.

"Let me ride my mare to Goats' Hill," she begged. "And as soon as we are in sight of the palace, I'll climb into the litter, so that Athelfrid won't see that I ride like a man."

The king frowned, and then shook his head. He sighed. "Why were you *not* a man?" he said, more kindly. "You *should* have been a man. Very well – ride your mare along the way, but you'll enter his palace as a princess, carried aloft in your mother's litter."

It only took a few days for the litter to be prepared and the gown to be remade. Precious food was measured out for the journey, an escort was appointed, baggage packed, tents made ready – and all too soon it seemed it was time to leave. Acha's sleep was troubled the night before they set out, so she woke early, dressed and went down to the stable to saddle her horse herself.

When at last she led her mare out into the courtyard, wearing riding boots, short tunic and cloak, she discovered the whole of Catraeth had risen from their beds, and were now gathering to take leave of her. Coifi watched from a distance, pale-faced and distraught, as helpless as she was to make things different. Edwin moved forward to present her with a gift; a small gold pendant in the shape of a sword. It was set with three tiny garnets and threaded onto a fine leather thong.

"I had it made," he said, "as your name means *sword-queen*. You should have become a queen," he added in a whisper. "And all I can do is to give you this."

She allowed him to fasten it round her neck and clung to him for a moment. Their father stepped forward and the small band of warriors that had been appointed to provide protection, mounted their steeds. She tucked the pendant beneath her riding tunic and sprang lightly onto her mare's back. Megan was helped onto a sturdy pony and Emma mounted one of the mules, taking charge of the baggage that would follow at the back.

"Be on your way daughter," Aelle said. "We need to know that our tribute is accepted before the first frosts come, then we can move south for the winter and have no fear that trouble heads our way."

With just one glance towards Coifi and Edwin – who stood together, jaws clenched against the unmanly emotion that they both felt – she rode away, uncertain that she'd see Deira again.

CHAPTER 3

THE CARLIN

Athelfrid strode out of the queen's hall, and headed for the stables, unable to bear his wife's presence a moment longer. It was not that Bebba complained or that he found her company undesirable, it was more that her quiet courage, her deep silent misery, made him feel as though he was treading on hot coals. He briefly inspected the latest season's geldings, which were newly broken to the saddle. The excellence of the equine stock he bred had become something of an obsession, ever since the fierce horsemen of the Gododdin had ridden south from Dun Eidyn and come close to wiping out the Anglian settlers, when they met in battle at Catraeth.

Now, he nodded approval at his horse-keeper, Duncan. "They look good," he said. "I'll take Midnight out."

"Shall I ride with you, master?"

"No – I ride alone."

He mounted his favourite black stallion and cantered out towards the lower slopes of the ancient sacred hill fort that towered above the palace. He rode unarmed, but for the sheathed dagger that he always wore strapped to the small of his back. Within the bounds of Goats' Hill, at least, he felt himself to be safe from the assassin's blade, for no one but a fool would invite the wrath of the ancient goat-headed goddess by committing an act of treachery on her land.

As he rode further from the settlement, he gave Midnight full rein and galloped for a while, startling the goats that wandered at will over the hillside. It was a relief to be away from the sympathetic loyalty of his hearth-companions, if only briefly. They never spoke of the great disappointment that he and Bebba shared, and tactfully kept their own strong, healthy children quiet and confined when in the king's presence.

Now Bebba was with child again – visibly pregnant and bravely enduring pain and discomfort, preparing herself to face yet another miscarriage or stillbirth. His chest tightened with frustration, and some pity too, for his long-suffering queen. How could it be that he could rule more land than any other man in the northern realms, receiving tributes from far and wide – and yet not be able to produce a living heir with his wife?

A fast gallop brought a touch of relief, but he slowed Midnight's pace as he approached a grass-covered dwelling built into the hillside. He was loath to offend the carlin who lived there. He hoped to avoid her, but the ageing prophetess rose up from the long grass where she'd been sitting amongst a group of bleating goats.

Athelfrid brought his steed to a halt close to where she stood and bowed, for even he was forced to treat this bedraggled old woman with respect. The beast-herders believed implicitly that she commanded the rain and snow that fell through the winter, which in turn allowed the goat-headed maiden to be reborn in the spring. It was the carlin's brief icy rule that brought fertility to the lush summer pastures – for without dark, there could be no light – to have plenty there must be dearth – and the carlin was believed to hold power over the very seasons. What's more, the settlers had come to understand that they'd be wise to allow their own goddess Freya to take on this strange goat-headed aspect from a far more ancient deity, who had once held sway in these lands.

"Greetings, lady," he said.

The carlin shook her head. "Too soon! Too soon! I will see you later!"

Confusion flitted briefly across Athelfrid's face as, without another word, the old woman turned and ran like a hare through the grass to her half-buried hillside home.

The sense of relief that the ride had brought to him vanished along with her – why did he have to tolerate such madness on his doorstep? He turned Midnight's head once again and set off back to the palace, feeling just as angry as when he'd set off.

***

Softly curving hills rose ahead of Acha, and it was difficult to know, at a distance, which one of them was the famous mountain sacred to the Bernicians called Goats' Hill. She'd heard a great deal about this revered spot, beneath which the King of Bernicia had built his harvest palace.

She and her party had travelled a good way past the great wall that stretched across the country, patterned with ruined forts and ancient crumbling palaces, left behind by Romans. Now, as the road broadened out, Acha scanned the landscape once again, hoping to catch a first glimpse of the royal settlement. At last she began to see that one of the hills rose above its neighbours and was linked to a second, slightly lower, knoll – as though two hills had grown together, bound like siblings. On a grassy shelf below she picked out the shape of a long palisade, set in the protective shadow of the huge twin-mounded earth mass.

She reined in her mount for a moment, thinking again of Edwin. Would he already be missing her sisterly care, or would he be beginning to enjoy the freedom and attention that would surely come his way now that he was released from her watchful eye? Lilla would never leave his side and Coifi would do his best to offer wise advice, for her sake if not for Edwin's own.

She pushed these thoughts away and urged her mare on again.

As they travelled further along the road, the pale thatched roof of what must surely be the mead-hall became clear, towering above an inner palisade. The whole settlement was large and solidly built; each one of the smaller halls grand by the standards of Deira.

Soon, they found that the path was joined by many others; it grew wider, as it needed to, for it became crowded. Cattle, sheep, heavily-laden carts and timber wagons all made their way towards the settlement beneath the sacred hill fort. She felt sure that the beasts and wagons must make up more of the tribute that Athelfrid demanded from his subjected kingdoms – and like the cattle and the timber, Acha was part of the tribute too. She swallowed hard. If her father's plan went well, this awesome place must become her home for at least some part of the year. If it failed, only shame and defeat lay ahead for her.

As they moved closer she saw that the gable end of the mead-hall was decorated with the carved shape of a huge torch, from which skilfully hewn flames appeared to flare. This was the symbol of Ida the Flame-bearer, Athelfrid's grandfather, who had come over the whale roads, just as her own father had done a generation earlier, to claim Bernician lands by force. The smaller surrounding halls were newly painted in bright colours. Acha stopped again and lifted her chin in the face of all this magnificence, reminding herself that *her* father had as much right to Deira, as Athelfrid had to Bernicia.

"Yes, Princess," Godric said with a quiet smile, as he reined in his horse beside her, having observed the determined tilt of her chin. "You are as good as any of them. This level stretch of grass would be a suitable place to set up your tent. It is time to dismount and prepare to ride in the litter."

He lifted his hand to signal that they should come to a halt.

Acha nodded, though her stomach knotted itself tightly at his words.

As Godric helped her down from the saddle, he omitted the usual light-hearted quip. Like a kind uncle, he'd always encouraged her riding skills, often comparing her to the warrior maidens of the gods who rode down from the skies to scour the battlefields for the spirits of brave, dead heroes. Now, as he set her down gently, she thought he avoided her eyes, turning quickly away instead to help Megan clamber down from her fat pony. The old woman's clumsy descent raised a chuckle amongst the men who formed their escort. Acha had known them all her life, and she felt suddenly desolate that they would have to leave her here amongst strangers.

Megan, at least, seemed her usual self as she grimaced and rubbed her bony backside. "Well… it seems it's time to set about you lass and turn you into a beauty."

This brought a sharp response from Godric, who frowned reprovingly. "Our princess is a beauty, just as she stands," he said.

A cheer of agreement rose from the men and a faint flush touched Acha's cheeks. The hopes and fears of all Deirans went with her – she knew that – and it was a heavy responsibility that she bore. If she succeeded, she'd become their saviour – however hard a road she might be compelled to tread.

The tent was quickly erected to give her privacy and a strong wooden coffer carried into it. Emma came bustling forward from the mules at the rear, her bags rattling with small horn bottles, and jars of salves, oils and face tints.

"We need water," Megan ordered. "And warm water too!"

For once, Acha's old nurse found herself in command of the men and even the surliest warriors hurried to obey her. But as they made a fire, a sense of awkwardness developed about all of their actions, for this was not the usual raiding gang or hunting party – this was women's work. Unease hung over the whole undertaking.

Acha dredged up a faint smile. "I think *you* are enjoying yourself," she said accusingly to her nurse.

"Hah!" Megan cackled. "I'm enjoying making that lot run at my command! I'll never get another chance like it," she admitted.

Inside the tent, Emma set out her work tools: clothing pins, brooches, tiny hogs-hair brushes and combs of different sizes.

"Now, arms up!" the girl ordered.

She and Megan removed Acha's girdle with all its useful hangers, though she insisted on keeping the plaited oath-braid that she took from her thread-box. They stripped her of her tunic and the boy's breeches that she wore underneath for riding. There seemed to be no way of avoiding these elaborate preparations, so despite her fear, Acha lifted up her arms and legs, docile and obedient. They fussed and fretted over her person and gradually a tiny seed of excitement began to grow, watered and fed by the extraordinary attention she received, for she'd never before been treated with such importance.

"Wrap her in a cloak… we don't want her shivering!" Megan ordered. "Now fetch the bowl of warm water, so that I can cast in the herbs, lavender, thyme and lemon balm; our princess must walk in a mist of sweetness."

While these ministrations lasted, the uncertainty of the encounter that lay ahead could be put off for a little longer. They washed her face, hands and feet, rubbed her neck and face with herb-scented oils, combed drops of rare, precious rose oil into her hair and finally dressed her in the new madder-dyed linen under-gown. Its sleeves and cuffs were decorated with delicate gold tablet weave that Acha had worked herself.

The smooth linen shift felt soft against her skin and it was good to be clean and cool again, for it had been a long, dusty journey from Catraeth to Goats' Hill. She tried to keep still while Emma painted her lips with berry juice, then delicately darkened her brows and lashes with soot ground smooth and mixed with flax oil.

"Do not blink and make your eyes water!" Emma warned.

"But – I have to blink," Acha said quietly.

Megan chuckled.

At last they lifted the gown from its coffer. It was weld-dyed to the soft gold colour of dawn. Dried rose petals fell to the ground as they unfolded it and held it wide for her to step into. Having drawn it carefully up to her shoulders, they fastened it with a matching pair of her mother's gold brooches from the jewel box that had been saved from the floods in Eforwic. Megan tucked the oath-braid down inside a small pocket in her shift, so that it couldn't be seen, understanding well its significance. They fastened a string of gold-coiled wire beads around her neck, from which was suspended Edwin's parting gift, the small sword-shaped pendant, and finally, they fixed a light woven veil over her hair that carried just a touch of rose madder in its delicate weave. Then they stood back to admire their work.

"My girdle!" Acha cried, feeling undressed without it.

"No girdle," Megan said firmly. "Would you ruin all this effort with a workaday belt?"

"But how will I eat without my knife?" Acha protested. "How will I manage without tweezers, comb and shears? I'll be helpless."

Megan folded her arms in determination. "As Athelfrid's bride you will be waited on. I'll bring your girdle and all your work tools in my baggage and they'll be there for you whenever you need them again. We don't offer Athelfrid a stitch-wife, we offer him a king's daughter and you must look like one."

Acha sighed. It seemed Megan would *not* be moved; if she failed to please Athelfrid because she looked like a working woman, she'd be shamed forever.

"Will I do?" she asked uncertainly.

"You *look* like a queen," Emma assured her.

Megan bent over the coffer again and brought out the polished bronze hand mirror that had once belonged to Acha's mother. "This is yours now," she said. "Your father told me to give it to you."

Acha took it in both hands, but then hesitated, afraid to look.

"You must *see* how beautiful you are, just like a queen," Emma insisted.

"But *not* a queen," Megan cut in, reprovingly. "We must not forget that Bernicia *has* a queen. If we hope to be accepted and live peacefully in this place, we must give Queen Bebba the respect she deserves."

Emma huffed. "Our princess should be queen, not a mere consort. They say Bebba is a Pictish barbarian, who eats her meat raw and produces neither sons nor daughters for her lord!"

"Stop it!" Acha ordered.

They both looked contrite, seeing that her cheeks had paled.

"Don't ever speak so again! This is hard enough for me, without you squabbling about it!"

They'd set her stomach churning and her mind running, once again, through the humiliation that might lie ahead. Would Athelfrid laugh at this extraordinary offer from the King of Deira? He would not be expecting to receive her for Aelle had refused to send a messenger ahead. And though the women had worked hard to remake her mother's gown, still the dyes had faded in patches that could not be disguised.

Megan took hold of the mirror and lifted it, forcing Acha to look into it. "I think you'll do," she said, her voice soft again.

Acha's mouth fell slightly open as she saw her own face. Then Emma took the mirror and stood back, tilting it a little so that gradually she saw herself from top to toe. She was amazed at what she saw, feeling little sense of recognition. An elaborately robed young woman stared back at her and, with a blossoming sense of pride, she saw that she looked both mature and beautiful.

With an astonished smile, she whispered. "Yes… I'll do."

There was a moment of quietness amongst them, and then the three women moved closer, wordlessly acknowledging their last moments of freedom.

Megan sniffed and wiped her eyes. "Your mother would have been very proud of you," she said.

Acha was touched by this unexpected expression of tenderness from her tough old nurse. "You'd better tell Godric I'm ready," she said brusquely, fearful that she too would weep if she didn't get on with it.

A hush fell over the men, as the women emerged from the tent and with one accord they dropped to their knees. Godric knelt creakily to kiss her hand.

"A true princess," he said, with a wry smile. "I'm missing my warrior maiden already."

Acha climbed inside the litter and then six of the strongest men lifted it with ease. The Deiran mission of peace set off towards Athelfrid's palace and very soon joined the wider path, busy with the tribute wagons that headed for the main gates of Goats' Hill Palace.

CHAPTER 4

BEBBA

Acha rode in the litter with the curtains drawn, as was correct for a princess. She hated the loss of control, compared to the freedom of riding on horseback, but knew that it would not be for long. The loose weave of the linen drapes allowed only light and sound to filter through, so that she could only guess that they'd reached the gates, when she heard the sound of running feet, followed by curious excited voices. She understood most of what was being said, but the Bernicians spoke the Angles' tongue with an unfamiliar lilt that would take some time to get used to.

The litter halted and was lowered to the ground. She heard Godric announce her arrival to the gatekeeper, and then again there came a babble of voices.

"Megan," she called. "Where are we?"

Her nurse briefly stuck her head in through the curtains. "Inside the outer palisade," she whispered. "They've let us through the gates. Hush now… you've caused a stir and this may be their king coming now. By Freya, lass, he's tall!"

The curtain dropped again and the voices faded into silence. Then Acha heard Godric speaking with polite formality.

"Aelle, King of Deira, greets Athelfrid, honoured King of Bernicia, Victor of Catraeth. Aelle sends, in lieu of a tribute of grain, the most precious gift Deira has to offer – the hand of our noble Princess Acha."

Gasps and hushed murmurs followed this courteous speech. Aelle had known what he was doing when he sent Godric as his emissary, for the man commanded respect. Acha's hand itched to pull back the curtains, curious to see the faces of those gathered around her litter and, most of all, to set eyes on the man to whom she was offered.

A hush fell and instinctively Acha knew that the king was coming to look at her. She dropped her chin at the sound of a footfall close by, and there came the faint sound of metal chinking. With a swish, the linen was drawn back and the sun shone into the litter and onto Acha's face… she felt blood rush to her cheeks.

"So…" the voice was deep and soft, faintly amused. "Aelle sends his little lamb into a den of wolves. I see that he does not come himself!"

Acha's head went up at once, offended at the slight to her father. She looked Athelfrid straight in the eye. "My father's health does not permit him to travel. He makes an honourable offer to a great warrior king."

Athelfrid's blue eyes widened at her sharp response – light blue eyes, set in a narrow, weather-beaten face. Suddenly he burst out laughing and Acha looked down again, flushing more than ever as laughter broke out all around her. The brief glimpse she'd had of the man had set a light thrill running through her body, for he didn't appear to be as old as she'd feared and he had the lean, muscular frame of a warrior.

The sound of laughter died as Godric moved to stand protectively close to her. His presence and voice brought comfort – she knew he'd give his life for her. "What answer have you for the King of Deira?" he asked firmly.

"Why, man," Athelfrid turned to clap Godric on the shoulder. "What sort of a king sends his child as a concubine?"

"No concubine," Godric answered forcefully. "The King of Deira offers you his daughter's hand in marriage… honourable, hand-fasted marriage by the rites of Freya as a secondary wife. Many a great king has taken such a consort and we offer you our princess in acknowledgement of the honour and esteem in which we Deirans hold you."

"Hmm…" Athelfrid paused thoughtfully. "You speak with courtesy man, but… *you* know that I have a queen, who might have something to say about this."

This comment was answered by smiles from amongst Athelfrid's hearth-companions. Acha could not help but pick up the light touch of humour in his voice – and though she still dreaded the humiliation of refusal, she found that she had to press her lips together to prevent them from twitching into a smile.

"Yes, indeed," Athelfrid went on, and the tone of his voice became more serious. "Queen Bebba will have something to say about it and I don't wish to displease her… certainly not at the moment. Grain is what I wanted from Deira; I have many men and horses to feed. What if I were to insist on grain? Have I been told the truth of the matter?"

"We regret that we have no grain to give," said Godric. "It is the absolute truth. Floods ruined Deira's harvest. We cannot give what we haven't got!"

Acha's heart thundered. Was this the moment she'd dreaded? Would she be refused, or worse? Only Godric's courage, there amongst so many threatening strangers, made it possible for her to wait in silence. It would be easy, so easy for her and her small escort to be slaughtered where they stood.

Quiet descended on the company again, and she gradually became aware that she was being scrutinised. Slowly, she lifted her head and looked up to meet Athelfrid's frank gaze. She saw that he was a man many women might find attractive, and she forced herself to stare calmly and appraisingly back at him.

The tension broke again as he smiled. "A young Deiran bride," he murmured, thoughtfully. "And sons, of royal Deiran blood."

Suddenly and shockingly he reached forward and grabbed her thigh, his grip strong even through the double layer of linen clothing. She gritted her teeth and tensed her muscles, but made no complaint.

"Strong thighs – strong as a mare," he said, smiling with frank enjoyment. "I think you'd better come to the mead-hall to meet Queen Bebba."

But Godric frowned and reached out to stay her. "Does the honoured king accept Deira's offer?" he asked, still stubbornly formal.

Athelfrid grinned wolfishly. "Yes, I accept."

A mild cheer was raised from the courtiers and relief briefly flooded through Acha, for it seemed she had managed to stride the first hurdle. Godric held out his hand to help her climb out of the litter and as she stepped to the ground, Athelfrid raised one eyebrow teasingly.

"I like tall women," he said.

He bowed and offered her his hand and Godric waved her forward. Acha took the king's hand, and finding his firm, warm grip not unpleasant, she allowed him to lead her forward.

Close up, the mead-hall was even more startling than it had been from a distance. The timbered pediment was carved into the shapes of fantastic beasts, fowls and fish, shaped by master craftsmen and painted in costly pigments. Goats' head emblems were everywhere. Small booths edged an open courtyard, stacked with food, live poultry, luxurious goods, dyes, fabrics, woven hangings and pottery. Wagons stood half unloaded, for many had stopped their work to stare with open curiosity at Acha's unexpected arrival.

"Come with me, young lamb," Athelfrid said.

She tried to keep her gaze steady and betray no fear before the gawping crowd. At the top of the steps that led up to the great hall she saw a fluttering group of bejewelled women, who stared momentarily in horror before fleeing.

To the side of the hall stood a sturdy double paling that curved and stretched away into the distance, and inside it she glimpsed the tossing heads and manes of horses. She stopped for a moment to stare at a totem that stood as high as the hall's gable end; it took the shape of a woman's body with a large belly and breasts, topped with the beast-like snout and curling horns of a female goat.

Athelfrid looked amused at her surprised expression. "Goat-headed Freya," he explained. "You will get to know her better, if you stay with us."

Acha said nothing but allowed him to lead her onwards, hesitating only when they reached the top of the steps.

"Yes – go inside, my sweet peace-offering," Athelfrid said. "What do you think of my palace?"

"I… have never seen anything so magnificent," she said, truthfully.

"No," he agreed. "You would not have seen such as this in Deira!"

He led her into the main part of the hall, which was furnished with trestles, benches and sleeping spaces, all fitted with luxurious skins and fleeces. Bright embroidered cushions lay on every bench. Slaves and servants bustled everywhere busy at their tasks – tending the hearth, sweeping, cleaning and mending. Hunting dogs growled and fought over bones, while house cats hissed and leapt warily around them. He urged her on past the long central hearth where a fire glowed, even though the day was warm.

She glanced upwards, impressed at the sight of the massive wooden beams that supported the lofty roof thatch, which was so high that small birds flew from post to post. The walls were covered with shields and finely stitched wall hangings. Some of the servants paused briefly in their work to stare, and then carried on polishing plates and cleaning pots in preparation for the evening meal.

"Go fetch the queen!" Athelfrid ordered, as the women that Acha had already glimpsed scuttled towards the far end of the room. They crossed a raised dais and vanished behind a tapestry curtain.

The King of the Bernicians stopped and glanced down at Acha, and, for an instant, she thought she sensed uncertainty. They waited in silence. Was he already regretting his initial acceptance of her father's offer? Then the curtain at the back of the dais shifted and an astonishing woman appeared from behind it – there could be no doubt that this was Queen Bebba.

If Athelfrid had been truthful when he claimed to like tall women, then he should have been delighted with his queen. Bebba was statuesque, with flaming auburn hair that curled thickly around her shoulders. Even more startling were whirling patterns like flaming wheels that adorned her cheeks. Despite this outlandish form of decoration, Bebba's face was still strikingly beautiful, though she must have been approaching her thirtieth summer. She was dressed in a tunic of green dyed linen, worn over a lighter lavender-tinted underskirt, both trimmed with purple silk. Her wide sleeves were neatly fastened back with elaborate golden clasps, while garnets mounted in gold hung round her neck. A delicate golden fillet bound her hair. Acha realised that she was staring. She hurriedly dropped her gaze and curtsied deeply, fearful that she might have appeared discourteous. She'd seen at once that the queen was pregnant and carried herself like a ship in full sail.

"Who is this?" Bebba asked.

Athelfrid smiled, all charm and mischief.

"It seems, my dear, that Aelle has sent us a sacrificial lamb," he said. "He advises me to take a secondary wife and offers his daughter, Princess Acha – in place of the grain we demanded as tribute!"

Bebba flushed at his words and gasped. Acha feared that anger would follow, and could find little blame for the queen if it did, but instead an expression of weariness flitted briefly across those startling cheeks.

Almost at once the queen had regained control again and examined Acha as though she were a young brood-mare for sale. "She is very young," Bebba said.

Athelfrid shrugged. "Young and strong?" he suggested.

Acha felt herself tremble before Bebba's gaze, as a mouse must tremble before a cat that is waiting to pounce. The queen sighed heavily, but her response, when it came, was courteous enough.

"Well then, husband… we must prepare a feast in honour of our guests – and you and I must speak in private," she added.

"Yes, lady," Athelfrid quickly agreed.

Acha glanced uncertainly behind her, and was relieved to see that Megan and Emma had followed her into the great hall and were waiting at a respectful distance. Bebba clapped her hands to call forward her own waiting women.

"Take Princess Acha to the guest chamber in the queen's hall. Make sure that she and her women have everything they need for their comfort," she added.

Remembering Megan's warnings, Acha curtsied respectfully first to Bebba and then to Athelfrid, feeling more like their obedient child than a possible second wife.

Two waiting women led them through a doorway at the back of the hall and down a few steps. They came out into a small but flourishing enclosed herb garden. Despite her anxiety, Acha exchanged a brief glance of appreciation with her nurse. The range and quality of the plants was impressive. Acha's mother had once kept such a garden at

Eforwic, but Aelle had refused to let anyone tend it after her death. Megan had acted as herb-wife at Aelle's court and would have given much for a fine, sheltered growing space.

They continued along the pathway through the garden to a smaller hall set directly behind the mead-hall. The reduced size of this building did not lessen its status in any way, for carved and painted on its pediment was a frieze depicting prancing goats and corn sheaves. As they entered the building they stepped into a sweetly scented, peaceful atmosphere, where the only sounds were gentle whispering, the crackle of logs and the light clack of weaving looms. The floor was laid with fragrant rushes and herbs, cosy bed-places were set around the walls, which were made warm with wall hangings worked in glowing colours.

A group of women looked up from the central hearth where they'd set up their looms, and their busy fingers and quiet voices ceased at the sight of strangers. They stared with critical curiosity. Acha realised uneasily that many such awkward moments lay ahead and she was grateful for the company of Megan and Emma, who trailed determinedly behind, carrying the baggage.

"This way," one of her guides ordered, hurrying with scant courtesy past the women. "That is the queen's chamber, and down this passageway is where you will sleep – for tonight at least," she added with a shrug.

Acha did not miss the oblique reference to her strange situation there, nor the disapproving tone of voice. She glimpsed rich wall hangings inside the queen's chamber, but the woman's cool words made her blush and turn away. Where would she sleep in future? Had Athelfrid really agreed to take her as his second wife, or was he playing some cruel trick? He was, after all, known as The Trickster. Even if he'd spoken in good faith when he'd accepted her in place of tribute, might Bebba still persuade him otherwise?

Megan bustled into the guest chamber and gave an approving grunt. It was small, but comfortable, with a wide feather-down mattress set on a wooden bed frame and another straw pallet on the floor. Woollen rugs and animal pelts covered both the beds and the floor, while patterned wall hangings excluded draughts and also made the space bright.

Bebba's waiting woman hovered beside the doorway, watching the newcomers with open resentment.

"You may go now," Acha said sharply, then hurriedly added, "but I thank you."

As soon as they'd gone, she heaved a sigh of relief and sat down on the bed. "Will he have me, do you think?" she asked.

"He said he would," Megan approved cautiously.

"Sweet Freya! He is not what I thought." Emma's eyes were bright with mischief. "He's not as old as we feared and I'd swear he has all his teeth!"

Acha sighed. "I don't care about his teeth or his age, I just want him to accept me and… and be courteous."

Emma nudged the nurse's elbow gleefully. "I'd not say no… eh Megan?"

"Less of that," Megan fixed her with a piercing glare of disapproval.

Acha turned away, ignoring Emma's teasing. "What should I do now?" she asked.

"We'll take off your overdress so that you can lie down and rest," Megan said. "You must be fresh for the feast they're preparing tonight. Meanwhile, we'll unpack your clothes and make ourselves at home."

"I cannot rest," Acha protested. "My stomach churns."

"You must try," Megan told her firmly.

Stripped of her over-gown, Acha lay down. As she pushed her toes into the soft-combed fleece that covered the bed, her thoughts strayed to her brother. Edwin would no doubt be impressed to see her in these lavish surroundings. And Coifi… how would Coifi fare? She could not let her mind wander in that direction.

She searched inside her shift to grasp the hidden plait of hair as Megan and Emma moved about, keeping their voices low so as not to disturb her.

Edwin would not go short of kindness with so many soft-faced, thane's daughters around, all eager to attract his attention as he grew older, but they'd never dare to offer him the frank advice that a sister could give. Coifi might take the role of quiet councillor though.

"Dear Coifi," she whispered, smiling sadly. The pain of parting was lessened now, overshadowed by the fear of failure in her mission. Still it was comforting to know that there was somebody who loved her devotedly, even though there was no chance of her ever becoming his bride. She must forget Deira – stop fretting about those she'd left behind – and struggle to make her own life bearable, here at Goats' Hill.

CHAPTER 5

ATHELFRID

Athelfrid stood in tense silence with his back to his wife, looking out through the open shutter. Bebba sat down heavily on her wide, soft bed, curling her fingers into a fist as though the sharp pains of labour had come to her already. The hurt was not to her body, not this time… it was her pride, her self-esteem that was wounded. As the sister of the King of the Picts, a man of standing and power, she was respected and honoured by the Bernicians, and her good opinion was sought by all of them.

What business had that strong-limbed, fresh-cheeked girl got coming here so brazenly, to offer herself to Athelfrid as a secondary wife? If Bebba complained to her brother of ill-treatment, she'd set the two kingdoms at war – like spark to tinder.

She felt as though a knife had been plunged into her heart… and yet she'd lived in fear of something of the sort for some time. She was no fool and she knew that something would have to be done to provide her husband with an heir. And of course this girl might fail as she had failed, and she would be easy to get rid of then. Maybe she could bargain at least to retain her power, if she accepted this Deiran proposition.

Dry-eyed and grim-faced, Bebba struggled to her feet and went to stand behind her husband. "I am your queen!" she said.

Athelfrid swung round, unable to disguise the bright excitement in his expression. "You are my queen," he agreed. "You will always be my queen; nothing will ever change that."

Bebba closed her eyes, an expression of misery on her face. "Do it then," she said.

***

Acha's women stowed the baggage while she rested, but the light was fading and it was soon time for them to dress for the feast. Megan went in search of a brazier, warm water, candles and a lantern, and these things were grudgingly brought to the guest chamber, although the servants retreated as fast as they could. Acha had no second gown of quality amongst her possessions, so they warmed up slick-stones to smooth the creases from her overdress and put it back on her again. They combed her hair and re-applied the rose oil, although they were uncomfortably aware of the rush of activity that was taking place in the queen's chamber down the passageway.

As darkness gathered, they noticed that the place had suddenly become very quiet.

"What is happening? Are they ready for me?" Acha fretted.

Megan marched out to investigate and hurried back quickly. "Godric is waiting outside to escort you," she said. "The queen will receive you at the feast."

They straightened her clothes one last time and followed her outside. A sweet scent of perfume hung in the air as they passed the queen's chamber, but the room was empty. The familiar sight of Godric waiting outside in the herb garden cheered them all.

"Princess," he bowed and took her hand.

"Oh Godric," she faltered.

"Princess, you've charmed him... I think."

"Is charm enough?"

"It's a very good start."

"You will not leave me yet?"

"No, Princess."

He began to lead her towards a small side gate, and she realised that they would have to go into the great hall by the main entrance once again. "Could we not creep in quietly by the back door?" she asked.

"No, Princess," he shook his head. "This is your chance to impress. We must make a dignified entrance, and receive the courtesy that is your due."

She paused and made herself remember the startling image of that proud young woman she'd glimpsed in the mirror as she dressed.

"Very well," she said. She braced herself, lifted her chin and tried to produce that haughty expression once again.

As she entered the hall she found herself momentarily distracted from her anxiety by the sudden rush of warmth, music, and chatter. The animal smells of hunting dogs mingled with delicious scent of meat and freshly baked bread. She paused on the threshold and all the noise died away as people turned their heads to see her. The musicians stilled their harps, and both Athelfrid and his queen politely rose to their feet.

Bebba gleamed with gold and garnets. Her gown had been twice madder-dyed to match the deep red hue of the precious stones she wore. She was a shining vision of mature beauty.

Athelfrid was an equally impressive sight, arms gilded with gold rings, his weld-dyed tunic trimmed with dark red cording, as he strode forward.

"Welcome Princess," he said.

He took her hand and gave it an encouraging squeeze, watching her closely all the time to judge her reaction. Could Godric be right? Had she charmed him? She feared he was amused, rather than enchanted, as he led her to the dais.

Godric was given a seat at the queen's right hand, and Megan and Emma were shown to benches much further away. Acha saw that an empty, high-backed chair had been placed to the left of the king's elaborate seat, but felt uncertain as to whether it was intended for her. Athelfrid presented her first to his younger brother Theobald, who looked older than Acha, but by just a few years. He bowed a little awkwardly, giving a warm smile that showed strong white teeth. She could not suppress a fleeting wish that she'd been sent as a bride for Theobald; that would have been so much simpler. Why had her father not thought of that? Surely marriage to Theobald would have secured Deira's safety just as effectively as this awkward secondary marriage to the king, which must surely bring with it the queen's enmity?

Athelfrid took his seat and with a flourishing gesture invited Acha to sit beside him on the empty chair. The queen, too, sat down, but almost at once she rose again to take an ornate drink-horn, patterned wonderfully with gold filigree around the rim, that a servant presented to her.

Despite her growing girth, Bebba carried the large vessel to Godric, graciously offering him the first drink, which he courteously accepted. She then carried the horn back to her husband, who drank deeply. Everyone clapped and cheered as Athelfrid sighed with satisfaction; the feast had begun.

Musicians struck up their harps and the buzz of conversation returned to the hall, though Acha was aware that both guests and servants stared in her direction with open curiosity. The delicious scents intensified as golden salvers were placed before the king, piled high with joints of succulent roast duck and goose. The roasted fowls were dressed with fragrant herbs and accompanied by a creamy mustard and sorrel sauce and soft white bread.

Acha was glad that the noise and commotion in the hall made conversation unnecessary. She was almost relieved when Athelfrid turned away from her to speak attentively to his queen, but the young woman who'd been placed on her left-hand side wasn't going to allow her to sit in peace for long.

"Well… it looks as though you're here for good!"

The girl spoke with a strong Bernician accent, but she was dressed almost as exquisitely as the queen, in a tight-fitting laced bodice trimmed with white fur. A red silk-fringed band adorned her brow, and her full lips and cheeks were reddened with berry juice.

"I hope that is true," Acha replied politely, assuming that she must be one of Bebba's waiting women or perhaps the young wife of an important thane.

"Are you a horsewoman?" the girl asked.

"Oh, yes," Acha answered, with a touch of enthusiasm.

"That's good," the girl said with warm approval. "Strong thighs… he likes that!"

Acha was shocked by these frank words, spoken loudly enough for the king to hear, but at least this girl seemed somewhat warmer towards her than the queen's waiting women had been.

"Are you…?" she began.

"Bree," the girl answered quickly. "They call me Bree."

"Are you one of the queen's women?" she asked.

Bree laughed and shook her head. "No, no… the queen would never have me, but… perhaps I could be one of your waiting women?"

Acha simply smiled, unsure whether she would have the power to make such appointments. Bree cheerfully picked up a joint of fowl and attacked it.

"Eat!" she invited Acha. "Who knows what tomorrow may bring."

Selecting a small wing, Acha tried to emulate Bree, but though the meat was cooked perfectly, nervousness took her appetite away.

It wasn't long before the bones and debris were cleared and replaced by fresh dishes of venison and wild boar. The roasted, honey-coated boar's head was carried aloft to the king's table and placed in front of Acha. Athelfrid cut into the golden crackling that covered the cheeks and offered the first crisped piece to her. She struggled with shaking hands to take it, crunch it appreciatively, and then to pronounce it to be delicious. The drink-horn was passed round again and voices grew louder as faces turned rosy.

Bree proved to be a useful companion, as she told Acha the names of the chief thanes and their wives, boldly pointing to them one by one. The men looked up as they heard their names mentioned and waved with warm amusement, but unfortunately most of their wives proved to be Bebba's unfriendly waiting women, who seemed to look away from her as though she were invisible.

Bree pointed towards a big man dressed in skins. "Priest of Woden, best avoided – even the king fears to cross him."

Acha glanced warily at the man as he sank his teeth deep into a haunch of wild boar, the juices running down his beard. It was best to know such things and beware, she told herself.

Athelfrid turned at last to speak to her and began by asking about her family.

"I hear that Aelle has named your brother heir to Deira's throne," he said, "but that he's not of age, as yet?"

"My brother is learning warrior skills," she told him warily.

Athelfrid looked thoughtful and glanced briefly at his queen with something of a thoughtful smile. "In the Pictish lands, the right to kingship passes through the mother. Were you of Pictish descent, a son of yours might inherit the throne of Deira."

She smiled and shook her head. "But I am not Pictish," she said firmly. "Since my older brother Aelric was killed, Edwin is named as heir. He will rule, when he has learnt the skills he needs."

"Ha! A loyal sister," Athelfrid nodded approvingly. "I remember Prince Aelric at Catraeth and the companions who fell with him. He would have made a strong and powerful king."

She nodded sadly, not needing to be reminded once again how much her older brother was missed.

"Eat up, Princess! A good brood-mare needs nourishment," Athelfrid said and he laughed and reached beneath the table to grip her thigh again with enthusiasm.

Acha forced herself to smile politely and picked up her mead cup. During the course of the evening her cup was re-filled often, and as she drank she found too that her appetite grew; it was a long time since she'd been present at so lavish a feast. There would be benefits to living at Goats' Hill.

As sweetmeats were brought to the tables, tumblers in gaudy tunics leapt into the hall; they turned somersaults and walked on their hands, while cymbals clattered and a drumbeat kept time. After their wild dancing the atmosphere mellowed a little and the king called for the harp-stool. The musicians and the king's companions vied with each other as to who should be first to entertain the company.

"What shall we have?" Athelfrid cried, raising his eyebrows in mock uncertainty, knowing full well what the reply would be.

"Catraeth," they cried, "the battle of Catraeth!"

"How the British quailed against the might of The Trickster!"

Acha was shocked to hear the king's nickname used openly to his face, but then she saw that it was Theobald, the king's brother who had been so bold. Perhaps he held a privileged position, for Athelfrid laughed at his audacity and called him forward to the harp-stool.

"Very well – sing to us of Catraeth, brother," he ordered. "But sing this night in honour of Aelric and his brave Deiran warriors."

Acha smiled at Godric, for it was a courteous complement to them and Theobald was quick-witted enough to include much praise of Deira in his song.

> *"Then came a warrior bright as his blade and brave,*
>
> *He feared no foe, and with him marched the flower of Deira's youth,*
>
> *Forward they came, giving no quarter,*
>
> *Shields and swords glinting*
>
> *These brave men marched to their deaths*
>
> *Into the drift of druid's mist"*

While Theobald strummed his harp and sang it seemed his gaze settled on Acha, and though at first she smiled back at him, she grew a little uncomfortable at this open admiration. Athelfrid appeared to be enjoying his brother's song, unaware of any impropriety, but before his ballad had come to a proper conclusion, Theobald's voice faltered unexpectedly and his gaze moved past Acha to the back of the hall.

The harp fell silent and the whole company turned curiously to discover who had interrupted such a thrilling account. Bree nudged Acha, and everyone rose to their feet to greet the newcomers, even the king.

"Who is it?" Acha asked.

"She is the carlin," Bree whispered, "the priestess who lives on the Sacred Mountain with the goats. You'd best please her or there'll be no wedding. She is a seeress; she knows all that has passed and all that is still to come."

CHAPTER 6

GOAT-HEADED FREYA

The carlin stepped forward from the shadows, into the light of the hearth, wearing a mottled, cream, high-domed, headdress. Her face was lined and thin, beneath the gleaming crown. Two young attendants followed her.

"Does Freya speak through this seeress?" Acha asked.

Bree shrugged. "They call our goddess Freya now, but we once worshipped a more ancient goat-headed she-god here. Even the king must respect her memory and please the carlin if he wants to keep his position."

Acha was fast coming to see that this strange goat-headed deity was somewhat different from Freya the goddess of love and fertility that she'd been raised to honour.

The queen's women got up from their seats and, with a rustle and swish of their gowns, bowed to the priestess and quietly left the hall as though acting on some previously arranged agreement. Bebba was the last to go; she spoke low to Athelfrid for a moment, and then swiftly followed her women from the hall.

The carlin's pale eyes moved around the gathering and to her discomfort, Acha realised that the old woman's gaze had lighted on her and stayed there. The priestess regarded her sternly and beckoned with a skinny finger.

"Go to her," Athelfrid said.

The hall was very quiet. The atmosphere of cheerful ease that had been induced by Theobald's singing had vanished. Acha got up and walked nervously round the high table to stand before the priestess. The carlin examined her from top to toe for what seemed a long time. Acha was somewhat surprised to observe at close quarters, that the priestess's headdress was fashioned entirely from curled goats' horns. She was even more startled when the priestess put out her bony hand and pressed it against Acha's chest, exactly where the concealed plait of hair was hidden. Could it possibly be true that this mysterious priestess really saw both past and future? She had heard of women who claimed such skills before.

The carlin leant forward and whispered in her ear, "Goddess preserve your oath, sword-queen!"

Acha blanched and gasped, but the priestess turned away from her to address the king in loud ringing tones. "This Deiran princess will bear sons for Bernicia, but there is a price to pay. The price is blood."

There were many low gasps followed by an awkward silence, as everyone looked to see how the king would receive the carlin's pronouncement.

Athelfrid looked annoyed for a moment, but then his expression quickly changed to amusement; he raised an eyebrow and smiled smugly at the priestess.

"The price of birth is always blood," he said and in response there came a light ripple of uneasy laughter. "I shall marry the princess tomorrow evening – a late Lammastide wedding. Our harvest celebration should bring fertility. Will Goat-headed Freya approve of that?" he asked.

"She will," the carlin agreed.

Close up to the woman Acha saw that her lined, old face remained solemn.

"We will speak again," the carlin whispered and then to Acha's surprise, the astonishing woman turned and imperiously indicated to her attendants that they should follow her. Just as abruptly as she'd arrived, she left – the young girls following in her wake.

Low whispers filled the hall, full of comment and speculation, and it was a while before the previous level of conversation resumed. Acha was left by herself in the central space by the hearth, wondering uneasily what she should do. She was relieved when Godric came to take her hand.

"You have the consent of their priestess," he said. "I think you should go to rest and leave the men to their drink – tomorrow will be a long day."

Megan heard his words and as she got up from her seat she signalled to Emma, who followed suit. They bowed to Athelfrid and led their princess out of the Mead Hall, well satisfied with their day's work.

Back in the guest chamber, they undressed her and put her to bed. Acha found that the down-stuffed mattress felt wonderfully comfortable after spending the last five nights in a tent, the plentiful wine and food soon sent her to sleep.

First to wake in the morning, she discovered bright sunlight streaming through the wooden shutters. Emma still slept soundly beside her in the bed, while Megan, snored loudly on a straw pallet on the floor.

For a moment or two when she first opened her eyes, Acha was puzzled by the unfamiliar, luxurious surroundings, but then the lavish feast came back to her mind, the king's acceptance of her as a consort and secondary wife, the approval of the strange priestess. Surely her mission was going as well as her father could have hoped it would.

Acha rose from her bed and crept to the door of the chamber, surprised that no servants seemed to be stirring out in the main hall. She opened the door and peered through the gap to find a brindled cat pattering towards her, mewing insistently as though it expected milk. Was there nobody awake even to stoke the fire? Megan's snores rose to a high pitch behind her and then stuttered as she began to wake up. Acha thought she heard the faint clack of a loom coming from the hall, so thinking that perhaps at least the websters were awake, she headed in the direction of the hearth, but stopped short outside the queen's chamber.

The door stood wide open and she could see at once that the great bed had been stripped of rugs and covers and the rich wall hangings she'd glimpsed the day before had vanished.

She stared for a moment, and then hurried back towards her own chamber to call her women. "Wake up – wake up!" she cried. "The queen has gone!"

Megan muttered as she struggled to get up. Emma rolled off the bed and came tousled and yawning to the door. "What… what do you say?"

"Come here! Come quick!" Acha cried.

The urgency of her tone brought them both sharply to their senses, suddenly wide-awake and worried.

"The queen has gone – Bebba has gone!"

"No," Emma murmured. "She cannot have."

"But she *has* gone and all her lovely things with her. Look – they have crept away and taken almost everything with them – her clothing, her jewels, even the wall hangings… no coffers left behind, no combs or pots."

Once again there came the light clacking sound of wood on wood from the hall. Without another word, they went to see what was happening there and found the space dark and cold; yesterday's ashes filled the long central hearth. In the gloom two women appeared to be carefully rolling up a strip of half-finished weaving that they'd taken from one of the looms. Another was unfastening the dangling loom weights and yet another stacking the weaving shuttles into a basket – that was what made the clacking sounds.

"Where is the queen?" Acha asked.

They glanced sourly at each other, as though they'd have liked to ignore her question. One woman shrugged. "Gone to Dun Guardi," she said. "And we will follow her there just as soon as we can."

Acha did not trust herself to make a polite reply, so she turned swiftly back to her chamber.

"Bebba is insulted – she *is* deeply offended by my presence!" she cried, as soon as they were out of earshot of the websters. "And who can blame her? I should never have come here. I could have been offered to Theobald instead!"

"Oh yes," Emma agreed enthusiastically.

Megan sighed and shrugged. "Yes, it seems that the queen is more offended than we realised," she agreed. "But we are here now, like it or not! And whatever Bebba may feel, we cannot offend the king. Your marrying Theobald would never bring Athelfrid the heir he clearly wants so much!"

"No," Acha agreed.

She was stunned and distressed at this latest slight to her person, for despite the coolness of the queen's women and Bebba's own icy civility, there'd been a sense of safety in the presence of those proud women. What would happen now that the queen had taken umbrage and left the court? Athelfrid had made it plain last night that his wife's wishes were important to him and everyone knew that she was the Pictish king's sister. Wars had been started over less than this.

"I'll go to find Godric," Megan said. "He'll know what to do."

Acha nodded. "Yes, go at once."

She hovered in the doorway of the empty room, with Emma nervous and restless at her side. It seemed a long time before Godric appeared with Megan and a nervous servant girl who carried a jug of milk, fresh bread and cheese on a tray.

"All's well," he told her at once. "I've spoken to Athelfrid and discovered that he and Bebba had agreed that the queen should leave for Dun Guardi. Bebba has an especial attachment to the fortress by the sea and will stay there while she awaits the birth of her child, but he was surprised that she'd gone so precipitously. She has no wish to witness your marriage festivities and I think we cannot blame her for that."

"She *is* offended, then!"

Godric sighed and shrugged. "It's a tricky situation," he agreed. "But Bebba has given her consent to your becoming Athelfrid's consort so long as she is always the acknowledged queen. Bebba knows her husband needs an heir and it seems she cannot provide one for him."

"But she is pregnant, is she not?"

"Aye, pregnant for the seventh time," Megan put in quickly, looking grim. "I learned as much last night at the feast. The queen has suffered stillbirth many times. I don't think even Bebba holds out much hope for this poor child."

Acha remembered her first meeting with the queen and the weary expression that she'd briefly glimpsed when the question of this new marriage was raised. Bebba had seemed all dignity and civility, but Acha could see that her proud veneer must surely have been hiding great suffering and bitterness. Yes, Godric was right – who could blame her for wanting to absent herself from the handfasting ceremony and celebrations?

Acha sighed. The role of peaceweaver was very complicated – a thin and difficult line to walk. "So... the queen is leaving the job of producing heirs to me," she said uncertainly.

"So it seems," said Megan.

Godric put a soothing arm about her shoulders. "This was what your father offered them – an heir-producer of royal blood. It was always there beneath the flattering words, my dear."

It was true and Acha knew it, but facing it so directly was not easy.

"Now... let's turn to practicalities," Godric said. "The king has sent this servant girl to wait on you for the time being, and he apologised profusely that you are left without the comfort and service that a secondary wife should expect. He asked that you call for anything you need and invited you to make yourself at home in the queen's hall. This building is now yours to command."

"What do you mean?" she asked, her interest piqued a little.

Godric nodded, smiling gently at her look of wonder.

"This hall," she murmured, looking around at the strong beams and beautiful carvings. "This hall even stripped of its fine fittings is much more than I could ever need."

"Well, enjoy it then and I will tell the king that you are content. The wedding is to take place at sunset. You must be ready to set off for the sacred hill as soon as the light begins to fade, and you must ride in your litter just one more time."

She looked perplexed. "I must go... up there?"

"Yes. You are to be handfasted on the sacred hill and the priestess will officiate. They do things a little differently here..." His brows were knotted with anxiety as he looked to Megan for aid.

"I believe they do," Megan agreed darkly. "But there is nothing in it to fear, I think. It seems they honour Freya in the ancient way of the tribes, by building a bower of branches and leaves – this too, I learned at the feast."

Acha flushed and caught her breath. "You mean I have to go to Athelfrid… up there on the hill… and lie with him in a bower of leaves?"

Emma turned pale at the thought of such a barbaric rite, but Megan saw it differently. "Does it matter where?" she asked.

"Will I not be shamed by such a thing?" Acha asked, faintly.

"Lady, we need to please them," Godric said. "They believe such rites ensure fertility."

Acha swallowed hard and nodded. "Megan's right. What does it matter where?"

"My warrior maiden is back – and ready to join battle," Godric added gently with a rueful smile. "This is just a different kind of battle, Sword-Queen. Have breakfast now, you'll need your strength."

The young girl he'd brought with him moved forward and began to put food and drink out on a trestle that was set up before the brazier, while more servants appeared with glowing charcoal and soon they were warm. She seemed pleased with her new role as maid to the Deiran bride; her name was Clover and she answered eagerly when Emma plied her with questions. She'd been a kitchen maid and her usual round of work meant serving food and scrubbing pots. Her friendly willingness to serve made a welcome change from Bebba's sour-faced women.

CHAPTER 7

A SKY-PRINCESS

With a full belly, Acha began to feel better, and she took pleasure in the thought that this beautiful little hall was hers to command, for a while at least. She took stock of what had been left there, and saw that if she gathered the pieces together there was more than enough to furnish one room. Pushing the evening ceremony from her mind, she set about putting the place in order.

"I shall take the queen's chamber," she announced.

Megan raised her eyebrows for a moment and then nodded, smiling at this touch of boldness. "Why not indeed," she said.

A flurry of activity followed, and by noon the queen's chamber was warm and cosy, with a brazier full of glowing charcoal, a bed piled high with skins and a small trestle set with tasty food that had arrived from the kitchens. Half way through their noontide meal Acha's appetite faded, as her thoughts began to dwell on what lay ahead.

"I suppose I will have to wear the same gown yet again," she said wistfully.

Megan shrugged. "Athelfrid should have presented you with a new gown. It's all such a rush – *a Lammastide bride* – no time to do things properly. Men never think of such things."

"And the queen has made sure that she left none of *her* finery behind," Emma added.

"But *she* couldn't know that I came with just one decent gown to my name," Acha replied, trying to be fair.

Clover had been listening to this exchange with interest. "I have a… friend who may be able to help," she said. "I will just see…"

They watched surprised as she bobbed a curtsey and hurried from the hall.

It wasn't long before she returned with Bree, dragging a heavy coffer between them.

"Bree will help you, Princess," Clover announced, delighted at her resourcefulness.

"No – no, that will not do at all," Megan was on her feet and shaking her head at once.

Acha stared at her nurse, puzzled by this sudden surliness.

"The princess is welcome to take her pick of my gowns," Bree offered with a charming smile.

Before anyone could say any more, Megan grabbed Acha by the arm and pulled her out of the chamber and into the main hall. As they passed the two women, Clover clasped her hands to her mouth, devastated at this reaction – while Bree folded her arms defensively and pouted.

"Megan? What are you doing?" Acha protested. "You will offend them!"

"I mean to offend," she said. "Do you not know who that woman is? When I found out I was sickened that he sat you next to her last night. *She* is his concubine – I had it from one of the women. Ask yourself, why has *she* not gone off to Dun Guardi with the queen's ladies?"

Acha's mouth dropped open. It did indeed make sense of Bree's strange informal speech and manners; she dressed like a queen, but behaved like a friendly goat girl.

"Yeees!" she murmured.

If this was so, why indeed had Athelfrid sat her next to his concubine? Was he testing her in some way? Was it to amuse himself or to somehow shame her? Was it to reassure the queen of her own position?

"You cannot dress yourself in *her* clothes!" Megan insisted.

Acha's first feeling was bitter disappointment, for Bree had appeared to be a potential ally. Apart from the maid Clover, she'd been the only Bernician woman to have spoken to her in a friendly manner. She glanced back into the room to see Clover red-faced and wringing her hands, distressed at her huge blunder. Bree stared resignedly up at the rafters, prepared for an angry dismissal.

"But Bree has shown me more kindness than any of the queen's women," Acha said stubbornly.

"So you are going to your husband in a gown his whore has worn?"

"Am I much more than a concubine?" she asked in a small voice.

"You are our princess, Acha!"

She replied in sullen tones, "And a brood-mare too!"

They stood facing each other in tense silence for a few moments, and then Megan relented and came to hug her. "Dearest girl… do as you wish."

Acha planted a firm kiss on Megan's soft, withered cheek. "Let us see what they have to offer," she said.

They went back into the chamber, where Bree and Clover waited glum faced, prepared for further rebuke.

"It's kind of you both to wish to help me," Acha said politely. "May we see your gowns?"

They stared at her startled for a moment, grinned at each other, then without further ado they flung open the lid of the coffer.

The bed was soon covered with under-gowns, over-gowns, tunics, mantles and cloaks. Most of them were dyed in the brightest colours and trimmed with furs, feathers and gaudy braiding.

Megan could not help but sigh and tut at the sight of the tawdry splendour, but Acha lighted on a simple linen under-gown, twice dyed with woad to a rich deep blue.

"This is a lovely colour," she said, "And the linen so soft."

"I have never worn it," Bree said, eager to please. "Nor this over-gown that was made to go with it… too pale for me, I think." She held out a feather-trimmed, lighter blue tunic, dyed to the soft shade of a sunny sky. "Try them, lady," she urged. "You are much of a height with me."

They slipped the smooth linen over Acha's head, and stood back to look at the effect. Megan shook her head and pulled a disapproving face at the downy white feathers that adorned the neck and ruffled with every movement.

"Wait," Bree commanded, growing bolder now. "It's not quite right for you, Princess, but if I do this…" She strode forward, took a dainty pair of shears from her girdle and began to snip the feathers away.

The others watched a little shocked at first, but then they saw that she was right: the simplicity that was now achieved brought out the beauty of the colours and the healthy sheen of Acha's skin and hair.

"Like a Sky-Princess," Clover whispered and even Megan nodded approval.

Bree fished again in the piles of clothing. "You need green, to go with that gown," she said. "I have a good green cloak somewhere amongst these things… then you will look like the goddess herself, spun from the grass and the sky. The carlin will approve; she has no time for gold and garnets."

Bree pulled out a cloak of felted wool, dyed to an earthy green and trimmed with silk.

Acha remembered the herbs that she'd seen outside in the garden, blue and green… rosemary covered in tiny sky blue flowers. "I'll wear a wreath of rosemary," she said.

Clover moved to the door. "I'll fetch some for you," she said, delighted.

Emma set to work with her slick-stones and smoothed the light linen weave until it was burnished like fresh washed sand. Acha invited Bree to sit and take a cup of wine with her, glad that she'd not dismissed the girl with angry words.

As the sun began to sink behind the sacred mountain, Acha left the queen's chamber, content in the knowledge that she looked more like a summer solstice dancer than a poverty-stricken princess. She knew that there could be no competing with Bebba's queenly splendour, so she had to offer something different; the simple look they'd achieved made her feel much more herself. Her only jewel was the tiny sword pendant that Edwin had given her – the precious oath-braid was hidden beneath the fresh-scented rosemary wreath that crowned her head.

She walked out to her litter, followed by Emma, Bree and Clover, also crowned with rosemary wreaths and dressed in simple smocks. If Athelfrid had meant to test her, or anger her, by sitting her next to his concubine, he would be disappointed.

"These are my handmaidens," Acha announced, presenting them to Godric, "the ones that I have chosen."

He glanced at Megan and the old nurse shrugged. "It is as the princess wishes," she said. "I think we must allow her this; there are few maidens left here for her to choose from."

"That's true," he agreed.

Acha's warrior band formed her escort, shuffling uncomfortably into place behind the litter, uncertain as to how they should behave in this strange situation. She knew they'd be glad to return home as soon as they possibly could.

"Will you be leaving tomorrow?" she asked, anxious at the thought of loosing him.

"I'll return when I've seen you settled, Princess; I'll not set out until you tell me you are content."

"Thank you," she said, as he took her hand once again, to help her climb into the litter.

She turned to send a brief, questioning glance to her old nurse. Megan answered with a reassuring nod, and then she stepped into the litter.

Acha was borne aloft – frustrated, as ever, that she couldn't see where she was going or what was happening outside the closed curtains. As they began the ascent of the Sacred Mountain, she braced herself against the tilting that was unavoidable. She thought she heard the whinny of horses in the distance and the sound of trampling hooves. Would Athelfrid and his thanes be riding up the hill? If so she envied them; she'd have given anything to be out on horseback, riding away from this peculiar duty that she must perform.

Megan lifted the corner of the curtain. "Wait till you see their holy place," she whispered.

At last the litter was lowered to the ground.

"One moment," Megan ordered them to wait, while she thrust her head inside the curtains. "Now is the time, Princess," she said quietly.

"Do you have it?" Acha asked.

"Yes – it's here, my darling." The old nurse took from her girdle a dainty drinking horn, plugged with beeswax.

Acha reached for it, her hands trembling a little. Megan broke the light seal and a strong spicy scent drifted from the rim of the horn.

"What's in it?" Acha asked.

"Golden root, angelica, a pinch of powdered kelp and sea-buckthorn berries, mixed with good mead. Oh, and there's hops to make you sleep afterwards. All you'll taste is spice and honey."

Acha sipped the drink while Megan chanted a magical charm under her breath.

"Freya of the midnight cats

Seed this woman like the barley,

Bring her pleasure from your rites, not pain."

The brew was sweet and fiery and sent comforting warmth running through her body, it even reached her fingers and toes.

"I thank you," she said, her eyes smarting with love for her old nurse. "Never leave me," she begged.

"I will not," Megan said and she gave her a warm kiss and a pat on the cheek. She drew back from the litter, her last important duty done.

Acha stepped out to stand on shaking legs and sought about her for the sight of a temple. But there was no stone altar as she'd expected, only an astounding view over the rolling hills that stretched away on all sides.

"But… but where is the building?" she asked.

"The whole of this hilltop is their temple," Godric explained. "They honour their gods on holy mounds, much as the ancient tribes did."

A rampart circled Goats' Hill and, on the highest point, by a stone cairn, stood the tall figure of Athelfrid. The carlin stood at his side and her dome-shaped headdress made her appear the same height as the king. Around them, in a huge circle, a crowd had gathered. The king's thanes, their servants and slaves were present, but so too were those who worked the land and reared the beasts. Everyone looked expectantly in Acha's direction. Quite oblivious to the importance of the occasion, the sacred goats foraged steadily, their neck-bells jangling as they moved.

The sun began to vanish behind the distant horizon, painting both the hill and those gathered there with a rose-tinted glow.

"Are you ready Princess?" Godric held out his arm to her.

Megan's fiery brew filled her with cheerful courage, and she looked at him with fondness, happy that he was here at her side, rather than her father. "As ready as I'm ever likely to be," she said.

Athelfrid, magnificent in his wolfskin cloak and gold armbands, watched them approach with a satisfied expression on his face, which only wavered briefly when he saw and recognised the fourth handmaiden. Acha noted his moment of uncertainty and smiled boldly back at him. Bree's eyes remained downcast; she was the very image of demure beauty.

The carlin stepped forward to greet them with approval. "Welcome, lady. You come to us looking like the goddess herself."

Acha flashed a small glance of appreciation back to Bree; only time would tell whether there might be the possibility of true friendship between them.

Dressed in what appeared to be her full regalia, the carlin wore a long lichen-dyed robe of shimmering goats' hair with a train trailing at the back. Around her neck hung a necklace of delicate, shining slivers of goat's horn that clattered faintly as she moved. As darkness fell, a steady drumming rhythm began, though Acha could not see where the sounds came from. The priestess threw a handful of herbs and spices onto a glowing fire, sending richly scented smoke drifting over the hilltop. A handful of tinder-dry kindling followed, sparking the fire into life. A torch was lit from it and passed on to the circling crowd. It seemed each person had prepared their own small torch, for as the brand was passed from hand to hand, many smaller flames jumped and flickered. At last the sun vanished behind the hills, leaving a faint pink glow in the western sky.

"Come!" the carlin commanded. "The time is right!"

She indicated that Acha should stand on one side of the cairn, while Athelfrid went to the other. As Godric led her to her place, the onlookers began a low, steady chant – the drumbeat grew louder.

"Who gives this woman to this man?" the carlin demanded, standing in between the bride and groom.

"I do," Godric was ready with his response. "In the name of Aelle of Deira."

He proffered Acha's right hand and Athelfrid too stretched his own right hand across the cairn to take hold of Acha's. Godric backed away and before Acha had had a chance to get used to the sensation of being held in the king's firm grip, the carlin flung a plaited rope over both their arms and began to bind their wrists together. The scent of rosemary hung in the air along with something else more potent and earthy that she thought might be hemp.

"In the name of Goat-headed Freya, I bind handfast this man and woman," the carlin cried. "Bless their union with increase! Bring sons and daughters for Bernicia!"

The crowd cheered in response and Acha felt a comfortable sense of acquiescence and contentment creep over her; Megan's herbs were doing their work. Then the carlin produced a goblet that smelled strongly of mead. Acha smiled dizzily at the sight of it and knew that she couldn't refuse to drink, whatever it was. She hoped vaguely, and with a touch of amusement, that she'd manage to stay on her feet as long as she needed to.

The carlin offered the goblet first to Athelfrid and then to Acha. It tasted slightly different from Megan's brew, but it too was sweet and strong. The drumbeat grew faster, until the sound of it seemed to match the beat of her own heart; she became dimly aware that people were dancing around them. They were turning – turning around to face the fire that was now blazing with flames the height of her thighs.

"Leap! Leap! Leap over the flames!" the priestess commanded.

"Still tied?" Acha asked. Holding up her bound wrist, she stumbled against the king.

"Tied forever," Athelfrid said. He put his lips close to her ear. "Trust me. When I say 'run'... run fast. When I say 'jump'... jump high. Can you do it?"

She looked at his excited face and laughed. "I can do it."

He grabbed her round the waist with his free left arm and braced his hip against hers, making her aware of every taut muscle in his leg, and then he gave the command: "Run now!"

Acha ran for all she was worth and when he shouted jump, she jumped. He took most of her weight, so that she sailed over the flames with him, only staggering a little as they hit the ground.

The crowd cheered wildly and parted before them, revealing the shadowy shape of a small shelter built of stout branches, and roofed with moss and leaves. Flowers and twisted stalks of barley adorned the entrance. This must be the bower she'd heard about. Two of the carlin's attendants held aside a curtain of loosely woven willow wands, disclosing a dark interior.

Acha allowed Athelfrid to lead her forwards, his left arm still round her waist. They had to bend down together to crawl inside, somewhat hampered by the binding of their wrists. As they struggled together in the dark, cramped space, Acha started to giggle.

"But we can do nothing bound like this!" she said, clutching at his knee to steady herself.

"Keep still, wench!" He laughed. "I shall unfasten you… I don't want an unwilling wife who is trussed like a pig."

She caught the glimmer of a blade and gasped, but with the flash came awareness that her wrist was free. He pushed her down onto something soft and faintly earth-scented. Dimly she remembered the advice that Megan had given her and stretched out her long limbs, letting her legs lie wide and slack.

She smiled as she realised that her worst fears were over, whatever came next. The King of Bernicia had accepted her as his wife. Deira would be safe and the whole of Aelle's kingdom must be proud of her.

CHAPTER 8

A MORNING-GIFT

Shards of sharp sunlight woke her, dancing down through the loosely woven roof of moss and leaves. For a moment she couldn't think where she was, but then dim memories of the ceremony and Athelfrid's unhurried, experienced lovemaking came back to her. She lay still for a few more moments, relieved that her wedding night was over. She seemed to have survived it and she felt no pain – in truth she felt warm and comfortable. When she tried to sit up, she discovered that Athelfrid's legs weighted down her feet, his wolfskin cloak covering them both. A short dagger in a gilded sheath attached to an ornate belt and buckle lay beside them. The king still slept, snoring lightly, while outside she could hear the gentle sound of goats' bells and also something else: the familiar sound of a horse whickering. Somebody must be out there, close by – surely they were not *all* still there, waiting for her to emerge from the bower?

She shifted cautiously, but her movement woke Athelfrid and he rolled away from her, with a surprised snort, then looked vaguely back at her and grinned.

"Greetings, my sweet Deiran bride," he said. "Are you well?"

"I am, sir," she said.

He grabbed her round the waist and pulled her to him. "I too am content," he said sleepily and kissed her. She wondered if he might wish to make love again and the thought was not unpleasant to her, but when there came again the sounds of a horse moving about outside, Athelfrid pushed her gently away.

"Time enough for Freya's rites this evening," he said. "You must have your morning-gift, to seal our union. Look outside – you will find it there."

She hesitated. "But – I can hear a horse outside," she protested.

He saw with amusement that she feared she might have to emerge sleepy and dishevelled to greet the whole gathering again. Reaching forward, he lifted the curtain of leaves so that sunlight flooded the earthy, confined space.

"That horse is my morning-gift to you," he said. "I took the advice of your good thane Godric."

Intrigued, she crawled on her hands and knees across the soft bed of dried moss to find four stamping hooves in front of her. Looking up, she discovered the most beautiful silver-grey mare that she'd ever seen, fastened by a leading rein to a stake that had been pushed into the ground. The horse was so light in colour that it brought to mind fresh fallen snow. Acha gazed at her in wonder. The beast's soft mane was thick and silky, falling over the most perfectly arched neck. It had been combed smoothly into place, but here and there it rippled where the light breeze caught it. The coat was smooth and shone to perfection, while the tail twitched and floated a little on the breeze, just as silken as the mane. The mare's hocks and fetlocks were encased in soft sun-bleached laced leather, and her saddle was wrought of sun-bleached leather to match.

"Do you like your morning-gift?" Athelfrid asked, his head appearing in the entrance to the bower.

"How could I not?" she whispered.

She struggled to her feet and instinctively went to stroke the soft muzzle. Blowing gently into her face, the beautiful creature accepted her caress with faint interest. Buckets of mashed oats and water had already provided her with breakfast; now she stamped her hooves, impatient for exercise.

Then Acha noticed that behind the mare's food stood a small trestle that had been set up with a steaming jug, a cup and covered basket. She glanced quickly around, but could see nobody else in sight, though somebody had certainly been there recently.

Athelfrid crawled out of the bower and stretched to his full height, groaning as he brushed leaves and twigs from his beard. He politely turned his back and walked away from her to find a more private space to pass water, while she too took the opportunity to relieve herself, feeling less abashed than she thought she might have having to do such an intimate thing in his company.

She stood up and straightened the blue gown as he walked back to her.

"Are you ready?" he asked.

"Yes, I am," she nodded, and they stood to face each other solemnly for this last, important part of their marriage agreement.

He picked up the mare's bridle and held it out to her. "Take her," he said. "This mare and her foals are yours for life."

For one brief moment she hesitated, knowing that once she'd accepted the morning-gift, the bargain was completed and sealed – there could be no going back. Most royal brides might hope for land or jewels, but this beautiful mare was indeed the perfect gift for her. She reached out and took the bridle.

"I accept this mare as my morning-gift," she said.

"Now you are mine," he replied, and gave the characteristic grin that she was beginning to recognise.

Acha smiled too and stroked the mare's silver withers. "What is her name?" she asked.

He shrugged. "It is for you to name her."

"She's as silver as a fairy steed," she murmured. "I shall call her Sidhe"

"Then Sidhe she shall be. Come, join me in a cup of warm mead; I see they've left bread and cheese for us, and when we've breakfasted we'll ride back down the hill together and announce that we are man and wife."

Acha found she *was* quite hungry, and ate the simple food with gusto. Athelfrid reached out to smooth back her hair from her face as she ate. "Pink cheeks and a good appetite… yes, I am content with my bargain."

"Even though I bring no dowry?" she began hesitantly.

"Your dower will be paid in full when you give me my firstborn son," he said. "A son is what I want, and I make no bones about it. It's a sorry thing for a great king to have no heir."

"I shall do my best," she said uncertainly, shivering a little. What if she failed to conceive, or produced only girls? What then? She pushed those thoughts to the back of her mind.

When they'd finished the mead, Athelfrid offered her a leg-up onto to Sidhe's back. She accepted politely, but as she leapt to sit astride the mare, he laughed.

"Little need for assistance there," he observed wryly. "Now you'd better help me to mount! This mare is strong enough to carry the two of us."

She smiled and held out her hand to haul him up behind her and as she felt the warmth of his muscular body at her back, she fleetingly thought of Coifi and the desperate ride away from Eforwic. They set off down the hill, Acha taking the reins. She found that she couldn't help but take pleasure in the magnificent view of the rolling hills and lush pastureland that surrounded the sacred hill. The sun was warm on her skin and the air smelled of honey and cut hay. Athelfrid grabbed her waist and she leaned back against the hardness of his chest, feeling a warm sense of satisfaction in a job well done.

As they followed the winding path that led down, they approached a small thatched dwelling built into the hillside.

"Stop here for a moment!" Athelfrid said, a touch of irritation in his voice.

Wondering why, she obediently brought Sidhe neatly to a halt just as the carlin emerged from the hut, dipping her head to get through the doorway. They did not dismount or speak, but the king bowed silently to the old woman and Acha followed his lead. She was surprised to see the meagreness of the priestess's dwelling. In Deira, the chief priestess inhabited a high-status hall attached to Freya's temple, on a hill overlooking Aelle's summer palace.

The carlin raised her hand in blessing.

"Ride on," Athelfrid said, but once out of hearing he chuckled and remarked irreverently, "We have old goat-face's approval, it seems."

Acha gave a small gasp of amusement.

"I don't complain," he added. "Goat-headed Freya asks little of us. I let these beast-herders worship as they've always done, so long as they pay their dues and obey Woden's call to arms. Tolerance of their ancient ways is the key to my success," he added. "That's where my cousin Hering failed. He thought openly to crush the old traditions, he had no idea how to deal with these fools, but I soon got rid of him."

Though his tone was humorous, a slight shiver ran down Acha's back – for the story of how Athelfrid had driven his cousin Hering from the throne after the fight at Catraeth was well known. Her father had also been ruthless in the way he dealt with rivals – a great warrior king needed to be without pity for those who'd take his place. She sat forward a little more in the saddle, recollecting that her new husband's nickname was The Trickster.

"You've not looked properly at the settlement yet," he said, seeing her thoughtful look. "You've done nothing but ride around in that litter of yours, with all the curtains closed."

"I'm glad to be free of it," she admitted, reassured a little by his return to gentle teasing.

"We will ride around the boundary," he said. "I shall show you Woden's temple and the rest of my morning-gift."

"The rest of it?" she asked.

"Aye… the rest of it!" he said laughing. "Come, put this mare through her paces and you will see!"

She skilfully urged Sidhe into a canter and Athelfrid barked with laughter and slapped her thigh again. They half circled the palisade and rode in through the main gate, only slowing down to a trot as a train of mares, with young foals amongst them, was herded out to pasture.

"These are the brood-mares. What do you think of them?" Athelfrid asked.

Acha watched them as they passed, delighting in the proud way they held their heads, the healthy whinnying snorts and the flashes of flying manes.

"The best I've ever seen," she admitted.

"Well, then – it is good that you say so, for they too are part of your morning-gift."

She caught her breath in surprise.

"The brood-mares and their stables are yours," he went on, "along with Duncan, my best horse-man. The colts are castrated, and then come to me for battle training. Let this gift symbolise our union and my hopes that you too will be breeding soon."

Acha turned back to watch the mares and their foals moving out onto the lush pasture land that surrounded the settlement. She felt a little overwhelmed as she came to realise the true worth of her morning-gift. Athelfrid had not stinted in any way and he'd taken the trouble to make a gift that was much to her liking, though it came with a heavy burden of expectation attached.

"I thank you," she whispered. "I am deeply honoured… and I pray Freya that I shall please my lord."

He kissed her cheek as she turned. "Tonight," he whispered in her ear and she looked ahead again, blushing. "Now ride over to the corral," he ordered, quickly practical once again, as he pointed the way ahead.

She brought Sidhe to a halt beside the stout double palings that were full of sturdy, jostling geldings, bridled as for war. As they watched, the young riders began lining up their steeds at one end of the corral, directed by an older man, mounted on a black stallion, and dressed in riding leathers.

"Cavalry," Aethelric explained. "This is where you will send the geldings. At Catraeth I learned, through bitter experience, that the most powerful battle weapon a warlord can possess is a horse. Hand-picked men and beasts, good riders, not too heavy in the girth, all trained by my chief thane and cavalry leader, Ulric."

"But my lord, you carried the day at Catraeth – you were the victor."

He nodded, but his face grew taut and angry. "We lost too many. There were three hundred of them – Goddodin they called themselves. We had five times their number, but your father lost his strongest men, – and he lost his son and heir!"

Acha didn't need to be reminded of her brother's death. She made no reply.

"They rode like Thor's lightening, dividing our ranks, smashing our shield wall and we were forced to reform again and again. Yes, we overcame them in the end by sheer numbers, but I saw what cavalry can do. To be certain of victory in battle a warrior king needs both shield-wall *and* cavalry. Since Catraeth, our horses are second to none."

She was silent, her mind full of the terrible image of young men and beautiful beasts falling amongst spears and swords. Athelfrid's gentle humour seemed to have vanished, and he too had grown sombre. The mare tossed her head impatient to be off, but Acha held her back, unsure whether to move on or not. The solemn moment was disturbed by the sound of faint cheering that rose from the courtyard behind them.

Athelfrid turned to see that a small crowd had gathered outside the mead-hall.

"They wait for us," he said, a touch of irritation in his voice.

Acha turned Sidhe's head and they trotted over towards the hall to find themselves pelted with flowers. It was impossible to remain solemn in the face of such warmth.

Horse boys vied to take Sidhe's reins and amidst cheers and catcalls they both dismounted. "I'll see you this evening," Athelfrid said, the wolfish smile back on his face again. "Tonight will be your bride-ale feast, so you must act hostess and order whatever you want. Take whichever servants you need – you are 'feast-mistress' while the queen is away."

Startled that he should expect her to take on the role so soon, she tried to protest, but Athelfrid turned away to speak to one of his thanes and vanished inside the great hall. He had dismissed her from his mind. Acha reluctantly handed Sidhe over to the grooms and stood for a moment in the courtyard, wondering where to start.

The serving women had hurried back to their work, and she was relieved to see Megan and Emma emerge from the herb garden. She strode towards them purposefully; it would be good to be away from public gaze for a while, to sit and talk with those she knew well and take time to gather her thoughts.

CHAPTER 9

A BRIDE-ALE FEAST

Back in her chamber in the queen's hall, Emma and Clover were full of nudges, winks, and sly grins. They served her a restorative herb drink and demanded to know how she'd fared through her wedding night. Smiling secretively, she avoided answering them but replied to Megan's direct questioning gaze with a swift nod, which told her nurse all she needed to know.

"Stop prattling about my wedding night," she told them, jittery with anxiety. "I have to order the food and act hostess tonight at the bride-ale feast!"

Megan nodded approval. "He shows respect," she acknowledged, but then her eyes narrowed as she went on. "And maybe he sets you something of a test. Luckily *we* know that you can conduct a feast properly."

"Yes, I think he tests me," Acha agreed, still anxious. "I've acted hostess for my father since I was ten years old, but here I know nothing of the kitchens or the servants."

"And what will you wear tonight?" Emma cut in. "Shall we call in Bree again?"

"No," Acha firmly shook her head. "Bree has given me enough. Tonight I'll make the best of what I have, and wear my mother's weld-dyed tunic over this blue under-gown. Please heat up the slick-stones and prepare it all!"

Emma helped her strip off her crumpled clothing and put on her old work-a-day gown; she smiled as she re-claimed her girdle with all its useful hangers and small tools; as soon as it was fastened about her waist she felt more herself again, more capable and in control.

"They'll have to accept me as I am," she announced.

She neatly coiled the precious plait of hair that linked her to her brother and placed it safely in her thread box, while Emma set to work to prepare her finery for the evening.

"You *must* wear a veil, now that you are a married woman," Megan insisted.

Acha pulled a face, but allowed her nurse to braid her hair and cover her head with a light veil and silver fillet to keep it in place.

"Is Godric still here?" she asked.

"Oh yes," Megan nodded. "He fusses about your safety like an old mother hen!"

She smiled fondly at this rude description of the man. "Please find him and invite him to the feast tonight, but tell him that he may prepare to leave in the morning. Say that I am content and delighted with my morning-gift."

Megan looked carefully at Acha. "Are you truly content, my lass?"

"Yes," Acha said firmly, and then she gave a small smile. "I shall manage here… so long as *you* do not leave me. But Deira will be waiting anxiously to know that its peace offering is accepted."

"I'll go and speak to Godric then," she said.

Acha sat for a while, frowning in thought and absently watching Clover as the girl came quietly to clear the remains of their small meal.

"Clover," she suddenly asked. "Were you ever there in the kitchens when the queen ordered a feast?"

"Yes, lady," she replied. "I was always there, but I like it better here."

"I trusted you yesterday," Acha said, her mind still working through the difficulties ahead of her. "I trusted you and you served me loyally."

Clover stopped her work and made a small curtsey. "You honoured *us* lady," she said. "Neither Bree nor I ever thought we'd be the handmaid of a princess bride."

Acha made a quick decision and got up. "Put down those pots," she said. "I need you again. Will you come with me to the kitchens and advise me what to order for the feast? I need to ask for everything the queen would order. Can you remember all the dishes, do you think?"

"I can," she said, smiling broadly.

The girl chattered cheerfully as they strode across the courtyard together, clearly relishing the role of adviser to the king's new bride, but as they entered the kitchens they found themselves greeted with smiles of wry amusement. The servants and cooks nudged each other and looked sideways at the stitch-wife's tools that hung from Acha's girdle.

At Clover's whispered suggestion, she began by ordering venison, wild boar, duck, goose and hare with all the trimmings. The food-wife nodded vaguely, but made it clear that she took little notice. A few of the older women who worked there exchanged glances of disapproval, offended that this young upstart should come from far away and think herself good enough to tell them what to do. When Acha added a few of her own favourite foods to Clover's list, the food-wife greeted the extra items with open contempt.

"We've none o' them," she said, and shrugged as though she'd never heard of apple dumplings or bread spiced with fennel and poppy seeds.

"I would be most grateful for your help," Acha said, her voice suddenly formal and sharp. "I fulfil the role of feast-mistress by the king's command, and though I am a newcomer here I will do my best to please him. I'm quite sure that none of you would wish to offend so great a man, so strong a protector."

All of a sudden they listened properly to her and responded with quick nods. It seemed their obedience was better won by veiled threats, than polite requests – well, it was a start.

"I look forward to tasting your dishes at the feast," she said bowing distantly, and left the kitchens quickly before her courage failed.

She let out a great sigh of frustration as they walked back to the queen's hall. "Will they do it, do you think?" she asked Clover.

"I think so," the girl nodded.

"For fear of the king!"

"Yes… for fear of the king," she said, with a smile. "You did well to make that plain to them."

"I'm not as inexperienced as they think," she confided. "Since my father had no queen, I learned to be hostess at an early age. But I have never carried the drink-horn in a hall as great as this before," she added uncertainly.

"You surprised them," Clover said with a satisfied smile. "They'll think twice before they ignore you again."

Back in her chamber Megan begged her rest again, but Acha was far too agitated – anxious that the feast should go well but helpless to do more to ensure that it did.

"Show me where the brood-mare's stables are," she begged Clover. "That building too is part of my morning-gift and I would wish to inspect it."

Clover caught her breath in surprise. "A valuable gift, my lady," she said. "But – Duncan the horse-keeper takes good care of all the mares. The king will not expect *you* to busy yourself with such things."

"Will he not?" she said with a smile. "If I am to own a stable full of mares, I will certainly wish to make myself busy there!"

Clover still looked uncertain, but nodded respectfully and led the way. They walked past the great corral and headed towards a long, low building that was set back amongst a glade of trees with its central doors open wide. The gables, patterned with carved wooden horses' heads, were painted just as beautifully as those on the two main halls.

She stopped for a moment, amazed. "This is the stables?" she asked.

Clover smiled. "It is the house for brood-mares and their foals," she said. "Built away from the courtyard, so the mares in foal can be quiet I think."

Acha smiled. "I wouldn't scorn to sleep in such a place myself."

They found three young men cleaning horse tack in a central area with a hearth and benches. An older man hurried forward.

"Duncan," Clover announced. "There's nothing he doesn't know about a mare in-foal."

"Lady, I am your slave," he said.

Acha saw that there was more than mere politeness in his words. His accent was unfamiliar and his head was shaved like that of a slave – but he wore good leather breeches.

"I would very much like to see the stables," she said.

The lads looked uneasy, but Duncan bowed and invited her to follow him. An airy stable block had been built on either side of the tack-room, with stalls lining the walls. It appeared to be empty of occupants, though a cheerful whinny of recognition announced that her Deiran mount was stabled near the door.

"Your mare knows her mistress," Duncan said.

Acha went to stroke her nose, feeling almost guilty for the new and instant love she'd felt for Sidhe. "Where is the silver mare – my morning-gift? I've named her Sidhe."

Duncan raised his eyebrows in interest. "An ancient British name," he said with approval. He led her through the tack room and into the farthest stable, where they found that Sidhe was the only occupant. She shifted her hooves at Acha's approach, eager for another gallop.

"Not just yet, my friend," Acha said as she turned to examine the building. The stable walls were fitted with shutters to allow air to circulate; the place smelled pleasantly of fresh straw, and was as clean and neat as the kitchens.

"Your management of these stables is excellent," she complimented Duncan.

"Thank you lady," he bowed.

"Where do you come from?" she asked.

Clover looked a little uncomfortable.

"I come from Dun Eidyn," he said quietly and his glance drifted away from them as though ashamed.

Acha saw at once that she trod on sensitive ground, and berated herself. His shaven head should have warned her that he was a captive, probably taken at the battle of Catraeth.

"The Gododdin!" she murmured. "Pray do not be discomfited. The king spoke of his respect for the Gododdin this very morning," she said, trying awkwardly to make amends for her clumsiness.

The man nodded, but said nothing more.

"A strong warrior *must* respect his enemies," she persisted, trying too hard to put things right. "I have often heard that said."

Duncan shook his head. "I was never a warrior, lady – only a horse-keeper – allowed to live, while my brothers were slaughtered, so that your husband might acquire the secrets of our beast-breeding. Had I behaved with honour, I'd have drowned myself rather than share the Gododdin's horse-skills with our enemy."

Acha could think of nothing to say. Many thoughts rushed through her head, until at last she spoke haltingly. "My brother died at Catraeth – but I for one am glad that you are here – and these gentle beasts must be grateful too. I see that my morning-gift could not be in better hands, and that you have no need of my advice."

"I shall call on you, lady," he said, smiling at last. "Do not doubt it."

Acha was quiet as they walked back across the courtyard.

"He's a good man," Clover said. "Whatever he said, he is respected here."

"Yes… a good man," Acha agreed.

For the last time, Godric led Acha into the feasting hall. The whole company rose to greet them, clapping and stamping their feet, as Athelfrid strode forward to greet his new bride. This time he led her to sit at his right hand, in the place previously occupied by Bebba, while Godric was placed at his left. When the drink-horn was ceremoniously carried in to the sound of more cheers, Acha rose gracefully to take it from the strong young man who bore it. She offered it to the king and his thanes smiled tolerantly as he drank from it and handed it back to her. She then courteously made her way around the table to offer it to the guests, her hands a-tremble from time to time.

"My brother is a lucky man… by Woden he is!" exclaimed Theobald, as she approached him. He stared at her darkly over the gold rim of the drink-horn; she curtsied hurriedly and moved quickly on to the next man.

She watched hawk-like as the servants presented the dishes, but it seemed that everything she'd ordered appeared, well-cooked and presented with even a few tasteful embellishments added, such as rose-hip paste, sorrel-cream sauce and a sprinkling of fresh chopped herbs. Even the apple dumplings duly arrived, served with rich golden cream and honey.

It seemed that her life as the king's consort might bring her many pleasant privileges, but when the court musician took up his harp to sing, she was reminded very thoroughly of the part she was expected to play. The first singer raised his voice in her praise and the king's hearth-companions thumped the trestles and joined in the chorus with gusto, but she struggled to keep the smile on her face.

"Praise a princess, blessed by Freya,

Quicken her belly with a lusty boy

Bring her to birth with a strong-limbed son,

A warrior brave, not a weakling."

The words left no doubt as to what was expected of her and she wondered whether Bebba had been subjected to these coarse incitements to produce an heir. As the feast progressed, and the singing grew bawdier, she almost began to miss the quieter, restrictive presence of the queen and her women.

At last Athelfrid put his arm around her waist. "It is time for Freya's rites sweetheart," he said, caring little that those around them heard. "Retire to your chamber and I shall join you there."

She blushed at the frank gestures of encouragement that followed his words.

"I hope a little mead is all we'll need tonight," he added, with a lifted eyebrow.

"Indeed," she whispered, rising hastily to her feet, blushing more than ever.

As her women followed her from the hall, she exchanged a fleeting glance with Bree, who sat on one of the lower tables; the girl looked away and Acha sensed her discomfort. What would the night hold for her? Would Athelfrid pass the girl onto one of his favourite thanes, now that their wives had followed the queen to Dun Guardi?

Back in her chamber, Acha nervously smoothed the thin linen of her shift, while the women combed her hair and rubbed lavender balm into her shoulders. They chanted more charms as they put her to bed and she slipped under the furs wearing only the shift and her gold and garnet sword necklace. The thought of Athelfrid's lovemaking held little fear for her, and she determined that she would try her best to keep her side of the bargain; many women would be pleased and honoured to be in her place.

As soon as he arrived, Athelfrid threw off his wolfskin cloak and started peeling off the gilt braided tunic beneath it. "Get out!" he snarled at the hovering women.

They fled.

He removed the jewelled dagger that was strapped to his back and placed it carefully on a wooden chest beside the bed.

Acha took a deep breath and threw back the bed-skins, a small seed of excited anticipation grew within her.

"Welcome, my lord," she said, as she gave an inviting smile.

CHAPTER 10

NEWS FROM THE NORTH

Godric left the following morning. Acha understood that he needed to return home; she knew too that the men were relieved to be taking good tidings back to Aelle.

Still she found it difficult to let them go, for once they'd vanished southwards she and her women would have no warriors of their own to call on.

Emma wept as they left, but Acha blinked back tears, frowning at her maid in irritation. "Stop it!" she hissed beneath her breath. "Do not shame me. We are well set up here, no need for tears. I'm happy with my lot."

Throughout Thanksgiving-month the weather began to cool a little and still more tribute payments flooded into Goats' Hill. Acha and her women could not help but enjoy the abundance of food and the comfort of their surroundings, and even Emma began to relish this luxurious existence.

Athelfrid presented Acha with more lavish gifts, including lengths of woven linen, fine woollen cloth, trimmings of braid and silk brought north by sea-traders from lands far away. She examined these costly rarities with much thought and a little uncertainty – and sent for Bree, who appeared in her chamber, looking apprehensive.

"You wanted me lady?" she asked.

"Yes. I need someone to take care of my clothing;" she announced. "Emma has many other things to do and I want someone I can trust to choose fabrics and styles that will suit me, someone who could find good stitch-wives and direct their work. Would you be willing?"

"You ask *me*?" Bree said, startled at the very idea.

"You chose well for my wedding and you have all the skill and knowledge to be a wardrobe mistress… is that not true?"

The girl took so long to answer that Acha feared she'd somehow insulted her, but at last Bree nodded. "Well… I suppose I could serve you in such a way. There's little else for me to do these days," she said with a sigh. Then suddenly she laughed. "You'd better be careful, lady… you come close to making a respectable woman out of me."

"And why ever not?" Acha said, with a lift of her eyebrow.

Megan who was watching, hid a wry smile, approving the light touch of craftiness in this appointment. If Bree was kept busy, well paid and out of the king's sight… well, maybe he would forget her, at least for a while.

The women set about making themselves comfortable in their new home. Bree produced a selection of elegant, well-fitting gowns. She also found good local websters who quickly set up the weaving frames, so that the gentle clack and swish of the shuttle could be heard in the queen's hall once again. They were making two new wall hangings, which were growing fast, and lengths of soft, fine linen, for the stitch-wives to work on.

Athelfrid presented Acha with a carved whalebone casket, decorated exquisitely with images of Freya riding in her chariot drawn by black cats. He smiled indulgently at her cries of excitement when she discovered that it was filled with bangles, enamelled sleeve clips, finger rings and expensive Frankish coloured glass beads. She examined each item with delight, astonished at the riches he had heaped on her.

The king continued to come to her bed each night, tolerating the crude encouragement of his brother and his hearth-companions, with excellent humour. He was in a benevolent mood and everyone gained from it – many nods, smiles and winks came Acha's way. She took pleasure in the growing intimacy that appeared to be developing between the two of them, and Athelfrid regarded her employment of Bree with mild amusement.

Acha visited the brood-mares stables every morning, welcomed there by Duncan, who made reports on how his charges fared. He discussed the beast's ailments and possible treatments, realising that she loved the creatures almost as much as he did. Sometimes Acha took Sidhe and rode alongside Athelfrid, to watch the progress of the cavalrymen.

Without the disapproving presence of the queen and her ladies, an atmosphere of freedom prevailed; feasts grew more lavish, and entertainment grew more wild and bawdy. Theobald and his younger companions in particular fought for the chance to seize the harp, inventing outrageously flattering songs in praise of the king's young bride. Acha had never received so much approval at her father's court; she grew to feel that her life in Bernicia held surprising prospects of happiness.

As autumn wore on the last of the tribute was counted in and war-gangs were sent out to harry those who were late in paying. Theobald rode northwards with his own warrior-band, to deliver messages to Bebba's brother, Nechtan of the Picts. Frost-month began, the nights lengthened and turned chill. As the Night of the Dead approached, Athelfrid seemed more attentive than ever towards his bride.

Megan surreptitiously examined the bed for bloodstains and as the days passed a gradual sense of excitement grew, until at last her nurse felt confident enough to speak the words out loud.

"There can be no doubt of it… you are pregnant!"

Acha smiled and stroked her still slim belly; it was no surprise, her own body had told her as much.

"Should I tell the king, do you think?"

Megan gave a wry guffaw. "The king can count days as well as any man."

Athelfrid was no ignorant youth – he must have watched Bebba many times for signs of pregnancy, and perhaps other women too.

"Lie abed, sweetheart," he suggested, when she made to get up and ride out with him. "Stay warm inside and save your strength. Stop this wandering out to the stables. Duncan is more than capable of seeing to your beasts."

He crushed her to him and kissed her fervently when she made her expected announcement. That night he called for a feast and proclaimed his joy to his companions, having presented Acha with a necklace of garnets, set in heavy gold. The deep red colour of the stones unfortunately brought to mind the carlin's warning – that the price of her bearing sons for Bernicia would be blood. Amidst wild cheers and thumping of feet, she fingered the thread box that contained the oath-braid, remembering how she'd sliced her finger when they made their oath. Edwin too had asked – "what is the meaning of the blood?".

She quashed her unease and tried to concentrate on Athelfrid's joy, making herself smile at everyone.

The musician brought forward the harp-stool and prepared to entertain the company with another raucous round of song. In the attentive hush that fell, the sudden sound of horse's hooves could be heard, followed by shouts. The celebratory atmosphere was broken as the guests looked up, uncertainly. Before the harpist had time to begin, Theobald and some of his men appeared fully armed in the mead-hall. They were unwashed and clearly saddle sore; making the king's companions stare with disapproval, for this was a huge breach of courtesy.

Athelfrid, full of mead and good tidings, overlooked their rudeness and rose from his seat to hug his brother and tell him of Acha's pregnancy. Theobald congratulated them warmly, kissed Acha and treated her to a friendly wink, but almost at once the two brothers fell into deep conversation and ominous looks flew around the hall.

Feeling a little offended that the jubilation had fled so fast, Acha retired with her women and left the men to talk and drink. She lay in the darkness waiting for Athelfrid to join her – but he failed to come to her bed that night.

Megan bustled around in the morning, offering unasked-for advice. "He fears to cause harm to the child," she said. "You must see his point of view and keep your dignity – this is no insult. I understand the king sat up all night talking to his brother."

A touch of nausea made Acha wince as she struggled from her bed. "Oh, I know," she said. "I'm just the brood-mare."

"You are more than that to him, I think," Megan said.

Emma was quiet and sympathetic as she helped Acha dress, making none of her usual teasing observations of signs of the king's passion for his new bride. This kindness made Acha feel worse. She steeled herself to be calm and think of the child, until another unsettling thought came to her.

"Where is Bree?" she asked. "Have you seen her this morning?"

"No, Princess," Emma replied quietly. "Nor Clover, either."

She failed to meet her mistress's eyes, as she straightened the bed and fussed with the furs.

Acha narrowed her eyes in suspicion. Why was Bree not here? Had Athelfrid taken Bree to his bed again?

"I need air," she announced. She got up and headed for the doorway.

Megan put down the bowl of herbs she pounded, ready to accompany her.

"No. I go alone," Acha said sharply.

"Wait," Megan ordered. She snatched up a warm cloak and fastened it about Acha's shoulders, before she reluctantly let her go.

As soon as she stepped outside the herb garden Acha knew that something had changed drastically for sounds of furious activity came from the courtyard. She gathered her cloak tightly around her and walked through the side-gate, just as a stable lad led a horse past at a steady pace. A wagon drawn by a carthorse rumbled to a stop outside the granary, and kitchen lads began hurriedly to load it with sacks of grain. As she watched, another wagon arrived at the kitchens, and was loaded with salt fish.

From the smith's workshops came the persistent, heavy clang of a hammer and smoke hung in the air. The very smell of the place had changed. Skeins of sparks sprayed wildly, steam rose in billows alongside the powerful hiss of tempered metal quenched in water.

As she stood trying to make sense of it, a gang of men came in through the main gateway. She could see from their clothing that they were shepherds, cattlemen and horse-breakers, though they bore roughly made weapons, instead of crooks and whips. Some of their faces were familiar from the fields she rode around, but they carried stout sticks with knives and spearheads bound to the tips, or bows slung over the shoulder and a quiver of arrows, along with rolled blankets on their backs. A second group, unknown to her, quickly followed them. Acha turned at the sound of clopping to find a stable boy leading a mule with empty panniers slung across its back.

"What's happening?" she asked him.

The boy looked at her in amazement, but said nothing.

"Tell me what is happening!" she repeated.

"The king goes to war!" he cried. "All able bodied men and boys are called to arms. The king has called for a war-hosting!"

Acha stared at him, unable to take it in. This was drastic; the fighting season was almost over. "He goes to fight… at this time of year?"

The lad shivered as though her words had chilled him. "When the king calls up all those who owe him arms, we must obey, whether it is summer warmth or winter chill." He looked past her impatiently to where the wagons were being loaded.

"Who does the king go to fight against?" she asked, as a wave of nausea rose in her throat again, her voice suddenly faint. Surely it could not be Deira? Athelfrid had seemed so pleased with her; he couldn't renege on their agreement!

The answer came quickly. "We go to war with Dalriada. Prince Theobald would not break into a feast fully armed for nothing. His scouts have seen a great army of Dalriads camped close to the Pictish border. That traitor Hering is acting as their guide!"

Acha was shocked.

"Nechtan of the Picts fights with us," the lad went on. "He'll fight for his sister's sake – our queen!"

The way he said "our queen" felt like a slap in the face, and the boy almost spat as he spoke the name of Hering. Acha now understood very clearly why Theobald had burst so rudely into the feast.

"I thank you," she said faintly.

The lad hurried off towards the stables, clearly relieved to be free of her questioning.

Acha clutched the gatepost, for she needed a moment to think. So – Hering meant to take back the throne of Bernicia with an army from Dalriada supporting him. Did he think to catch Athelfrid unawares, just as he was settling down for the bitter months? It was frightening to think that the peaceful harvest feasting could be so suddenly replaced by preparation for war. But she saw that Athelfrid could not ignore this open challenge to his throne – no king could.

She looked up and glimpsed a familiar figure coming out from one of the smaller thatched halls, carrying a heavy hempen bag. It was Bree.

"What are you doing?" Acha called to her.

The girl stopped for a moment, but then disregarded the question and marched on towards the main stables where the geldings were kept.

"Do not ignore me!" Acha shouted. She strode after the girl and when she caught up with her, she grabbed her by the shoulder. "Why, Bree?" she asked more softly now.

Bree turned to face her, sweating and pink-cheeked.

"Do you think I want to go with them?" she asked, her voice brimming over with anger. Once she'd started, the words flew from her mouth. "Do you think I want to lie in a freezing tent, unwashed and stinking, rough-handled by men who are crazed with bloodlust, when I could be sitting by your hearth, stitching braid onto your gowns?"

Acha gaped at her.

"*He* is my master," Bree went on, "*him*…not you. The idea that I might be a princess's waiting-woman was only ever a game for his amusement! He has ordered me to pack up my belongings and be ready to go with them and I have no choice but to obey. I was only set aside while he got you pregnant," she added scornfully.

Cold fury washed over Acha. "I shall see about this," she said. "I shall see."

She rushed out of the stables, shocked and furious, only to discover that a long train of her best mares trotted out into the wide corral, caparisoned in war gear, as were the young men who rode them.

She closed her eyes in horror. What of those young foals they'd leave behind? How dare he do this? What had all those promises meant? Where now were her brood-mares, to do with as she wished?

CHAPTER 11

A BREACH OF COURTESY

Acha strode across the courtyard and up the steps that led into the great hall, where she found Athelfrid sitting at a trestle with Theobald, Ulric his chief thane, and two of his hearth-companions.

"Am I not to go with you?" she demanded, without waiting for invitation or acknowledgement, unable to control her anger. "Am I not even to be *told*? You have taken my brood-mares – my morning-gift without my permission!"

The men looked, appalled, and the king answered with icy disapproval. "You forget yourself, lady! Go back to the queen's hall at once; I shall speak to you later."

She struggled to get her breath. She wanted to shout, to scream at him, but she'd caught a touch of cold steel in his voice and the flash of a warning in his eyes. What had she done? What had she said? Where was her place in all this? No honourable queen would speak to her husband so – not in front of his friends and followers. She'd committed an outrageous breach of courtesy! It took a great deal of effort to do it, but realising the enormity of her offence, she forced herself to turn away quietly and leave them.

As she walked back down the steps and across the courtyard to the queen's chamber, she found that she was trembling. She was still shaking when she arrived. Megan became anxious and made the servants bring a hot drink and a brazier packed with glowing coals.

"What has happened?" she demanded.

"They go to war," she gasped.

"War? With whom?" Megan turned pale, and Emma looked up, aghast.

"No," Acha said. "Not against Deira – they take up arms against Dalriada. Theobald has word of a vast army of Dalriads heading this way, led by Hering son of Hussa. They are taking my mares with them – and Bree rides with them too, though it seems *I* am to be left behind."

Her voice sounded pathetic and whining, even to her own ears.

Megan gaped for a moment, but then recovered briskly. "Well, what did you expect?" she asked. "You cannot follow the king to war, especially in your condition. You knew that the purpose of all this horse-breeding was always war."

Her sharp words cut through with an awful clarity and Acha saw that the pleasant days of honeymoon had somehow lulled her into a soft, dreamlike vision of the future. She'd drifted into believing that she'd live in peace and comfort with an affectionate husband at her side, once she'd become the honoured mother of the longed-for heir. It was a vision that bore no resemblance to reality. This was what exile meant: to be powerless and friendless in a strange land.

"I thought he would stay with me… at least until the child is born," she whispered.

Megan took her into her arms. "A king is a war leader first and foremost, you know that. He took Bernicia from his cousin Hering by the sword and now he must keep it by the sword."

Clover entered the chamber, carrying a pitcher of water.

"Did *you* know that the king prepared for war?" Acha demanded.

The girl looked somewhat offended by her tone. "Yes," she said. "Hering son of Hussa leads the Dalriads against us. The king has no choice but to meet him in battle. My mother remembers when the Picts and the British tribes raided our borders every spring, but now – since Athelfrid – we live in peace. The son of Hussa *must* be punished and the Dalriads too for helping him. How else can Bernicia stay strong?"

Acha felt sick and suddenly faint. "It is true that Athelfrid is a great warrior king," she managed to say.

"A weak king is no king," Clover said, her voice full of feeling.

"I've shamed myself," Acha admitted, suddenly tearful. "Will he send me back to my father, do you think?"

"No!" Clover looked appalled at the idea. "You carry his child."

Megan shrugged. "You will plead delicate state of health… a breeding woman is known to take strange fancies. He won't want you upset, it could harm the child. Now sit here in the warmth and compose yourself!"

Acha sat, but struggled with her injured feelings, still shocked that the sweetness of honeymoon had melted away so fast. It wasn't long before Athelfrid appeared his face pale and taut with anger. Emma and Clover scuttled fast away, but Megan stubbornly stood her ground, arms folded across her chest.

"Leave us," he said curtly.

"Our princess is distressed… not good for the child," she warned. Then she bobbed a curtsey and followed the others at a steadier pace.

Athelfrid took a deep breath and turned away for a moment; when he faced Acha again his expression was calmer. "You are young and have much to learn," he said.

She nodded, not trusting herself to speak.

He pulled up a stool and sat down in front of her, carefully taking her hands in his. "My cousin Hering makes blatant challenge for my throne," he said. "I was a fool to let him live and should have killed him when I had the chance. Now he leads the Dalriads to Bernicia and I cannot sit here waiting for them to come, nor can I even wait to celebrate the Night of the Dead."

"But my mares?" she whispered.

"I have told my men to take no pregnant mares, only the ones with foals well-grown. I would have explained it to you, but there was no time…"

"But they're not battle trained like your geldings."

"They are broken and used to riders," he said sharply his patience fading. "I need every steed I can lay hands on – and any loyal wife would willingly offer her morning-gift to defend the kingdom."

She hung her head, her cheeks burning and her chest so tight that her breathing felt laborious.

"Now listen to me," he went on in a gentler tone. "Your welfare is of great concern to me and I've appointed you your own protective warrior band. You will remain here for one more day. Then you travel to Dun Guardi."

"Dun Guardi?" she gasped, more shocked than ever.

"You will travel in your litter and your warrior band will escort you."

"But, I can ride Sidhe."

"No… no more riding for you until the child is born," his voice was sharp again.

"Not to ride… but that will kill me!" she cried, her words spilling out impetuously.

He looked away for a moment and when he turned back to her his icy expression made her shiver. "Give me your word on this, or I shall take your mare to war with me. Your word!" he demanded.

The threat to Sidhe brought Acha swiftly to her senses.

"I will not ride," she whispered. "You have my word."

"Very well then – you will go to Dun Guardi and present the queen with cattle, grain and gifts for the winter stores; all this will be prepared for you."

She answered him coolly. "I am your servant sir."

"You will help the queen in any way you can – her own babe is due and she…"

He hesitated, and his steely expression suddenly changed to one of distant melancholy. It seemed that he too took it for granted that another such tragedy lay ahead for Bebba. Simple decency brought a more thoughtful response from Acha.

"I will do my best," she said.

There was a moment of silence and when he spoke again it was as though he addressed an errant child. "Bebba knows her duty – she will receive you courteously. You will stay safely in my stronghold by the sea until I return. Do you understand?"

She nodded, barely able to believe this was the man who'd lain with her two nights ago and woken her at daybreak to make love again. He'd kissed her fingers one by one and then the palm of her hand, before he left her to ride out with his men.

"Come," he said, taking her by the shoulders, his voice warmer now. "Your job is to care for the coming child – we will part friends."

"Must Bree go with you?" she asked.

He drew back, his expression cold again and she knew she'd been mistaken to speak out.

"Bree always comes with me when I go to fight," he said, gruffly. "This is the way it has always been and you will have to get used to it… there have been many others. The queen tolerates the arrangement; she is not such a fool."

He got up and strode to the doorway, then turned back to give her one last command. "My warriors gather in Woden's temple tonight. You and your women will stay inside the queen's hall; Woden's rites are not for women's eyes."

That night the women supped by their hearth, disturbed by the muffled shouts and snatches of song that drifted to their ears in waves from behind the hall.

"What are they doing?" Emma asked wide-eyed.

Clover took pleasure in sharing her knowledge. "They slaughter oxen and drink the blood! They mix it with secret magic herbs," she told them.

Acha put her hand to her mouth as yet another wave of nausea rose at the back of her throat.

Clover continued, enjoying their shocked looks. "Woden's priest wears a huge horned headdress to make the sacrifices. He casts the runes too and they say he learns who will live and who will die, but he doesn't tell."

Emma shuddered. "Who'd want to know?"

A low sound like thunder rose in the distance, growing louder.

"What is that?" Emma whispered.

"They beat their shields with swords, as the games begin. My father served them last year – only men may wait on them and you *must* keep secret what I tell."

"What games?" Acha asked, fearful of the reply.

"War games – they throw knives and spears, while the youngest warriors leap to avoid them, almost naked!"

"Naked?" Emma looked more interested.

Acha frowned and her stomach lurched again, for she knew well what that meant. Her father too had held bloody ceremonies in honour of Woden whenever war threatened. She and Edwin had whispered of it together, their eyes wide with horror. Soon enough Coifi would follow in his father's footsteps and be named priest of Woden, but she couldn't imagine the gentle boy she'd loved conducting such rites.

"The high priest marks out a young warrior," Clover whispered, her voice dropping low as though the boy himself might hear. "He won't know until the last moment that he is to be the sacrifice."

The women were shocked into silence.

"My father once held such rites," Acha admitted. "But since Catraeth we have had peace in Deira."

"Your peace is due to Athelfrid's strong rule," Clover reminded her, and she wondered for a moment why she'd ever taken this loud-mouthed kitchen wench as her servant.

"To me it seems a waste of a young life," Megan said sadly. "Enough of them will die in the battle that lies ahead, whether they win or lose in these games."

"To be the chosen one – the sacrifice – is an honourable death," Clover insisted. "The young warrior will go straight to Woden's Feast-Hall. Our king claims descent from Woden himself and this sacrifice will ensure his victory."

"My father claims descent from Woden, too," Acha said.

Clover's eyes grew round. "Then lady – this son of yours will be twice Woden-born… he will surely be a great warrior."

Acha shivered. "But it may be a girl," she said. "And what then? I grow weary. Let us leave the men to their games – it is time for us to go to our beds."

Despite her tiredness, Acha spent a restless night and Clover came early to wake her. "The king is calling for you," she said.

Acha struggled from her bed, feeling alarmed. "You are not going with them too, are you?" she asked.

Clover shook her head firmly. "No. My orders are to serve you in any way I can. And I'm glad of it," she added warmly.

Acha managed a small smile, for despite her brief irritation with the girl, after a good night's sleep, she knew she'd feel safer with Clover at her side.

Her women followed, as she wandered out into the sharp morning sunlight, to find the men already mounted and ready to go. Many of them wore helmets, their brightly painted shields, short swords and axes swung from their belts.

Theobald smiled boldly at the women as they approached. "Keep our beds warm, sweethearts," he ordered.

He was answered with a hearty laugh from most of the king's companions, but the distant ranks of men who'd spent the summer beast-herding stood quietly behind the mounted warriors, pale and blinking in the morning light. Their eyes were bloodshot, and there was a remote, excited fire in their glance... it seemed the rites of Woden had continued through the night.

"Lady, you must offer the farewell mead," Clover whispered, nudging her arm.

Acha took the heavy horn from the king's cupbearer and reached up to hand it solemnly to Athelfrid, who bent down from his stallion to take it.

"May you ride with Woden at your side," she managed to say.

"The gods grant victory," his companions bellowed.

"And Freya protect you – and the child within you," Athelfrid replied formally. He handed the horn back to her with just a touch of his old, wry smile.

With Clover at her elbow issuing quiet instructions, Acha carried the mead amongst the Bernician thanes, hesitating only when she came to Woden's high priest. He reached down and curtly took the vessel from her. She suppressed a shudder as she caught the scent of blood on him – and worse. His ceremonial robes were marked with dried entrails, his hands and nails still caked with dark blood. She took the horn back and returned to Athelfrid, who waved forward one of his elderly thanes.

"This is Selwyn of Yefrin, who will escort you to Dun Guardi," he told her.

The old man bowed over her hand and winked cheerfully. "Have no fear, Princess... I shall take good care of you." She sensed that Selwyn was somewhat relieved to have a gentler task ahead of him.

Athelfrid seemed edgy and distracted, eager to leave. He glanced back down the ranks, all ready and waiting for his command, and without further ado raised his hand as the signal to move off. "To the north... against Dalriada!" he cried. "So perish all enemies of Bernicia!"

A loud and eager roar answered him.

"To the north!" they yelled.

As his hand fell, the vanguard-men moved off. Then without another backward glance, Athelfrid led the cavalry forward and his great army set off to war.

The women stepped back to watch them pass, forgetting their own anxieties in their fears for these men, some of whom were unlikely to return. Many of the young cavalrymen were those who'd cheered Acha on her bridal morning, and since then she'd watched them in training while she rode at Athelfrid's side.

Now they surged forward on their magnificent beasts and in their wake marched an army of trained foot soldiers, well-equipped with shields, axes, swords and spears. Behind them rode the older men, along with blacksmiths and carpenters, whose sturdy horses were hitched to wagons loaded with weapons and supplies. The pale-faced farmers brought up the rear, along with shepherds, tanners and thatchers, who were all clutching spears and staves, as though they were herding crooks or working tools. Finally, at the very back, rode a small contingent of women mounted on ponies or mules, well muffled and wrapped against the cold. They passed Acha and her women grim-faced and stoical. Bree rode amongst them, her usual bright finery replaced by a thick woollen cloak and fur-lined hood, her expression blank. Their eyes met briefly and somehow, despite her misery, Acha managed to raise her hand, pinching together her thumb and first finger to make the rune-sign for a safe journey.

Bree looked away unsmiling, but just before she'd vanished from sight she shifted slightly in the saddle to look back, and raised her own hand to make the sign for friendship.

The ghost of a sad smile touched Acha's lips, as she caught the brief gesture and her eyes brimmed with tears. Though she grew stiff and cold, she insisted on watching until the last wagon had rumbled away, and only then did she turn back to the queen's hall.

CHAPTER 12

DUN GUARDI

An uneasy quiet hung over Goats' Hill. Gore lay congealing in the gullies below Woden's temple, forcing the women to lift up their skirts as they returned to the queen's hall. Three fresh ox heads could be seen nailed just below the pediment of the building. Even more sinister, there appeared to be a strip of earth beneath the doorstep that was newly dug, onto which dark blood from the severed heads dripped freely.

Was Clover right? Did the body of some young man lie beneath the strip of earth? Acha looked away, trying to take her maid's practical attitude to such a death; this victim was only the first. And maybe Woden *did* demand sacrifice before he would grant victory.

She shrugged such disturbing thoughts away and turned towards the queen's hall, dwelling once again on her own concerns. How would she be received by Bebba? Did a lifetime of humiliation stretch out before her, now that Athelfrid's ardour was satisfied and maybe cooled for ever?

While Megan took charge of the packing, Acha allowed herself one last visit to the stables. Duncan was there with two of the horse-boys, too young to be marched off to war. Half the stalls were now empty and the young foals that remained were restive at the loss of their dams. The two lads struggled to feed and settle the beasts.

Acha greeted Duncan uncertainly. "Did you know that I am ordered to go to Dun Guardi?" she asked.

"Yes, lady," he said. "I have tack and blankets ready for your mares."

"I would rather stay here to help you," she said regretfully. "This house with all her mares and foals – my morning-gift – is precious to me."

Duncan nodded. "Lady, there is much we would wish, but cannot have," he said.

She smiled sadly. "You are not the only foreign slave here," she whispered.

He boldly touched her arm in sympathy. "I will take good care of these foals and mares that are left to you," he said. "We have a large supply of oats, now that…"

And he looked away, not wishing to finish his words and stress her loss.

"…Now that their dams are gone," she finished for him.

But she had found comfort in his kind words and the knowledge that though she spoke unwarily, he would be discreet.

"May your goddess go with you," he said.

"Thank you," she said, with a smile, feeling somehow calmer. "And now I will leave you to your work."

She found her women almost packed and ready for the journey.

"Try to rest for a while," Megan insisted. "We must rise early in the morning and be on the road."

Suddenly, overwhelmed by weariness, Acha went to lie on her bed, while the women tiptoed about her, their voices hushed.

They set off soon after dawn the following morning, escorted by Selwyn and the warrior band. Acha felt sick as she climbed into her litter. She sat back as it was lifted, and tried hard to ignore the irksome rocking that must come with it. The other women were mounted on mules, and a groom rode Sidhe.

They headed eastwards and as the journey progressed the morning chill lifted and the sun came out, the nausea faded as she became accustomed to the swaying movement of the litter. Once the warmth of the sun penetrated the clouds, she pulled open the curtains to observe the pleasant, green, gently rolling hills. Having crossed the

River Glen, they stopped at noon to eat beside an ancient Roman road, and then travelled on in a north-easterly direction through the afternoon, the sun now warm on their backs. They came in sight of Athelfrid's great fortress by the sea, just as the light began to fade.

Despite her anxiety as to the reception she'd receive from Bebba, Acha found her spirits lifting at her first sighting of the sea. Dun Guardi stood high on a wide rock, surrounded by a double wooden palisade, the outer one built on top of a sturdy stonewall. A substantial settlement sprawled in the shadow of the fortress, but beyond it, smooth golden beaches stretched as far as the eye could see, both to the northwest and the southeast.

As they moved on the sun sank lower still, mottling the vast stretch of sand with patches of pink and gold. The sea was calm and still – deep lavender blue darkening to charcoal grey along the line of the horizon. The stillness was broken only by flocks of gulls and terns and a few sea eagles soaring high above intermittent patches of white foam.

"What are those shapes out there?" she asked, Selwyn.

"They are the Islands, lady," he said with a smile, relieved that his young charge seemed less gloomy than when they'd set out.

Acha and the other women stared at the vast, flat horizon, for this long, low shoreline was nothing like the towering cliffs that bounded most of the Deiran coast. Even Clover gasped at the wide-openness of it.

"I never seen anything like it," she murmured.

"But Clover, surely you've seen this place before?" Acha asked.

"No, Lady," she said. "I've never come *this* far."

As they approached the outer palisade, the keeper opened the gates for them and they rode in, expecting some kind of reception. Instead they found the place very still and quiet. The many huts and stalls that clustered about the inner gate were empty of goods and appeared deserted. Even Selwyn looked a little uneasy as he brought his horse to a halt and dismounted. Acha glanced at Megan and braced herself for more humiliation. Had the queen vanished once again, leaving an empty fortress behind her? Or even worse – might she find herself locked out?

At last there came the sound of running feet and a small flurry of activity followed as the inner gates were hastily opened. A well-dressed man, his belt heavy with keys, hurried out to meet them, flanked by a few guards. They could see at once that he was agitated.

"The reeve," Selwyn told her. "I will go forward to announce you lady."

He dismounted and both men conferred for a moment and then turned anxiously to look at the women. Selwyn came back to help Acha as she stepped from the litter. "This is Bron, the reeve," he told her. "I'm afraid the king's message arrived rather late."

Bron bowed twice in quick succession. "I'm so sorry Princess," he said. "Please forgive this rude welcome… you see the queen is very ill."

Acha was stunned for a moment, but then reminded herself that the birth might be imminent or even overdue. Uneasy at the thought of witnessing her rival's suffering, she stood uncertainly by her litter, wanting only to get back into it and flee.

"But where are all the servants?" she asked at last.

The man bowed again and looked apologetic. "By the time we got the message that you were coming, the queen's women had set off across the sands to celebrate the Night of the Dead, leaving only my wife and a small number of servants to stay behind. The queen herself told them to go, and so you see…"

Acha looked blank for a moment.

"The Night of the Dead," she murmured. "I had forgotten the day. It was all so sudden… the preparation for war and the king's departure. But did you say they have gone over the sands?"

"Yes. Over the sands to the sacred island and the queen has taken a turn for the worse. I knew I shouldn't have let them go, but the queen herself insisted…"

He looked so forlorn, his manner so anxious that Acha felt forced to respond politely. "It cannot be helped," she conceded. "Do not distress yourself."

"The queen has given orders for you to be welcomed and given the guest chamber in the queen's hall. She wishes to see you first, but cannot leave her bed. Will you come this way, lady?"

Acha nodded and followed him, but her heart sank to her boots. Surely a sick, vengeful queen might be even more dangerous than a healthy one.

She glanced fearfully at Megan, but her nurse whispered low to her. "This might be for the best. You will meet Bebba without those sour-faced women crowding all around."

The courtyard, mead-hall and booths were empty as they passed through, and only a little light and activity showed in the open thatched area where cooking pots hung over two smoking fires.

"You say they have all gone over the sands?" Acha asked, desperately trying to understand the situation.

"Yes lady… every year they do it. They go to the Isle of Metcalfe, sacred to Hella, Queen of the Dead. The high rock is her holy place; they light a bonfire there and sing and dance. Once there, they will stay until the tide ebbs in the morning, for the island casts its own strange magic and briefly holds them prisoner there. They'll be wandering back across the sands in the morning, but they won't reach here till late in the afternoon, and I fear they will only be fit for their beds, when they get back."

A shiver ran down her back. "I've heard of this," she said.

And as she followed the reeve she dug deep into her memory. Yes, she'd heard of an island temple, where the goddess held her worshippers with the power of the tide – a place of powerful magic.

"Do you celebrate such feasts?" Bron asked.

"Oh yes," she said quickly. "My brother and his fellows will be flocking to the temple close to my father's summer palace. They'll drink and dance all night out there on the hills. But we have no enchanted isle," she admitted. "The haste to go off to war made us forget the importance of the day. I suppose the king will celebrate as best he can, wherever they make camp, on their way to do battle with the Dalriads."

Bron opened the heavy wooden door for her and smiled. "The king usually leaves such things to his queen," he said vaguely – and Acha sensed that Athelfrid might secretly scorn the island celebrations, just as he privately scorned Goat-headed Freya.

"Woden is his god," she murmured.

Bron nodded and Acha thought she caught some subtle meaning behind his words as he answered softly. "Yes Woden – and Loki!"

He led them past a smoking hearth, empty trestles and benches, then up the few steps that led to Bebba's chamber. "The Queen wishes to see you alone," he said, glancing meaningfully at her women. "I will take your servants to the chamber that's prepared for you."

Suddenly fearful, Acha caught hold of Megan's arm.

"I must keep my nurse with me," she said. "She is used to seeing women close to birth and will not even speak unless I tell her to."

"The queen may be displeased," he warned, but he opened the door and ushered them inside.

Bebba's room was as rich and comfortable as might be expected and Acha recognised some of the bright wall hangings that she'd glimpsed briefly at Goats' Hill, before they were so hurriedly snatched away.

The queen herself had certainly changed since they last saw her. She was formally dressed, but lay propped on cushions on the bed, looking hot and uncomfortable, with just one woman to serve her. She struggled to rise as Acha came into her room.

"Please don't get up," Acha begged.

But Bebba insisted on struggling to her feet, supported by the woman, who Acha realised must be Bron's wife.

The queen carried the baby high. She did not have the look of a woman about to give birth, but her face was pink, her hair undressed and slightly dishevelled. The whorls on her cheeks appeared as dark mottled patches against the unhealthy flushing of her skin.

"I trust your journey went well. I have made arrangements for your comfort," Bebba said, unsmiling and formal. "Please forgive our lack of servants; they will return tomorrow night."

"It's no hardship," Acha said, curtseying rather late in the day. Then to fill the awkward silence that followed, she added, "I have brought gifts and supplies of stock and grain with me."

"Of course, as my husband promised," Bebba added quickly, reminding her where the power lay.

The queen sank back down to the bed with a small gasp of pain and Acha wondered if she should slip away, but Bebba recovered her dignity almost immediately. "You may go to your chamber," she said, dismissing them. "Edith, show them out."

They left quickly, relieved that it had been so brief a meeting, to find Bron waiting outside ready to take them to their room.

The guest chamber was large and comfortable and Emma and Clover were already unpacking some of the coffers that they'd brought. Megan sat down wearily, looking distracted, unusually oblivious to their new surroundings. Almost at once two young girls arrived to serve them a simple meal of bread, cheese and smoked mackerel, washed down with mead, followed by honeyed sweetmeats. They fell on the food, as they were hungry after their journey, all but Megan who still seemed to have her mind on something else.

"That's a breech," she whispered darkly, once the servants had gone.

Acha frowned. "What? You mean Bebba's child?"

Megan shook her head ominously, "A breech and riding far too high."

Acha shrugged, pushing away concern, she'd surely find herself in a strong position once Bebba miscarried – as everyone thought she must – so long as Acha's child survived.

"So – you are saying that this one is likely to go the same way as the others?"

"Aye," Megan agreed, and she gave a small shrug. "And in some ways, it would be better still for you, if Bebba were to die."

Acha looked up, startled. "What did you say? She might die? But surely a breech birth need not mean the mother dies?"

Megan's expression remained grim. "Carrying a babe so high and the wrong way round, at her age will likely kill her."

Acha was stunned at this new possibility and she could not help but see that it offered quite a different vision of the future. If Bebba died, might *she* become queen of Bernicia in her place? If she bore Athelfrid a healthy son and Bebba died, surely then she'd become the most powerful woman in the northern lands? The bitter humiliation, the rivalry – it would simply be wiped away with one death, two if you counted the child. Was this what the carlin had foretold when she warned that blood would be the price of Acha bearing sons for Bernicia?

And yet her heart sank stone-heavy at the thought. She swallowed hard and forced herself to ask the question uppermost in both of their minds.

"Could anything be done to save her or the babe?"

Megan huffed and shrugged. "Without getting a closer look it's hard to say, but an experienced midwife might manage it, with the co-operation of the mother. The turning of the child would not be comfortable for her… but yes, I think I could probably do it. I have done such things before."

Acha frowned. Clover and Emma glanced up at each other and stirred uneasily at this whispered talk of life and death.

"I've nought to gain by letting you help her and much to lose," Acha admitted. "You should have left well alone and never mentioned it. If I bid you try to help her and you fail – then *I'd* be blamed for her death!"

"I only said *perhaps* I could help," Megan told her roundly.

They sat in angry silence for a moment, but then Megan's face grew more thoughtful. "Maybe you *would* have something to gain by offering help," she said at last.

"What could I want from *her?*"

Megan smiled softly as she answered. "Perhaps you'd gain the queen's gratitude – a touch of kindness towards you – even friendship maybe."

"Gratitude," Acha almost spat it out. "Do you think I'd get gratitude from that barbarian?"

Clover looked shocked, but Megan used to Acha's brief flares of temper refused to be cowed; she carried on making her opinion plain. "A woman in childbirth is a desperate creature," she said. "She does not forget the midwife who brings her comfort in her time of need. But if you are set against it – I could cast the runes and ask Freya for guidance."

"You do what you want… I'm going out for air," Acha said, as her nurse began to fish in the rune-pouch that swung from her girdle.

She was somewhat unnerved to discover that she was trembling as she got to her feet. Emma moved to escort her, but the angry glance she flashed in her maid's direction made her back away.

CHAPTER 13

BETWEEN LIFE AND DEATH

Lost in the unfamiliar hall, Acha strode down the passageway, only knowing that she headed in the opposite direction from the queen's chamber. Very soon, she found that a fresh, cool, draught of air led her not to the outside of the building as she'd expected, but onto a small space, open to the air and built high above the palisade. As she stepped out onto it, she caught the sound of rushing waves beneath her. A wooden handrail had been built for safety and she clung to it, as she took in great lungfuls of the salt-laden air.

A bonfire flickered in the far distance and she wondered if that could be the strange island where the living met the dead. She took a few more steadying breaths of fresh air as the moon emerged from heavy clouds and almost magically a shimmering-silver pathway appeared across the waves, a pathway that led far away and out to sea. Faint, haunting cries drifted on the breeze; they came and went, and put her in mind of babes that wailed in hunger. The ethereal sounds sent shivers running down her spine – could the mewlings be the sad, lost voices of the dead? She thought of the babe in Bebba's belly, poised between life and death.

Megan's frank words had forced fresh hopes and fears to leap and tangle in her mind. Could she stand by and let Bebba die without lifting a finger to help? Acha scorned mean-mindedness, but the offer of aid in this dire situation must certainly carry risk with it. What if she interfered and Bebba died? Might she stand accused of murder? But, how would it feel to stand by and watch a woman's life ebb away, knowing that she could have tried to help?

She'd been raised as most kings' daughters were, to have knowledge of herbs and healing, of birth and death. Under Megan's expert tutelage she'd assisted at birthings and knew that Megan's assessment of the situation rang true. As her father's hostess, she'd dispensed both medicines and special foods to those who were sick. She and Megan had only ever once refused to give help, and that was when they regretfully left Eforwic. The distant whimpering that now drifted across the sea echoed the terrible cries of the drowning children. She'd left them then because she'd had little choice in it. Now the choice was hers – and what of this child?

Why couldn't Megan have kept her mouth shut? Acha would soon be in need of the goddess's aid at the birth of her own child, and that too was an uncomfortable thought.

She took a last deep breath of salty air, gritted her teeth and walked back inside, her mind made up, whatever the outcome – she would never again leave a woman or child to die, not if she could do anything to prevent it.

Instead of returning to her chamber, she hurried down the dimly lit wooden passageway until she found the queen's chamber. Standing still for a moment, she caught the sound of a small bleat of suppressed pain, just as Edith hurried through the doorway carrying a slop pot. The woman stopped, astounded to see Acha standing there in the shadows.

"What are you doing here… Princess?" she asked, suspiciously.

"The servants should never have gone to the island and left the queen like this," Acha said fiercely.

Edith answered defensively, carefully keeping her voice low. "Do you think the queen wants an audience for what is to come?" she said. "It was the queen herself who sent them away."

They stood awkwardly facing each other and Acha knew she must somehow or other make her intention clear. "I know you hate me," she began. "And I understand well why you do, but…" Then she spoke the words that she knew must change their lives for good or ill. "But… I think I can help the queen if she will let me. My nurse Megan is the most skilled midwife in Deira… that's why I brought her here with me."

"What?" Edith stared as though she thought her mad. "You'd offer the help of your woman – you think we'd trust you?"

A deep groan of suppressed anguish issued from the queen's chamber, and they both shuddered.

"You will see!" Acha said, and she pushed impatiently past the woman, almost making her spill the contents of the slop pot, as she marched into Bebba's chamber.

The queen was curled up on the bed, eyes closed, her face grey and trickling with sweat in the candlelight. A string of small sheep-like bleats came from deep within her throat.

Edith rushed after her and hastily deposited the pot on a chest in the corner. "How dare you? How dare you force your way in here?" she cried. "You – who are no better than a concubine!"

Acha ignored the insult and turned to Edith, trying to think calmly. She needed to win this woman over if anything was to be done – and she struggled to see what argument might carry weight with her. "This child cannot be born," she said. "Not in the position that it's in. I think you know it too, if you are honest and truly have your mistress's welfare at heart."

Edith opened her mouth to give a furious reply but hesitated for just a fraction of a moment and Acha saw that her words had somehow hit home.

She rushed on, seizing the advantage. "The child could perhaps be turned by a skilled midwife."

"No! My mistress needs nobody but me! Your woman is the last person we could trust." There was a moment of tense silence, but then Edith looked down at the queen and spoke again in quieter, more reasoned tones. "How can we trust you?"

Acha could think of nothing that might convince the woman, so instead she dropped down onto her knees beside the bed and spoke directly to Bebba. "Let me bring my nurse to help you," she begged. "She is highly skilled as a midwife and will do you no harm. I promise you."

Bebba struggled to open her eyes. "Why… why should you help me?" she whimpered.

Acha stretched out her hand and gently touched the lank, damp hair. "I would not wish to stand by and watch any woman die, or her babe," she whispered. "I think you know what is at risk – what have you got to lose?"

"It is… too late," Bebba panted.

"Let me bring Megan!"

Suddenly, much to Acha's surprise, Edith too dropped down on her knees beside the queen. "Lady, perhaps we should let this midwife try," she said.

Bebba gritted her teeth as a strong pain came and, for a few moments, she was lost to them and could only moan, like an injured beast. As the spasm ebbed away, she nodded. "Bring your woman," she whispered. "You are right – what have I got to lose?"

Acha got to her feet and fled back down the passageway, shouting wildly for Megan. She had a moment of confusion, not sure where the chamber was, but Megan appeared through a doorway looking flushed and anxious.

"I have cast the runes for you," she said.

"No time for that," Acha said, grabbing her arm. "Come! Do your best for her… and save the babe too, if you can. I will help."

They hurried away, leaving Clover and Emma staring after them, their faces pale and terrified.

Edith was waiting anxiously and now seemed willing to do anything to help. "Shall I fetch mead?" she asked uncertainly.

"Yes," Megan said, "I have poppy juice, but we cannot give too much of that." She patted the little horn bottle that swung from her belt alongside the rune-bag and – practical at once – began rolling up her sleeves.

"Now Lady, let us see what we can do for you."

She approached the bed, lifted the covers and, without any hesitation, pulled up Bebba's shift. She proceeded to examine the swollen belly with gentle, confident hands and the queen made no protest. It seemed she was past caring what they did to her now.

"Yes," Megan said addressing the queen in a business-like manner. "See here lady… this is the back of the child's head, a little to the side and high beneath your breasts, and here are the feet down below; I can feel them trying to kick."

"Is it not too late?" Edith asked.

"I think not," Megan said, her hands roaming once again over Bebba's belly. "Have the waters broken?"

"No," said Edith.

"Then it's not too late." She bent over the bed so that her face was close to Bebba's. "Lady, I am going to push your babe's little backside upwards and his head and shoulders down where they ought to be. It will be painful, but it may save you both."

"Painful? Do you think I care about pain?" Bebba responded, with a growl and a touch of her old fire. "I have had years of pain. I only care that you do not harm the child. If you kill it, I shall have *you* killed... both of you," she said, turning to include Acha in her glance. "Do you hear that, Edith? If I die and the child dies too, they are both to be slaughtered."

Megan pulled a wry face. "Well then... we'd best be very careful. Here now take a sip of this; it will help to keep you calm."

Acha rolled up her own sleeves, ready to assist as best she could.

"Lay her flat!" Megan ordered, having administered a few drops of poppy juice.

Edith helped Acha remove the cushions and pillows from the bed and they soon had the queen lying flat on her back. They took their places on either side, ready to help.

"Freya guide my hands," Megan whispered and she began digging with the heels of her hands into the taught flesh of Bebba's belly. Deeper and deeper she went, while the queen gritted her teeth and groaned.

"My poor lady," Edith cried, trying to soothe the queen by stroking her hair and forehead.

Deeper and deeper into the tight flesh went Megan's hands, rolling and pushing. Deeper and deeper – until it seemed as though she'd cupped the babe's small rump in one hand, while she searched for its tiny skull with the other, grunting with the effort of it all.

The queen grabbed hold of Acha's wrist and gripped it tightly. It hurt and she flinched, but didn't withdraw her hand.

"By Goat-headed Freya... I shall hurt *you* as much as I can!" Bebba growled and gave a great beast-like roar, as Megan dug deep again and pushed the head firmly downwards.

"Oh lady… lady," Edith cried. "Sweet Freya, help us!"

Megan grunted with the effort of her work. "Go on little one, get your head down!" she urged.

Bebba bared her teeth in a snarl and then flopped back, inert, releasing Acha's hand. Megan worked on regardless and Acha watched wide-eyed, holding her breath, as the smooth bulge of the baby's head vanished, swiftly to be replaced by the gentler curve of the rump.

"That's it," Megan said giving one last push, which settled the babe into a better place.

Acha gasped. "A somersault," she whispered. "That babe has done a somersault."

Megan wiped sweat from her forehead and grinned. "Aye, that's exactly it," she said, allowing herself a huge sigh of relief.

Edith was speechless with dread, for Bebba lay still and white upon the bed. The three women watched in silence, but after a moment or two the queen's eyelids fluttered and a faint flush crept back into her cheeks.

"Is it done?" she murmured.

"Yes, lady," Edith whispered, her throat constricting as though she fought back tears.

Megan gently patted the bulging belly that now protruded much lower down and respectfully pulled the queen's shift down to restore her modesty. "The little backside is where it ought to be and the head well down in the proper place," she said firmly.

Clover appeared in the doorway, with Emma behind her. "Can we help?" they asked.

Megan nodded. "Fetch the queen some mead."

Acha picked up the pillows and cushions that they'd tossed aside, and began to replace them. Bebba struggled to sit upright again, but before she'd managed to get herself comfortable she gave a small cry. A dark watery stain grew between her legs, marking both her shift and the fine linen sheet.

"Ah, lady…" Edith began.

But Megan refused to be harassed.

"Aye – I thought that might happen – nowt to be fearful about.

Turning the child has set you off and released the waters; you'll be seeing your babe very soon, lady. Rest now while you can. A sip of mead will help, before the pains return."

Bebba sat up against the cushions and when Clover arrived with the cup, she took a few sips of mead. As she handed back the cup, her face contorted. "The pains…" she announced, then gritted her teeth.

Acha backed away towards the door, but Bebba caught her movement. "You will stay," she cried, "both of you!"

Megan simply rolled up her sleeves once more, while Acha moved reluctantly back to the bed.

"What can *we* do?" Clover asked.

Megan replied briskly. "We need clean cloths, warm water, my bundles of herbs and a pot and brazier with glowing coals."

"I'll show you where," Edith offered, and the three of them scuttled away

All through the night Megan and Edith worked together to ease Bebba's suffering, while Acha sat by the bed doggedly offering her hand when the pains came. Her women fetched and carried from the kitchen and the well.

"You should go to your bed," Megan whispered to Acha during the early hours of the morning, seeing her pale and weary face.

But Acha shook her head, for she could never have gone back to her chamber and slept.

A baby boy slithered out of his mother's body and into the world, as shards of light came creeping through the wooden casement. Megan cut the cord and rubbed his body with soft lamb's wool and goose grease. He gave a piercing cry as they laid him on a clean shawl.

Acha experienced a moment of triumph. She went to stand at Megan's elbow. This child was a boy and he was strong, curling and uncurling his little fists at her, and waving his legs in the air.

"You must present him to the queen," Megan whispered.

"Not I," Acha murmured.

"Yes. It must be *you*," Megan insisted. "Or we'll lose all we've worked to gain this night."

"I've gained nothing," she whispered.

Megan put the child unceremoniously into Acha's arms. "Look at him," she said. "Maybe he is what the fates intended."

Acha swallowed and looked down at him, while he regarded her solemnly. He was perfect, pink-skinned with a faint fuzz of golden hair covering the fragile bones of his skull, so delicate and vulnerable. How could she ever wish him harm? She took a deep breath, swallowed hard and carried him to Bebba, who was lying exhausted on the pillows.

"You have a beautiful, strong son," she said, putting him carefully into his mother's arms.

Bebba looked at the child bewildered. Her mouth began working frantically as she tried to speak, but for a moment her emotions were so powerful that speech was impossible. Then, suddenly, the queen saw how deeply she'd marked Acha's hand with her nails when she had gripped it so hard in her agony.

"Have I done that to you?" she cried.

Acha backed away, but the queen snatched her hand.

"It's nothing," Acha said.

"Not nothing!" the queen managed at last. "It is everything! You should have left me to die, but you came to my aid. I have a child and he lives."

Acha glanced across to Megan. "It was my nurse's skills," she acknowledged.

"But the decision to help was yours," Bebba said. "And you sat beside me all night to comfort me."

Edith opened the shutters and the morning light flooded in; she smiled warmly at them all. "Name him, lady," she said.

Bebba's lips trembled with emotion again and it was hard for her to form the words. "Enfrid. I shall call him Enfrid… a son at last by the grace of the gods."

"Enfrid is a good name," Edith agreed.

"Princess Acha, will you sit here a while, beside me?" Bebba asked. It was not an order, more a plaintive request.

Acha pulled forward a stool and sat down beside the bed and this time Bebba patted her hand gently.

Sensing that this could be the best moment for her to make her own situation plain, she said "I too am with child."

The queen turned briefly away, composed her face, and then looked back and nodded. "Then, when your time comes… I shall help you, as you have helped me," she said.

"Thank you," Acha murmured.

A sense of relief came and then exhaustion washed over her. Bebba suddenly saw the girl's pallor. "You are pregnant and I must let you go to rest," she said. "You have watched with me all night and I am grateful for it, but now you must go to your chamber and sleep."

This time it *was* an order. Acha got up, curtseyed and went to her room. The runes were lying where Megan had cast them and as she drifted off to sleep she wondered vaguely what the outcome had been, for she'd never learned to read them herself.

CHAPTER 14

BY THE GRACE OF THE GODS

It was noon before Megan came back to Acha's chamber, pale and exhausted, her apron still stained with birth blood.

Acha roused herself to greet her.

"You did a good job, and you did it for me," she said. "You must rest now, but tell me first – what did the runes say? There was no time to ask."

Megan sat down heavily on her truckle bed and frowned. "The runes said – 'what you give, you will receive!'"

"What does that mean?"

She shrugged. "You know the runes speak in mysterious ways. Perhaps it means that you too will get what you have given… a healthy son."

Acha got swiftly up from her bed and kissed her nurse. "You lie down here and sleep," she said. "And when you wake, I shall wait on *you*."

So Megan slept and, while Emma bustled about their chamber, Acha went with Clover to see if she could find the lookout spot that she'd discovered the night before. Now, in daylight, the view over the islands and down the coast was breathtaking; the tide had retreated and the Sacred Isle was part of the mainland once again – the vast stretch of sand that linked it spread out along the coast.

Sea eagles swooped overhead, startling flocks of noisy gulls, while in the distance dark dots like ants moved across the pale golden miles. It was the palace servants returning along the safe pathway that lay far to the west.

"It will be a while before they get here," Acha murmured.

"And I daresay they'll be stunned when they do," Clover replied, with a wide smile.

Later that afternoon, the palace servants began straggling back to Dun Guardi, some on foot, some pulled in carts, some mounted, but all of them pale-faced and puffy-eyed.

Bebba's women were no less affected by their night of celebration and hurried to their beds, to sleep until the following morning. When they did at last appear in the queen's chamber, ready to take up their work again, they stared open-mouthed at the astonishing sight that met them there.

The queen was weary but elated and on her lap rolled a baby boy, who roared loudly and fed fiercely at his mother's breast, for no wet-nurse had been engaged, so sure was everyone that the queen's pregnancy would end in miscarriage or stillbirth. A queen giving suck to her own child was almost unheard of, but the sight of the hated Deiran bride at the queen's bedside was the most bewildering thing of all. And when Bebba grew so weary that she had to fall asleep, it was to Acha of Deira that she passed her child to be soothed and cosseted.

"What has happened there?"

"They are sharing a mead cup – see!"

"They say she saved the babe somehow!"

The servants walked about in a stunned daze for the very core of their world had changed while they caroused on the Sacred Isle.

***

Athelfrid lifted the heavy flap of his tent of skins and growled. He'd just made camp, but it was growing cold and a light sleet was falling. If it continued this way they'd soon be wallowing in mud. His heart rose at the thought of battle, but nobody could relish fighting in these conditions. Utter fury that his cousin Hering had dared to make this challenge drove him on. He knew that his men would resolutely follow him, however much mud they marched through and however much hail rained down on them.

He turned at the approach of one of Nechtan's scouts. The man greeted him with the news that King Aidan's army of Dalriads and Ulstermen was camped on the far side of the Dawston Burn, just over the hill on the horizon.

"Are they as large a gathering as we thought?" he asked.

The scout hesitated, apprehension clear on his face.

Athelfrid knew that look. "So… there are many?" he asked.

"Yes, my lord."

"Have they horses?"

"Yes, lord."

"And do they know that we are here?"

"I think not yet, but they soon will."

"Just so," he agreed. "We will be seen by them as we breast the hill."

"Yes, lord," the man said, picking up the king's thoughts. "But you will come from the higher ground and the Dawston brook is shallow, easily crossed."

"Ah!" Athelfrid's eyes glinted with fire. "So if we lead our cavalry to the top of the hill and ride down on them at dawn we might take them unprepared? Our foot soldiers will swarm down after the cavalry."

The man hesitated for a moment – the action his leader proposed was not an honourable one – but he recalled that they were brought here by the treacherous plans of a traitor. He quickly recovered his wits.

"Aye," he nodded. "The Dalriads argue with your cousin Hering, not trusting him I think. They will not expect…"

Athelfrid smiled fiercely, and let the tent flap drop. He clenched his fist. "So maybe their distrust of a traitor will be their undoing. Could you lead us to the brow of the hill in darkness?"

"Yes, Lord, I know this land well!"

"Then we will do it," Athelfrid said. "Fetch Theobald to me!"

Excitement and anticipation blazed afresh in him. If against all the odds, he could catch Hering and the Dalriads unawares he might slaughter them into submission. And then… he would not just have won security for his own throne, but the right to demand tribute from all the lands of the Dalriads. Was Loki on his side again? His heart and courage leapt at the thought of it. More power – more power than any of the invading Angles had gained since they came across the sea to look for land.

When his brother arrived, Athelfrid clapped him on the shoulder. "We move tonight. The cavalry will ride down on them at dawn!" he said. "They'll have no chance to form a shieldwall."

Theobald stared at him, astounded. "No negotiations?" he asked.

"Do those who listen to a traitor's lies deserve a chance to negotiate?" Athelfrid demanded.

Theobald hesitated, thinking fast. Woden was known to walk the earth disguised – his all-seeing eye watching what men did and that was a troubling thought. But Hering's action in leading the Dalriads towards Bernicia was dishonourable and went against all rules of kinship. At last Theobald smiled – Loki, the trickster was Athelfrid's god.

"Brother, we are here to win!" he agreed at last.

"Our men are fresh and eager now," Athelfrid said, "but if this filthy weather goes on they'll lose heart. We will set out in darkness to take the higher ground while the Dalriads sleep, and wait for dawn. The burn is shallow enough to cross. Our horses will set them running unawares from their tents, then our spears will follow. Our axemen and swords will be waiting. Nechtan's household troops will be ready too."

"It is a wild plan, brother," Theobald said, his eyes now gleaming with reflected fire. "You are The Trickster – truly The Trickster!"

"Together. We must be completely together," Athelfrid thumped his clenched fist upon the trestle. "That is the only way that we can beat them, brother. Let us get this done and return to Dun Guardi, where we have a warm hearth and women waiting!"

"Aye," Theobald answered with a laugh. "And some of us have more than most!"

***

At Dun Guardi, Blood-month brought the slaughter of cattle and goats. Haunches of meat were smoked above every hearth and the kitchens were well stocked. No messages arrived from Athelfrid and even though Selwyn and some of the other elderly thanes warned that the Dalriads were reputed to be skilful fighters, Athelfrid's reputation as a warrior kept spirits high.

Bebba recovered from childbirth and her joy at the delivery of a healthy son spread through the fortress, cheering the servants and townsfolk. There was much talk of celebration when the king returned victorious, as he surely would.

Gradually Acha found her feet in these new surroundings; her progress was hastened by the change in the queen's attitude towards her. Thanes' wives and waiting women, who'd once treated her with icy coldness, now approached her with courtesy, addressing her respectfully as "Princess", some even going so far as to present her with small gifts of jewellery, fine clothing and sweetmeats.

Megan became smug. "Didn't I tell you that you'd gain from the bairn's safe arrival?" she whispered, when yet another dish of honeyed nuts arrived in their chamber early one morning. "Didn't I say it?"

"Yes, you have said it many times," Acha agreed.

One morning early in Yule-month Edith appeared in Acha's chamber. "The queen wishes you to wait on her," she announced. "It is a matter of great importance," she hinted, but would say no more.

Clover and Emma bustled about, looking to find a suitable gown and warm the smoothing stones.

When Acha arrived in Bebba's chamber, she found her having her hair elaborately braided, while Enfrid slept contentedly in her arms. The queen wore a linen gown, twice dyed to a deep gold, trimmed with green and gold tablet weave, a heavy gold and garnet pendant about her neck.

Acha curtseyed respectfully, sensing that a certain formality might be attached to this occasion, whatever it might be.

"Is there news, lady?" she asked.

"No, no word from the king," Bebba said absently. "But today I go to Hella's temple on the Sacred Isle. Even though I missed her sacred rites on the Night of the Dead, still the goddess smiled on me, so now I must make my offerings and give thanks. I wondered... if you'd accompany me?" she said, with just a touch of hesitation.

"Yes, lady," Acha said, surprised and pleased at the invitation, which must surely be yet another sign of the queen's continuing warmth towards her. What was more, she'd wanted to go to the strange half island, but hadn't been sure how she might arrange a visit.

Bebba nodded. "Good. If you can be ready before noon, we'll take a boat across at high tide and stay overnight. The priestesses offer accommodation in simple shacks, but I think you will find it satisfactory. You should make your own offerings and beg that the goddess brings you too safely through childbirth."

Acha nodded uncertainly. "I will be guided in this by you, lady. What offering should I make?"

"Hella has no love of gold or sacrificed animals. Fruit will be most acceptable," Bebba said.

Acha returned to her chamber and, while her women prepared her clothes, she wandered down to the thatched apple stores, outside the kitchens to spend time carefully choosing a small selection of the most perfect fruits.

The two wives of Athelfrid left the fortress together and rode down to the wooden staithe in the queen's litter, where the royal barge *Flame-Bearer* was waiting for them.

Before the sun reached its zenith the sea had crept into the bay, reclaiming all the sandbanks. The place was popular with many grey seals, who dived into the advancing waves when the tide rushed in. A row of cormorants lined the staithe, and performed their cheerful wing-drying dance.

The ship's captain, had rigged an oiled canopy for the queen's protection and provided snowy lambskin rugs for warmth. Bebba insisted that Acha sit beside her under the shelter, and Enfrid slept warm in a soft woven basket at their side, for he too must be carried to the Isle to be blessed by the goddess. Edith and Megan settled themselves further along the boat within call of their mistresses and fell comfortably into a discussion of the various benefits of herbs.

"But would you use thyme for a fever?" Edith queried.

"For a fever with a dry cough," Megan nodded, "and for milk fever too."

As the barge pulled away from the staithe the queen sat in silence, nervously fingering a small leather bag that hung from her girdle. Acha judged it best to remain quiet, nursing the basket of near perfect green, gold apples she'd chosen from the apple store, as her own offering to the goddess of the otherworld.

Twenty pairs of slaves pulled on the oars, setting the boat to dip and lift a little as the waves battered its prow. Sharp-beaked terns soared about them, making tiny peeping cries as they dipped into the surf. Once they were out into the deeper water, Bebba seemed to relax a little and recall that she had invited company. "Have you had communication from your father, Princess?" she enquired politely.

Acha shook her head. She'd heard nothing from Deira at all and though she longed for news of Edwin and the others, she told herself it would be a costly thing for Aelle to send a messenger.

"No, lady," she replied. "Do you hear from your brother?"

Bebba shrugged. "Rarely. I send a messenger every harvest with presents and news… and the messenger usually brings me a reply before Yule. Perhaps I will hear from him sooner this year, as he rides with the king, against the Dalriads. I've sent messengers to announce the birth of Enfrid, but the news will take a while to reach their camp – wherever that may be."

There was another silence until Bebba spoke again. "*I* could send a messenger to your father if you wish!"

"Oh yes, lady!" Acha was eager. "I should be very glad to let him know that I am well and I'd be relieved to hear that he and my brother both thrive."

Bebba nodded. "You should tell him that you are with child – and I daresay he'll be pleased," she added with a soft sigh. "I shall see it done."

Two fat seals surfaced beside them and regarded them intently before vanishing once more beneath the waves. Emboldened by the queen's kindness, Acha determined to say something she'd had in mind since the night of Enfrid's birth.

"I… I would not have come to Bernicia, Lady," she began, falteringly.

Bebba's head jerked up sharply and Acha feared she'd given offence, but she went on with her speech, determined to finish what she'd started. "I would not have come to Bernicia, offering myself as a bride, if it were not for the ruined harvest… and my father's fears for our kingdom."

The queen gave a sharp nod. "The choice was not yours," she acknowledged. "I see that your father was in a difficult situation – too old to lead a war-band himself and your brother too young, I hear. You were sent as a peaceweaver bride to hold off trouble and you are not the first; I, too, was given to Athelfrid in just such a way. My brother now rules in Dun Eidyn, only with Athelfrid's permission."

Acha stared, astonished.

"Oh, yes," Bebba smiled wryly. "My father sought to protect his kingdom from Athelfrid by offering me as wife. I thought I'd failed them all, but… now I have Enfrid," and she looked down fondly at the sleeping babe beside her. "Did you know that the Picts choose their king through the mother's line?"

"I think I have heard of such a thing," Acha admitted, and suddenly her eyes widened as she realised the full significance of this. "So – your little Enfrid could be heir to the Pictish throne?"

Both women smiled as he opened two sleepy blue eyes and regarded them for a moment, just as though he knew they spoke of him, and then closed them again.

"It is possible," Bebba said.

They sat quietly again, contemplating the potential power of a prince who could unite the Bernician kingdom with that of the Picts.

Then Bebba spoke again. "I heard you had an older brother?"

Acha nodded sadly. "Aelric was the child of my father's first wife. He led the Deiran forces to Catraeth and was killed in the fighting there; it was a bitter blow and my father has never ceased to mourn him."

Bebba looked thoughtful. "Families of king's have such tangled kinships; two of my cousins were married to princes of Dalriada… they were my girlhood friends, and now *my* husband goes to slaughter *their* husbands."

The hairs crept up on the back of Acha's neck and she shuddered. "That must be hard for you to bear, lady."

Bebba's look hardened. "The lot of a peaceweaver bride is harsh," she said. "You too will find it so."

"Yes, lady," Acha whispered.

Enfrid set up a hungry wail and Bebba's face softened again as she leaned over to pick him up. "I mean only to speak to you in friendly warning," she said. "We have much in common, after all."

They sat in comfortable silence, smiling at the loud sucking noises that came from the hungry babe as he fed at his mother's breast. Acha looked up to examine the small coastline that they approached. As they drew closer she saw that parts of the island were hilly with ragged patches of rocks that almost formed other tiny islands, but the boat headed for a curved sandy cove that formed a natural harbour. Edith and Megan grew excited at the sight of precious samphire growing at the water's edge.

Suddenly the oars were lifted, and the keel ran into the sand with a soft, scraping sound. A strong scent of seaweed surrounded them, as the captain rushed to help them disembark.

CHAPTER 15

THE TEMPLE OF HELLA

There was no mistaking the temple of Hella, for a pathway led straight from the harbour to the high rock, topped by an ancient standing stone that caught the sun. Small huts surrounded the lower part of the rock. Acha turned her head to look back at Dun Guardi, but a soft mist had crept over the surface of the water and blurred the outline of the fortress. She knew that Athelfrid's stronghold was there, just a brief gull's flight across the sea, but the enveloping mist made it seem a world away.

Bebba removed the soft kidskin slippers that she wore and hitched up her embroidered robe. "We step barefoot from sea to land," she explained. "When we greet the goddess we must respect her customs. As you step from the sea onto the island, you step into the Otherworld; it is like a little death."

Acha shivered, but she removed her slippers and hitched up her skirt. The captain leapt out into the water, ready to help the royal women down. The queen turned back for Edith to hand the now sleeping baby down to her. She dropped a kiss on his forehead. "Come, little one," she said. "It is time for you to meet the others."

Acha solemnly paddled her way through shallow wavelets and out onto dry sand.

"You may put your shoes on again," Bebba announced as they reached the pathway. "We've completed the first rite. Now we follow the ancient processional way."

Acha turned back one more time to look at Dun Guardi, but the fortress had completely vanished in the mist. She understood why the local people connected this strange place with a dreamlike sense of stepping into the Otherworld?

As they walked on a small procession emerged from the base of the rock to meet them, led by a stout older woman. Bebba picked up speed at the sight of them, her face alight with joy. Acha dropped behind feeling uncertain. Edith saw her doubt and spoke up with reassuring kindness.

"This is Cara coming to meet us – the high-priestess of Hella's temple."

Acha watched in astonishment as the priestess picked up her skirts and began to run towards the queen. Dispensing with any attempt at formality, she hooted with pleasure and threw her arms about mother and child.

Edith chuckled. "They are old friends," she explained. "I don't know how Bebba would have born it all without Cara's help."

Acha followed shyly, but found herself swiftly introduced and enveloped in an earthy, warm embrace. Cara could not be more different from the austere priestess of Goats' Hill. Six young female attendants, who surrounded the baby, cooing and laughing until he wailed at them, followed her.

"Welcome – welcome all of you!" Cara cried. "We missed you so much at the Celebration of the Dead."

"It is not too late?" Bebba asked; a touch of anxiety in her voice.

"No… never so. Come back to my hall, we'll eat and drink before you make your offerings."

The priestesses' home was a modest wooden hall set on the small promontory, close to the sea at the base of the rock. A fire was burning in the hearth and cushioned benches were set all around. The young priestesses bustled noisily in and out, providing them with a simple meal of bread, cheese and plums dipped in honey, served with sweet warm mead. They sat down to eat without ceremony. Everyone talked and drank and helped themselves, but once hunger and thirst were satisfied the company grew quiet. A sense of expectation hung in the air.

Cara rose to her feet and addressed Bebba. "Come now, dear one, the time is right."

The queen got up, the colour rather fading from her cheeks. She picked up Enfrid from Edith's lap and turned to Acha, her expression plaintive. "Will you come with me and bring your offering," she asked.

Acha rose and took up her basket of fruit, touched by the manner in which the words had been spoken. They followed the priestess out through the back of the hall and walked side by side in silence following the processional way as it looped around the base of the rock. Mist rolled in from the sea, making their surroundings appear hazy. They hadn't gone far before they turned northwards along a pathway that led to a small stockade, the line of which was broken only by a low gate guarded by two priestesses. They bowed deeply as the queen approached and opened the gate – Acha got a glimpse of foliage ahead of them, as she followed Bebba into a neat, private garden planted with herbs, still green despite the early frosts. Stout palings protected this garden from the windswept shore, so that it seemed to possess a gentler climate all its own

In the centre of the garden stood an ancient stone, roughly hewn into female form. It was a representation of Hella herself, goddess of the Otherworld. A moon was carved upon her brow, and a few incised lines shaped the face. Acha had seen similar carvings set amongst the crumbling walls of Eforwic, and more on her journey north, when they'd passed the decaying townships close to the old Roman Wall, but as she gazed at this stone face, she recognised that none of the others had quite the same calming sense of tranquillity.

A stone altar stood at the goddess's feet, with six small cairns in front of it.

"You may place your offering to Hella," Cara said and Acha set her basket of fruit on the altar, gave a respectful bow and stepped back, hoping she'd behaved as she was expected to.

The queen moved forward with Enfrid in her arms, the child now awake and fretting. She began to fumble at the bag that she'd clutched so anxiously on the boat. Acha hesitated to intervene, fearful that she'd make a wrong move; but Bebba turned to her.

"Will *you* take him for me?" she asked. "He is used to being held by you."

Acha took the child and began shifting her weight from side to side to create a rocking motion so that he settled in her arms.

Cara stepped forward and began to blow gently into a bronze dish that contained smouldering charcoal; her breath made it spark and glow into life. Bebba produced from her bag a handful of rare and costly beads of resin. She fed them one by one onto the glowing charcoal. A delicate coil of sharp scented smoke was released into the air, to drift and curl around the rounded curves of the goddess and up into the sky beyond.

Bebba opened her bag again and this time she brought out a handful of white stones that gleamed with crystalline facets, just like the ones that formed the cairns. The dark whorls that had been pricked into the skin of her cheeks and rubbed with dyes, in the Pictish style, stood out against her pallor, and all the while she chanted softly in the Pictish tongue as she added the stones to the cairns. Gradually, Acha came to understand the significance of the six small cairns.

These were the "others", the queen had spoken of. Each cairn had been made from glistening white crystal stones, to mark the places where the tiny bodies of the six children that the queen had lost had been laid to rest. Enfrid lay still, watching the curls of smoke as they twisted upwards.

Bebba remained dry-eyed, but Acha found that she wanted to weep.

At last Bebba turned to see her distress and reached out to take her child back, her expression almost fierce. "I have shown you what it is to be married to Athelfrid," she said. "It is a harsh thing."

Acha nodded, her throat constricting so that she couldn't speak.

Cara watched them silently.

"I must give thanks for the boy," Bebba whispered, turning back to Hella's graven image.

Acha felt a little calmer as she watched the queen give silent thanks, with bowed head, for her living child.

"Now it is your turn," Bebba said. "We will both ask that your child be allowed to live."

Cara stepped forward and stood between them for a moment. "You have now done all you can," she announced. "The goddess is not ours to command and her ways are not our ways. Let us go back inside."

They walked back in silence, the way they had come, but just before they entered the hall the queen turned to Acha. "Never speak of what you saw there," she said. "I've never taken anyone else to my sacred spot – only the priestesses may go there."

Acha was moved. "I… I thank you for this honour," she whispered.

"Yes. It is an honour," Bebba agreed, still somehow unbending. "I have put my trust in you – for you saved my child."

Acha closed her eyes for a moment, uncertain whether to laugh or cry. She felt as though a she-wolf had leapt to the attack, but then merely licked her hand. When she opened them again, Bebba had gone ahead into the hall and Megan was hurrying towards her, concerned at the emotion in her face.

"What have they done to you?" she hissed.

"Nothing," Acha shook her head and forced a small smile. "They have done me no harm. Quite the opposite, I think. The queen has honoured me, and I am touched. You were absolutely right when you urged me to save the child."

Megan nodded and said no more

Back in the hall it seemed the solemn atmosphere had lifted. Acha was approached by one of the young women who curtsied and smiled. "I'd love to show you our island, Princess, and then take you to your sleeping hut where you may rest awhile. The queen and Cara will wish to speak alone."

Acha and Megan followed her out of the hall, surprised that Edith came too. Outside, they found the mist was lifting. The island was a small world of its own. The priestess led them through stretches of marram grass that edged vast sand dunes; startled pipits and warblers rose at their approach, along with a few late butterflies. Then they returned back again to the sheltered cove where the royal barge was beached, just as the sun began to sink. Fat eider ducks and graceful curlews waded at the water's edge, while skeins of lapwings looped and soared above the receding tide and cormorants danced on the edges of the wooden wharfs. Acha's spirits soared.

"If you are not too tired, we may tread the pathway to the summit of the sacred rock," the priestess offered. Acha agreed at once, filled with renewed energy as they followed the trod. From the summit there was now a fine view of the fortress and the rolling hills beyond. As the sun dropped to the horizon, it painted the landscape with a soft rosy glow. Grey seals had gathered on the sandbanks again as the tide uncovered wide stretches of sand. Soft wailing cries rose up into the darkening sky.

Acha shivered, uneasily. "I heard that sound on the Night of the Dead," she said. "I thought it was spirits from the Otherworld crying out to the living."

The young woman smiled. "It is nothing but the singing of the seals," she said.

Acha laughed softly then, feeling foolish, for she could see the grey shapes as they gathered on the sandbanks, each creature adding its own individual pitch to create a plaintive, ethereal chorus.

Suddenly the blare of a horn disturbed the peace.

"Feast-time!" the priestess announced, and she turned to lead them down again. "Our evening meal is ready."

Acha sat beside the queen at the table, and they talked comfortably together once again of their kin and their homes, while Cara watched with quiet approval. When at last they rose to go to their beds, Bebba caught Acha's arm, her expression suddenly serious.

"Our husband is a great king," she whispered. "He's feared and respected as a follower of Woden, but I would say this to you… those close to him know he worships Loki."

"Loki!" Acha shivered, she understood the meaning, for Loki was the sinister trickster of the gods.

Bebba watched as her words sank in. "His men call him The Trickster and he enjoys that reputation, it amuses him. What I am saying is that you and I should not forget this in our dealings with him." She released her arm. "That is all… just a gentle warning. Now sleep well!"

Mulling over her words, Acha went off to her tiny sleeping cell, where she slept more soundly than she could remember.

Next morning she woke to shouting in the distance, soon followed by running feet. She struggled to dress herself and hurried outside to find the young priestess running along the path towards her.

"Come, lady, come," she shouted, waving her hand frantically. "Come up to the top of the sacred rock – they have all gone up there."

Megan came yawning from her hut next door. "What – so early?"

Edith appeared, carrying Enfrid.

"I think we'd better do as they ask," she said.

They struggled up the pathway to find Bebba already on the summit with Cara, who was talking fast and pointing to Dun Guardi. Flames could be seen leaping high into the sky.

"What does it mean?" Acha asked breathlessly.

Bebba turned to her with a quizzical smile. "It means our husband has returned from Dalriada – and the beacon's flames proclaim victory. We must return as soon as the water is deep enough!"

They hurried back down the hill and tried to eat, but everyone was filled with such excitement that eating was a mere necessity. *Flame-bearer* set off to carry them back to Dun Guardi as soon as the tide made it possible.

Acha and Bebba sat side by side, the queen smiling happily down at her child, while Acha pondered uneasily what her place at court would be. Bebba would take her rightful queenly role as hostess, while the humble consort must surely sit in the shadows.

As they approached the shore, it seemed the whole town had come to meet them. The captain brought *Flame-bearer* steadily to the quayside, crowded with warriors still dusty from the road. Ropes were thrown and snatched and the barge was quickly secured.

Acha's stomach churned as badly as when she'd arrived at Goats' Hill, but suddenly Athelfrid was there, looking leaner than ever. A raw scar that stretched from eye to jaw now marked his weather-beaten face. His glance travelled fast, taking in the situation. As it lighted on the babe he leapt aboard the boat and strode towards them, his hands outstretched, greedy for the child.

"A boy? It is a boy?" he asked. He must have been given the news, but it seemed he needed to hear it from the mother's own lips.

"A strong boy," Bebba confirmed. She smiled proudly as she handed the baby over to him.

"Blessed Freya!" Athelfrid cried. He grasped Enfrid awkwardly. "I could not believe it, but now I see it with my own eyes, I know I'm truly blessed!"

The child opened his eyes, pulled a face and began to howl loudly.

"Hear him roar!" Athelfrid shouted in delight. He held the tiny struggling body aloft and a great cheer went up.

Acha watched it all silently, trying to look pleased, but her brittle smile did not deceive Bebba. She leant close to whisper. "Your time will come."

The king kissed Enfrid's downy head and passed him carefully back to his mother. "Ladies… we shall feast tonight!" he announced. "The son of Hussa is dead! This little one need fear no usurping uncle when he grows to manhood."

Images of bloody battle and death rose in Acha's mind, as well as guilty relief that the vanquished need not take the face of *her* father or brother or anyone else *she* loved.

But Athelfrid too turned solemn, and he went on reluctantly to speak. "The price of victory was high; my brother fell in the thick of battle, with many of his companions at his side."

The women gasped.

"Theobald? Oh my lord, a high price indeed," Bebba whispered.

Acha was saddened at the thought of life-loving Theobald dead on the battlefield. She knew she'd not be the only woman mourning him tonight.

"And my brother? What of Nechtan?" the queen asked, a new fear rising in her breast.

"Nechtan is safe and back in his palace. As for Theobald, we built a pyre at the place of victory and buried his ashes beneath a mound. They call the place Degastan. Tonight we feast to honour our dead, as well as this shield-worthy, living son."

The king grimaced and all at once his mouth began to work wildly. He snatched up his cloak to cover his face, for it would be unseemly for a warrior to weep in front of women. He strode fast away to vanish amongst his men, and the women stood together, shaken and sad.

CHAPTER 16

DALRIADS

The captain helped the queen and her women from the boat and into the waiting litter. The crowd dispersed quietly, for the brief moment of joy and hope had faded. Everyone knew that the price of victory had been very high.

Bebba clutched Enfrid tightly. "They'll take him from me," she whispered. "They'll make a warrior of him, and then…."

Acha could think of nothing comforting to say. They sat in silence as the slaves carried them up the hill, their spirits flagging. Acha's hand strayed to her own softly rounded belly and Bebba saw the movement.

"Pray you have a girl," she whispered.

"They take the girls too," Acha murmured. "They take them and send them far away to a strange land."

Bebba reached out to press Acha's arm. "But we two can be friends, at least," she said, her tone unexpectedly soft and pleading.

Acha nodded and smiled. "Yes – we can be friends," she agreed.

The courtyard was full of wild activity, smoking fires and the smells of butchered meat. They climbed out of the litter and returned to their respective chambers in the queen's hall. Acha found Emma and Clover in a state of bustling activity, already preparing clothing for the evening. Clover's pride in Bernicia had been bolstered by the victory – so much so, that she could not keep her tongue still.

"Those Dalriads got what was coming!" she cried. "Now they can pay tribute to Bernicia. Who would ever have thought it? The Dalriads must bow to us!"

Acha found she couldn't share this enthusiasm. "But the king has lost his brother and many Bernician warriors are dead," she said.

"Yes, lady," Clover said. She looked downcast, suitably reproved.

"I'm weary," Acha said.

Servants brought food and drink and a brazier of coals, but as she lay down to rest, Acha became aware of whispers. Then she heard Megan snort with disapproval.

"What are you saying?" she demanded.

Emma blushed and shook her head, clearly wishing they'd been more discreet, but Megan gave her a straight answer. "You'll know soon enough, so you'd best hear now from us. They are searching for a wet nurse for Enfrid… the king has ordered it."

Acha understood. The king intended to return to the queen's bed, while she, the secondary wife, would be left alone, like a breeding sow – who'd successfully visited the boar.

She sank down onto the soft furs that covered her bed. She should have known this would happen, but it would be hard to bear it with dignity.

"You can put your slick stones away," she said peevishly. "What do *my* gowns matter? They'll only have eyes for Bebba and the babe and I've no one to blame but myself, or my nurse," she added with a resentful glance at Megan.

Her nurse was unperturbed. "Take off your overdress," she ordered. "You'll be more comfortable. Things always feel worse when you're tired. Last night you were thanking me. The queen has offered you friendship and she's a powerful friend to have. I'll make a camomile simple and sweeten it with honey… you'll rest and feel a great deal better after that."

Acha slept for a while and woke feeling better, as Megan had predicted. As the sun went down, her women dressed her and brushed her hair till it gleamed, braiding it ready for the feast. The women's excited, breathless chatter served to rekindle her spirits, for despite the loss of Theobald, this would be a feast to end all feasts.

She turned from examining her reflection in her mother's mirror at the sound of a commotion outside her door. Athelfrid walked into her chamber unannounced, flashing a wide, appreciative grin at the sight of her.

"Leave us!" he commanded and the women fled.

He strode across the room and kissed her tenderly on the mouth. "Lady, are you as well as you look?"

She curtsied and nodded. "I am well my lord, but deeply saddened by your brother's death."

He pinched her cheek and raised one eyebrow, showing no sign now of the emotion that had threatened to unman him. "And yours is not the only woman's heart to grieve. How is the babe?" he asked, putting a hand on her gently rounded stomach.

"Well I think, and the morning sickness has faded, but I fear that *my* child may not be needed now."

"A great king cannot have too many heirs," he protested cheerfully, but then he grew serious. "The queen has told me of the aid you gave her at the birth. That was well done and will not be forgotten."

"I was glad to help," she murmured, faintly surprised and touched that Bebba had so quickly acknowledged the role she'd played.

"And your woman, the one who acted as midwife… she shall be well rewarded."

"I thank you, sir, on her behalf."

He clapped his hands and a slave strode forward carrying an ornately decorated box, gleaming white in colour. Athelfrid lifted the lid, and presented the contents for Acha to view.

"These are no spoils of war," he said. "They were especially made for you, by the same Frankish jewellers that came with the Kentish king's bride. I sent messengers to Kent, and they have only just arrived. Here are gold and garnets, just like those worn by the Queen of Kent."

Acha lifted out a gold brooch wrought in the form of a galloping horse, the eye embellished with a bold red garnet. Beneath it she discovered a diadem, the centre part moulded to the shape of a horse's head with a curling mane and rich red garnets again for the eyes. The box itself was decorated with horses, cut and shaped from the pearly lining of seashells.

She could not help but smile. "Thank you," she murmured, overwhelmed.

Athelfrid set the diadem in her hair. "I do not forget that I have two royal wives." He stood back to admire the effect, then kissed her again, but when she responded warmly he pulled away.

"Lady, this is not the time. Your babe *is* precious and must not be risked. Tonight is Bebba's night, but I am pleased indeed with my Deiran bride. Your day will come."

He bowed formally and was gone, leaving Acha feeling faintly foolish and reproved for her eagerness.

The feast that followed was lavish. Acha found that after all she was content to sit in the queen's shadow between Bron and Edith, who both treated her with friendly warmth. She enjoyed the glances of admiration that came her way, decked as she was in her new finery – clear tokens of the king's esteem.

Bebba looked magnificent in an over-gown dyed to a rich ruby red and stiff with embroidery and trimmings, her hair and arms glistened with gold and garnets. Acha wondered if they too had been made by the Frankish goldsmith. When the queen rose from her seat to carry the gilded drink-horn, wild cheers broke out in her honour and the whole company rose to their feet.

"I salute the bravest warrior of Bernicia!" Athelfrid cried. "I cry drink-hail to Theobald my brother, who feasts this night in Woden's Hall!"

"In Woden's Hall!" they responded.

A moment of respectful silence followed, but then Athelfrid smiled at Bebba and the atmosphere changed. "Now I cry drink-hail to my queen! For love of Bebba, Nechtan of the Picts fought at my side."

There were wild cheers and stamping of feet.

"And Freya has softened our loss by giving me a son! A prince!"

Shouts echoed around the hall. "A prince! A prince for Bernicia!"

"From this day forward," the king went on, "this place shall be called Bebbanburgh; for this fortress is my gift to you. My queen shall have a stronghold of her own!"

The response was deafening. Athelfrid's companions stamped their feet and banged on the tables. Bebba looked tearful, proud and happy, her chin held high.

Acha joined in the applause, feeling little envy. *My day will come*, she thought, *the king himself said those words*. But she frowned a little and shook her head. How could her day come? Surely she was now put firmly in her place as secondary wife and any son *she* bore could inherit nothing.

Extravagant dishes of boar, swan and venison were carried into the hall while the queen continued her stately progress, carrying the drink-horn round to all her guests.

Acha searched for some familiar faces in vain and realised that Theobald was not the only loss; many of Athelfrid's company were missing and some who were present were not so easily recognised for their faces bore still-raw wounds. Others ate awkwardly with heavily bandaged limbs and others were completely unknown to her.

Glancing down towards the lower trestles, Acha looked for Bree but could see no sign of her. Would it be proper for the royal consort to inquire after the concubine?

A servant appeared at her table with a smaller drink-horn and whispered to Bron, and then they both turned to Acha.

"Princess," he said, "the queen asks that you honour the Dalriads by carrying this horn to them. There are many at this feast, and Bebba fears she cannot manage to serve everyone, but she doesn't want *certain parties* to feel offended at her neglect."

Acha was puzzled but got up at once. "Dalriads, you say? There are Dalriads at the feast?"

She followed Bron's glance towards a trestle set somewhat back from the central hearth in a shadowy corner. The reeve bent close and whispered in her ear. "The boy is Prince Donal Brecc Mac Bude, better known as Freckled Donal. He's here with his tutor and retinue."

"I've heard that name," she pondered.

Bron nodded. "Prince Donal is grandson to the King of the Dalriads and, after his father, now heir to the throne."

A chill ran down her back as she came to understand. "A hostage?" she whispered.

"Yes, Princess, he's a hostage. He's to be treated as a royal foster child, but of course should his grandfather fail to pay tribute or the army cross the borders again... well," he dropped his voice, "that would be the end of Freckled Donal."

The boy looked young, much younger than her own brother. "Does he understand, do you think?"

Bron shrugged. "Lady, it is the way of war!"

She nodded. Hostage-taking was common enough, a clever means of keeping enemies subdued.

"Come," Bron said. "I'll announce you, so the Dalriads will know that they have a princess serving them."

Acha crossed the crowded hall at his side, carrying the drink-horn carefully. The boy was blue-eyed and sandy-haired, no more than ten, with a grand crop of freckles sprinkled over his nose. A swarthy young man who sat next to the prince rose to his feet and laid a protective hand on the boy's shoulder.

"This is Brother Finn, the prince's tutor," Bron explained. "He speaks our language, though the prince does not."

The man was tall and striking, his head shaved at the front like a slave but left long at the back. He wore the undyed tunic of a shepherd, with no adornment save a silver pendant in the shape of a cross, but a useful looking meat knife was tucked into his belt. Acha had heard of some austere Christian priests who came from Ireland, and she guessed that this man must be one of them. She also saw that Freckled Donal tried manfully to hold back tears, the food in front of him untouched.

Bron presented her as a Deiran Princess, honoured secondary wife to King Athelfrid. The priest listened carefully, then translated the Bernician greeting into the Gaelic tongue.

Donal regarded Acha with a little more interest when he heard that she was a princess. Dropping down on one knee, she offered the boy the drink-horn as respectfully as though he were a full-grown warrior. Donal gawped for a moment, but when she smiled warmly he recovered his dignity and leant forward to take a good gulp of mead. The prince's companions smiled tolerantly and encouraged him in his own language, and the gloomy atmosphere that hung about the dark corner lifted a little.

As Acha rose to her feet the priest whispered a thank you over the prince's head, and though he spoke with an accent she found she could understand him. "That was well done," he added.

She smiled wryly at him; for it was the second time those words had been spoken to her that day.

Freckled Donal asked something in Gaelic, watching Acha all the time. She waited to see if an answer might be required, but the tutor only shrugged in reply. Somewhat cheered by the warming mead, the boy began picking at a honey roasted leg of goose and Acha turned her attention to his companions. Though she knew nothing of their language, she offered each man a smile and a nod as she worked her way around the table. They responded politely and by the time she had served them all, she felt confident enough to whisper a question to the tutor-priest.

"Did the prince ask about me?" she said. "I would help in any way I could, for I too am something of a stranger in this kingdom."

Brother Finn smiled politely.

"But what did he say?" she repeated.

She saw that he was discomfited by the question and feared that she might be breaking some rule of courtesy. She made to move away, somewhat crestfallen, but then he spoke. "As you ask – I will speak truth. The prince wished to know if *you* were also held hostage at this court."

Acha's heart sank. Despite her effort to behave with cheerful courtesy, the boy had perceived that she was little better placed than he. She saw too that he'd given up any pretence at eating, and was sunk once again in gloomy despair.

"He meant no dishonour lady," the priest hastened to add, his dark brows knit with anxiety.

She gave a sorrowful smile. "And I am not offended," she said frankly. "Your prince is right; I too am a hostage of a kind."

The priest regarded her with new interest. "You speak truth," he said, "uncommon in a hostess."

She nodded. "A royal child sent far from home must keep a careful tongue – be they son, or daughter," she admitted. "But at least the prince has been able to bring his companions and his tutor with him. I have my old nurse, who I trust with my life."

The man looked thoughtful. "I am a Christian, sent from the Island called Iona to be the prince's tutor. Perhaps now, I should become his friend, perhaps his bodyguard too," he added, and he lightly touched the meat knife at his belt. It would be a weapon in the right hand.

Acha couldn't deny the truth of his statement.

A huge burst of applause suddenly filled the hall behind them, as the king rose to sit on the gift-stool. This was the moment Athelfrid's warriors had been waiting for, when they'd be acknowledged and honoured with gold in return for their courage and loyalty in battle.

The Dalriads glanced uneasily at each other, but made no comment – they could play no part in this ceremony, but must keep still and silent as those who'd slaughtered their friends and kinsmen were rewarded.

Acha felt for them. "I will try to be the prince's friend too," she said quietly to Brother Finn.

With that, she bowed and carried the empty drink-horn away, to be filled again, somehow touched by the brief, honest exchange that had taken place between them.

CHAPTER 17

FRIENDSHIP

That night, as she settled to sleep, the thought of Athelfrid and Bebba together in the great bed in the queen's chamber troubled her for a while, but when she woke in the morning the first image that came to mind was the vulnerability in the face of the boy – Freckled Donal. She smiled, thinking of her exchange with the Christian priest. She doubted that anyone would ever dare to speak so frankly to the priest of Woden. But then Coifi's lovelorn face came to mind, and she felt the loss of him again. She knew that she would always be able to speak to Coifi about anything, were she ever to see him again.

She dressed herself and left her women to sleep a while, as she wandered out onto Bebba's walkway that overlooked the island-patterned sea. As she stood there enjoying the fresh breeze, she noticed the slender figure of a man, standing still as a fishing heron at the water's edge. It was only when at last he turned and walked quickly back towards the fortress that she realised it was Brother Finn.

She too turned back to her chamber with a sigh.

Later that morning the queen sent for Acha. There was no sign of Athelfrid in the queen's chamber and Bebba dismissed her women and invited Acha to sit with her.

"Are you well? Are you content?" she asked; her strong features unusually soft with solicitude.

"Yes, lady," Acha replied.

"I feared it might be hard on you. But I do assure you that I will do all I can to make you comfortable here as secondary wife."

Acha realised that Bebba was concerned that she might be feeling neglected now that the king had returned to the queen's bedchamber.

She smiled and nodded. "I am quite content as secondary wife," she said.

"But… the gift," Bebba said. "A fortress!" And she shook her head, eyebrows raised in astonishment.

Acha smiled warmly. It was true that she'd never heard of such an extraordinary gift being made to a queen before, but she found that she felt no envy. "Oh lady, I am pleased for you," she said. "The king did you great honour, but you are worthy of it. You've suffered much to give him an heir. I know that better than most and I'm well content that he rewards you so."

Bebba sat back then, smiling with relief, as Edith came to announce – "They're here!"

The queen nodded. "Offer drinks and sweets," she said. "And sit them by the hearth; I'll come through to them in a moment."

Edith went off to do her mistress's bidding and Bebba rose, picking up her hand mirror to straighten her veil. "Will you come with me?" she asked. "Prince Donal and his tutor are here and I wish to do my best by them. The boy is distant kin to me… the tutor too."

Acha was amazed. "The Christian priest is your kinsman?"

Bebba sighed. "Finn is the youngest son of a Pictish Princess."

"So they took two royal hostages!"

"Yes. The younger sons of royal Dalriads are often given to the Christian God. And there is another thing I must tell you, I'm afraid these Christians disapprove of a man possessing two wives, even a great king like Athelfrid. They call us pagans, and barbarians. But Finn must learn to accept our ways," she added with a little toss of her head. "And I shall try to keep young Donal safe."

Acha nodded.

"I'm grateful that you attended them last night," the queen went on. "Would you be willing to serve the Dalriads again?"

"Oh yes, lady," Acha answered willingly. "I'll do anything I can to help."

"There you are," said Bebba, as she took her arm in a friendly manner. "You see. I think, after all, we shall do well together."

The two women entered the hall, where they found Prince Donal and Brother Finn waiting. They bowed as the women approached and Acha saw the monk's gaze flicker over her and back to the queen with a touch of unease. If he truly believed it wrong for a man to take a second wife, might he feel it an insult to his prince to be greeted by both of them together?

Prince Donal regarded Bebba with wide, frightened eyes, but she would allow no ceremony, and spoke to him fast in Pictish. She enveloped him in a warm embrace, which he tolerated patiently and even appeared to understand something of what she said.

"But this is wrong," Bebba cried. "You must learn to speak as the Angles do, and then you will feel much better, much happier."

Finn translated the queen's words, but Donal didn't look enthusiastic.

"I had to learn to speak their way when I married Athelfrid," Bebba said. "Princess Acha might teach you, for it is *her* native tongue. You must come each day to the queen's hall and we'll speak together. That way you will learn fast. We'll have no more Pictish and no more Gaelic, hey?"

The boy looked dismayed and an awkward silence followed.

Remembering the pleasure she and Edwin had once taken in such things, Acha walked over to a fine polished granite merrills-board set on a chest. "See here," she said. "We could play merrills."

She made to pick it up, but Brother Finn stepped lightly forward and lifted it onto a low table for her, then he pulled up a chair for her too.

Donal watched with a flicker of interest, seeming to recognise the game. When she'd set up the board, Acha turned her warmest smile on him. "I will beat you," she challenged.

For the first time he smiled and with a shaky flash of humour, he replied – "No! I… beat… you!"

Acha laughed. "Dalriads against Deirans!"

The boy looked round for a stool and joined her in a rather tricky game of merrills that required a great deal of signing and repetition of simple words. Bebba and the monk sat by the hearth and spoke together quietly in Pictish, the queen's hands busy embroidering a soft linen wrap for Enfrid.

When at last the two royal hostages left to return to their quarters, Acha turned to the queen. "Oh lady, I don't know *how* to teach our language. Is it right for me to do this?"

"All you have to do is speak with him," Bebba relied, "the game was a clever idea." She raised her chin and looked determined. "This fortress is mine to command. Did the king not say so? A king's wife must entertain her husband's guests and make them welcome – it is her duty. Poor Donal is my kinsman and though he's here under threat I'm determined to make him comfortable. And Finn? What do you make of him?"

Acha hesitated. "He takes his duties seriously," she said at last. "He'd give his life for the boy."

"You are right," Bebba agreed, wistfully. "Pray Hella it will not come to that!"

That evening, as Acha was dressing for the feast, she turned to Clover. "Have you seen Bree?" she asked.

"No," the girl shook her head. "But then I wouldn't expect her to come here; she'll be back at Goats' Hill, I think. Bree's never been to Dun Gaurd… or Bebbanburgh, I suppose we should call it."

Acha sighed, sorry for Bree – discarded once again. She wondered how the girl had fared in amongst the blood, filth and mire that must be the lot of any woman, on the edge of a battlefield. No doubt she'd have had to go to the aid of the wounded and she'd seen for herself that there were many badly hurt. Had Bree helped with the dead and the smoking pyres? Acha shuddered. In contrast she knew her position was privileged.

During the days that followed the feast, there were more deaths from wounds. The queen and her women did all they could to treat them with salves and clean bandages. Some of those wounded fell into a fever and Bebba refused to let Acha help with the work of caring for them, for fear that the child within her might be harmed.

"Look after the prince," she begged. "He is much in need of your care."

Acha reluctantly agreed; her role was clear enough.

Through the days that led up to Yule, the young Prince and his tutor appeared each morning in the queen's hall, and Acha contrived to lift Donal's spirits with challenging games. His knowledge of the Anglian tongue grew fast. Finn watched them, always alert to danger, intervening calmly if the boy became too wild, or too melancholy.

Yule came and went, and night after night there were genial gatherings in the mead hall, where bards who vied to flatter the royal pair with evermore outrageous praise would entertain the company.

The night before Yule was Mother's Night, on which depended all hopes for fertility in the coming year. A boar was sacrificed and then roasted and eaten. Chains of bawdy revellers danced outside and along the beach, circling the great fortress rock with wild songs in praise of the goddess Freya.

Hale to you, earth mother!

May you ever be growing

Filled with food and fruit and bairns!

Aloof from such wildness, Athelfrid's wives took Freckled Donal and his tutor back to the queen's hall, aware of Finn's discomfort with ribald, pagan celebrations. Acha and Bebba sat on cosily by the hearthside, when at last the monk led his charge away to bed. They chuckled together at the snatches of riotous singing that reached them from below. Bebba smiled at the astonished expression on her sister wife's face, as Acha's child moved for the first time in her belly. The strange fluttering sensation brought a touch of joy and hope for the future.

"You have a healthy babe," she said, with warm approval. "The goddess blesses you."

After the exuberance of Yule, Bitter-month brought sleet and snow and wild crashing seas. Bebba had kept her word and sent messages and gifts to Deira, via one of the sea captains whose boat travelled up and down the coast. Though she longed for news of home, Acha knew not to expect a reply while the worst of winter weather reigned.

Finn continued to bring his charge to sit by the queen's hearth.

One particularly cold afternoon the prince hinted, casting a crafty eye towards his tutor. "I wish I could do my writing here, by the queen's hearth!"

Bebba looked up with interest. "I have heard of this skill," she said. "By all means bring your writing to my hearth, I wish to see how it's done."

When the monk arrived the following morning he carried a leather satchel, from which he produced a pot of dark ink and sharpened goose feathers. He unfurled a strip of vellum made from stretched, dried calfskin and set it out on Bebba's trestle.

"I can write names," Donal announced.

Under his tutor's supervision and much to the women's amazement, Donal began to produce a pattern of neat marks.

"Like runes," Acha said. "Do they tell the future?"

Donal smiled and shook his head. "Not magic, just words. I am a scribe – this is my name and now I shall write my kinswoman's name."

They watched fascinated as he dipped the quill into the ink and more neat marks appeared.

"Are these Gaelic words?" Bebba asked.

"No," said Finn. "This is Latin, the language that came from Rome. On Iona a prince may be a warrior, a scribe and a Christian too."

The queen called Edith in to admire the magical patterns the prince was producing and Acha took the opportunity to speak more privately with Finn. "So *you* are warrior trained," she said, for she'd guessed as much.

He smiled grimly, "I hope never to use those skills again."

"I pray you will not need to," Acha whispered. "Here in Bebbanburgh you are free to come and go. Could you not take your prince and ride for Dalriada any day?"

"I could," Finn agreed, his face suddenly taut. "But Athelfrid would follow at our heels and more Dalriads would die as a result."

Acha regretted that she'd led the conversation in that direction.

"I saw it all," he whispered, his brow knit with pain. "I saw the slaughter, the anguish, the waste of life."

"And the prince?" she glanced up at Donal. "Did he see…?"

Finn shook his head.

"I'm sorry to bring dark thoughts to you," she whispered.

But he looked up at her and smiled again. "Do *you* never wish to take your sylvan mare and ride for Deira?"

She stroked her growing belly, nodding gently. "We are all hostages to the safety of the lands and the people that we love."

Mud-month arrived and all but the slaves and the lowliest servants huddled about their hearths. Athelfrid enquired politely from time to time as to Acha's health, but mostly he left her alone. The two wives sat at their looms in the queen's hall with Donal working at his scribing by the light of a lamp, and as time passed Finn took to wandering alone onto the sands, no longer fearful of leaving the prince in the queen's good care.

***

As the earliest touches of spring sunshine shone down on Bebbanburgh, the old, familiar restlessness came to Athelfrid. It did not suit him to sit by a blazing fire for long, however well fed and comfortable he might be. Too much time to think – to grieve for his brother – and dwell on what might have been, had he not broken Woden's battle laws. Had Theobald's death been his punishment?

The apparent harmony that now existed between his two wives did not make him feel as comfortable as it should have done. At moments, he felt almost an outsider in what had once been his own hall. He paced his chamber, hall and courtyard, eager for the comradeship and excitement of the war-trail once again.

One bright morning at the beginning of Easter-month he came across his two wives watching with Donal from the little walkway that looked out over the sands. He moved behind them quietly, curious as to what engrossed them. They were watching the Dalriad monk. Finn strode out into the freezing sea, moving without a flinch of hesitation and wearing nothing but a loincloth, to stand chest-high in the water.

"How can he do it?" Acha murmured.

"Why does he do it?" Bebba asked curiously.

"Is he testing his will to stand the cold as warriors do?" Acha asked.

"No." Young Donal shook his head, standing between them. "He is praying. See his palms turned up to the sky. That means he's praying."

Bebba watched, bewildered. "Would you do such a thing?" she asked the boy.

"Not in the freezing sea!" he said.

Athelfrid broke suddenly into their conversation. "The man's a fool!" he cried.

They all jumped at the sound of his voice behind them.

"What god would take pleasure from that?" he asked. "What does that achieve, when a god may receive a sacrifice of blood and slaughtered beasts?"

Donal could give no reply and Athelfrid watched with a vague, but growing, sense of hostility. He didn't understand this quiet magic. A man who could stand so still in freezing water, making no sound or movement… what else might he be capable of?

CHAPTER 18

BLOOD-PRICE

Once Mud-month was behind them the clang of the smith's hammer could be heard all day in the courtyard, and as the warmer days of Easter-month approached horses were shod, blades honed and mail-shirts and helmets were welded and shaped. The bustle and preparation signalled to all that the king and his warriors would soon be leaving to patrol their borders, issue demands for tribute and accept the lavish hospitality due to them.

Acha worried constantly that the king might demand tribute from Deira, if the child in her belly were not born live and strong. And of course, it must be a boy.

One morning towards the end of Easter-month, Donal and Acha were arguing cheerfully over a game of tafl in the queen's hall. Athelfrid appeared from Bebba's chamber having slept late after an evening of heavy drinking with his companions. He stood quietly on the threshold, watching through blood-shot eyes, as they moved the twelve light and dark antler pieces around the board.

"I have your dark king trapped in the corner," Donal crowed.

"But why are two of my gaming pieces on the floor?" Acha asked.

The queen stitched away at her embroidery by the fire, listening to them with motherly tolerance. Enfrid slept beside her in his wooden cradle while Finn sat quietly in the shadows, an open vellum scroll upon his lap. It was a peaceful domestic scene, and yet Athelfrid felt somehow irritated by the harmony of it.

Acha became aware of the king's brooding presence and hushed her young opponent, willingly admitting defeat.

"You win… you have my king trapped," she conceded.

At last Athelfrid strode forward to speak to Bebba. "Lady, we ride for Dalriada tomorrow," he said, "if the weather holds fair."

"So soon?" Bebba said.

"No point in delaying – we'll discover whether this boy's grandfather has gathered the gold he promised in the autumn."

Bebba and Acha exchanged a glance of concern. Donal looked up fearfully, dropping a gaming piece as Finn moved silently from his seat to the boy's side; the cosy atmosphere had vanished.

"We've trespassed on the queen's hospitality long enough," the monk said courteously. "I will take the prince back to his quarters."

Athelfrid nodded curtly. "The boy will stay here in Bebbanburgh with the queen," he said. "And if his father and grandfather behave with honour, all will be well."

Finn quickly rolled up his scroll and took Donal by the arm.

"And you, Princess," Athelfrid continued, turning unexpectedly to Acha, "will tell your women to pack at once."

Both women looked startled and Finn hurried the prince outside.

"Have your litter made ready," he went on. "I shall escort you to Goats' Hill, where you'll await the birth. Messengers will ride ahead to see the queen's hall prepared for your arrival."

There was another shocked silence, in which Bebba appeared more astonished than any. "But, my lord," she said. "I wanted the princess to stay here with me. I'm in her debt and must help her when her time comes."

"No need," Athelfrid said curtly, his tone brooking no argument. "Acha will have her woman with her. You said yourself. It was the nurse who saved our son." Then he turned to Acha. "See that it's done!"

"But husband…" Bebba started after him as he strode across the hall and vanished through the doorway.

Acha got shakily to her feet, her face drained of colour. The truth of her situation had been laid bare in those brief, sharp words: she was just as much a hostage as Donal was for Dalriada, and must obey.

Bebba returned, defeated and distressed. "Princess," she cried. "I cannot change his mind. I don't understand why you have to go, when I wanted so much to be with you! But the king is adamant!" She took both Acha's hands in hers. "I wanted us to be together, as sister wives."

Acha nodded. "I know… I know you did," she said, her throat constricted as she endeavoured to keep her voice calm and level. "Perhaps this is something of the harshness you spoke of?"

They embraced and stood for a moment cheek to cheek. "Never trust him," Bebba whispered. "He is a great king, but his god is Loki – never forget it. I fear we have been too open in our friendship and unwary in our doings."

Acha kissed the queen's cheek sadly. There was nothing for it but to pack and get ready to move.

The litter rocked from side to side, in the wake of the king and a good-sized Bernician war-band. Acha felt humiliated and physically weak, but she made no further attempt to argue with him, and could only guess at her husband's reasons for separating her from Bebba. Had he found his wives' friendship threatening? Would he rather they quarrelled over him? Did he object to the women's growing closeness to Prince Donal and the Christian monk? It did seem that their presence in the women's hall had angered him.

She glanced wearily out at the rolling grassland, glad at least that the journey would not be long. Her eyes lighted on Megan, who rode close to the litter on her own steady pony, gaily caparisoned with a soft red leather bridle. The old woman wore a hooded fur-trimmed cloak, part of the riches presented to her, in reward for Enfrid's safe delivery. Athelfrid had kept his word on that score and the thought cheered Acha – as long as she had Megan at her side, she would never be alone. Then Emma too came into view, mounted on Sidhe, Clover nervously riding pillion. She was not without friends that she could trust.

"Gentle on the bit," Acha instructed.

She smiled as she remembered how much she'd dreaded her last journey, fearing that the queen would humiliate her, or even worse

– perhaps attempt to poison her. It was better to feel as she did now and to regret their parting than to burn with resentment as she'd done back then.

Just as the sun was setting, they arrived at Goats' Hill, its summit shrouded in mist. Faint lights flickered up there, marking the carlin's meagre dwelling. Acha wished it was the open-hearted priestess of the Sacred Isle that presided here, as the carlin's fierce warning rose in her mind again. "The price is blood… the price is blood!" What had it meant? And why had the king not let her stay with Bebba, safe by the sea?

She drew the curtain, shutting out both the cold night air and the sight of the carlin's lights. With an effort, she turned her mind to happier thoughts, as she realised that she would be glad to find Duncan in the stables. Many of the pregnant mares would be ready to foal, and those that had returned safely from the battlefield might need special care.

When they arrived they found the servants had set a good fire in the queen's hall and prepared an evening meal. Acha suppressed her surprise as the king came to eat with her; she made an effort to be polite and cheerful, though she longed for her bed. His courteous manner and sudden attentiveness made her think wistfully of their honeymoon, when she'd believed he'd do anything to please her.

As soon as they'd finished the meal he stood up and bowed to take his leave of her. "I shall endeavour to return before the child is born," he told her. "Give me a healthy boy and you shall have glory heaped on you."

Acha caught her breath. "But what if the child should be a girl?"

"She'd suffice for now, and there'd be time to get a boy." He stroked the hair gently back from her face. "Remember Princess, all honour will be yours."

Two days later, Athelfrid set off for Dalriada with a good-sized warband. There were no bloody rites this time to see them on their way, and Acha was glad to see that Woden's priest rode with them. In the earl morning, the men lined up outside the palisade: gold arm rings and brooches gleamed in the sharp spring sun, a display of wealth and power this time, rather than an open threat of war. Acha struggled to present a dignified image as she passed around the horn for the farewell drink. As the cavalcade moved off, she caught a glimpse of Bree amongst the women followers. The girl rode behind the wagons, wrapped in a fur-trimmed cloak and this time she was the first to raise her hand in salute.

Acha reflected that a long ride in good weather, and with the prospect of hospitality in the Dalriads' comfortable palace at the end of it, must be a better prospect for Bree than a winter war campaign. She returned the brief gesture of friendship with little envy. She wanted only to relieve her aching back and return as soon as possible to the comfort of the queen's hall.

Acha tried to push away her growing fears, as the birth came close. The sharp, spring sunlight showed up many cobwebs in the queen's hall, so to distract herself she ordered it to be cleaned and refurbished. New lavender-scented rushes were laid on the floor and the wall hangings were aired, cleaned and repaired.

When she went to the stables, she was saddened to discover that many of her precious mares were scarred from the battlefield, and – like the men – more than half had not returned. Duncan worked tirelessly to nurse the survivors back to health.

"Lady, it isn't fitting that a princess so near to giving birth should spend her time in the stables," he ventured one morning, when Acha appeared, unattended.

"But the stables is where I feel happiest," she confided. "None of these gentle beasts will hurt me and even the fresh smell of their bedding lifts my spirits!"

He chuckled. "You should have been a warrior maiden," he said.

"That is what my kind guardian, Godric, always said."

As Three-milking-month began, the child inside her began to kick and roll.

"Is it growing as it should? And is it in the right place?" she asked Megan, fearfully remembering Bebba's pregnancy.

Megan gave sturdy reassurance. "Yes, the head is down and you carry low. It may well be a boy."

"Do not say it!" she protested. "If it's a girl, what shall I do?"

"If it's a girl we'll take good care of her, just as I always did of you."

She dared not speak the worrying retort that sprang to mind. *But you are getting old Megan and the carlin spoke of blood-price.*

"Gentle exercise is what you want, my lass, for a quick and easy birth. Sitting all day by the hearth will make you soft – get out and walk."

"I wish I could ride!"

"But you cannot ride – so walk!"

So Acha walked and tried to enjoy the fresh Goats' Hill air, but found that her feet took her unbidden in the same direction every time: towards the Sacred Hill, to catch a glimpse of the priestess and her women as they tended the goats. Then one evening, the carlin herself appeared in the queen's hall. She came alone, without ceremony.

Clover admitted her while Megan helped Acha to her feet.

"Welcome, priestess," she managed to say.

"Leave us!" the carlin ordered, speaking with the authority of a king.

The women hastened to obey her.

"Now sit, Princess!"

Acha sat, but the pervading scent of goat made her want to retch.

The carlin helped herself to a stool. "I see more than you think from my hillside home," she said at last. "You are troubled, and I don't need goddess-sight to tell me that."

Acha could only acknowledge the truth. "I cannot sleep," she admitted. "Now that the birth approaches I am afraid. I came here as a peaceweaver bride to protect Deira, willing to give my life to that cause, but I fear to take the journey to the Otherworld and you said… when…"

"Ah, I spoke of blood," the carlin cut in. "I spoke of blood, but it was not yours. When the goddess speaks, I cannot be certain what she means, but this I do know… the blood will not be yours."

“Not mine?” Acha gasped as the thought of something even worse came to her. “The child, then?”

“We will see.”

The priestess came close and pressed her hands onto Acha’s stomach. She struggled not to retch as the rank, earthy smell surrounded her, but then quickly the warmth in the pressure of the carlin’s hands calmed her and the babe within her settled too.

The carlin closed her eyes and her voice grew soft and breathy, as though a younger woman spoke. “Wanderer,” she pronounced. “Born strong, bold warrior, wide-ruler.”

Acha looked astonished.

The priestess removed her hands and spoke again in her usual voice. “I told you, I can’t understand all the goddess tells me, but for now what matters is this: he will be born strong.”

“A boy?”

“Yes, a boy. Sleep well, Princess. Goat-headed Freya has blessed you tonight.”

The carlin left the hall as quietly and as swiftly as she’d come and the women waiting outside rushed back to Acha.

“Are you all right?”

“What has she said?”

“Has she frightened you?”

They fretted and fussed, but Megan observed a new sense of quietness and calm in Acha’s answers.

“Leave her be,” she said. “Let her go to bed.”

CHAPTER 19

OSWALD

Acha slept soundly through the night and early next morning her birth pangs started.

"I can't give birth yet," she protested. "The king is not here and he said..."

"Better this way," Megan pronounced. "Women's work... we don't want men hanging around."

"I didn't know it could hurt so much," Acha gasped, astonished at the powerful cramps that came to her muscles. "A monster grips my belly! Oh... oh it comes again."

Megan smiled and soothed her brow with lavender brew.

"They all say that when first they feel it, but you are young and strong, your body knows what to do. Let the child come, and he will. You know that you have Freya's blessing."

Acha bit her lips as another pain came. "I have the goddess's blessing," she murmured. "I have her blessing."

She laboured through the day, and as dusk approached she was delivered of a healthy boy, who squalled loudly in protest at his expulsion from the safety of the womb.

"What is he like? Is he whole and hale?"

Megan tied and cut the cord, wiped him with soft sheep's wool and held him up for Acha to inspect. "See for yourself," she said.

The little mouth gaped wide. "Waah..." he yelled.

Acha stared in disbelief. He had the same soft golden downy head as Enfrid... but yet he was not Enfrid, he was totally himself. How could she have done it? How could she have given birth to this tiny person, so complete, so perfect, so very much himself?

"Take him!" Megan said, laying him across her belly.

Acha reached for his naked body and, sensing familiar warmth and scent, the babe grew quiet. She stroked the soft down that covered his head, and longed for Bebba; how cruel that she could not be there.

"Can we send a message to Bebbanburgh?" she asked.

"I'll see to it," Megan promised. "And we must try to inform the king, I think."

The sound of soft, rhythmic, squelching, made Acha look down; one tiny thumb had found the rosebud mouth and the babe was contentedly sucking. "He is so clever… he knows just what to do!" she cried, dropping a kiss on his head. "Tell Clover I shall feed him myself. No wet-nurse for him!"

Megan nodded, smiling broadly with satisfaction, hands on hips. "What is he to be called, I wonder?"

Acha sighed and held her son a little tighter. "I suppose the king should name him."

The messenger sent in search of the king had barely set out when he returned, Athelfrid riding fast behind him, eager to see the child. He found Acha sitting up in bed, cheeks pink and healthy, hair brushed and gleaming, suckling her son.

"Blessed Freya!" he cried when he saw them. "What have I done to be so blessed? Two healthy boys!"

He strode to her side and kissed her on the lips. "Since you came to me I have been truly favoured by Freya. You shall have all you wish for."

Acha seized her opportunity. "I wish to feed him myself; no wet-nurse for me."

He shook his head, but smiled wryly. "You'd feed our son like a slave girl?"

"I am his slave. And Megan swears that his mother's own milk is the best for him. Remember how Enfrid thrived."

Athelfrid nodded. "I can deny you nothing."

"But you must name him," she said with a smile.

He reached for the babe who'd now fallen asleep at her breast and she handed him over willingly. The child opened his eyes sleepily and reached for the golden fillet that circled the king's brow.

"Hah!" Athelfrid raised one eyebrow, smiling wryly. "He grasps the symbols of power in his little fist already – he wants to be a king. I shall call him Oswald, God-given ruler. "

"Oswald," Acha smiled. "A good name!"

"We've brought a fortune in gold and jewels back with us," Athelfrid said. "The Gaels gave us all we asked – you shall be decked in gold and garnets. But for now you must rest and I will order a feast in honour of my new son."

"May I beg another favour?" she asked.

"Anything," he said.

"I wish to set Duncan free – free to return to his homeland."

Athelfrid frowned for a moment and then laughed carelessly. "He is *your* slave – you may release him. But he will not go."

"But still I would like to offer him freedom."

Athelfrid shrugged. "Do as you wish," he said.

As he left her chamber Acha felt suddenly weary. Oswald lay quietly sleeping in a crib at the side of her bed. The sight of him was sheer delight, but some small thing troubled her in her husband's joy. Oswald could only become ruler on Enfrid's death – and she could never wish Enfrid dead. She told herself not to take the naming of her child so seriously: many a slave was named Coening – little king.

Athelfrid and his companions dined and drank heavily that night. Acha was relieved that they did not expect her to rise from her bed to serve mead. The whole of Goats' Hill slept late the following morning and Acha woke to hear bustling activity outside her chamber. Clover appeared looking flustered.

"Lady, riders have come to warn us that the queen is on her way. They say she wishes to see the child."

Although Acha's first response was of joy, she also understood why Clover looked so worried. "Ah! And here I am in the queen's bed!"

"Yes, lady," Clover said, her brows knit with concern.

"And there you stay," said Megan firmly.

"But it was you that warned me never to disrespect the queen!"

"I did," Megan admitted grumpily.

"Then send a servant to take a brazier to the guest chamber and make up a bed for me there," she ordered.

"I have set them to do it already," Clover admitted.

"I suppose it cannot hurt to move you there once the bed is warmed," Megan conceded.

Bebba arrived at sunset just as the king emerged from the mead-hall, still red-eyed from carousing all day. He managed to welcome her courteously and, at once granted her request to see the new baby. He escorted her there and Bebba hugged Acha warmly, forbidding her to get out of bed, and only then did she go to the crib to admire the child.

"Greetings little prince," she said. "Ah see… he's like my Enfrid. He wakes to greet me… may I pick him up?"

"Of course," Acha said.

Athelfrid hovered awkwardly in the doorway watching for a moment as the two women settled themselves on the bed with the child between them. When they began comparing details of their different birth experiences, he left them alone.

Bebba glanced up as he went. "I refuse to be cut out of your joy," she whispered. "I'm powerless to change the big things, but in these small things I shall have my way."

"You are his queen," Acha said.

"I am his queen," Bebba agreed.

"Have you brought Enfrid with you?" Acha asked.

"No, I left him in Edith's good care, but I've brought Freckled Donal and Finn with me. It seems the Dalriads have paid the tribute asked of them."

"Are they both well?" Acha asked, uncertainly.

"Donal frets at his captivity," she said. "I would wish that he might be returned to his kin."

"Yes, indeed," Acha agreed.

That evening Acha got up and dressed and went to join the king and queen in the mead-hall. It was not a formal feast, just a hearty meal with the king's companions. She was greeted with warm cries of welcome and the company looked on with approval as the king's two wives sat happily at board together. Acha noticed Bree sitting at one of the lower tables, further down the hall.

The bards sang of Athelfrid's victories and of the Deiran bride who rode bravely north to bring fertility to the land and to their king. Bebba clapped generously as the song ended, smiling in agreement at the sentiments expressed.

As the women rose to go to their beds, Athelfrid stood up and raised his hand for silence.

"I'm favoured by the gods," he began. "But we cannot sit at home feasting every night! In two days' time we ride for Rheged."

"Aye! Now it's Rheged's turn to pay!" his companions responded.

"Rheged maids and Rheged pies!" one daring wit cried out.

Athelfrid smiled tolerantly. "Bebba will accompany me, for a queen of Pictish descent, decked in gold, brings honour to her king."

Acha caught Bebba's intake of breath and saw her hand curl tightly into a fist. The pleasant expression on her face, however, did not waver.

"Indeed the presence of the queen would honour us," Ulric cried, with a courteous bow towards Bebba.

"And her smile persuade reluctant payers!" another added.

The king held up his hand for silence again. "Prince Donal shall ride with us," he announced. "Before he returns to his kindred, we'll make a warrior of him!"

Donal looked startled, as did Brother Finn, but they too managed to put a brave face on it. Those around him thumped the prince heartily on the back.

Acha realised that Finn might have a harder job to keep his charge safe, in such a situation, but at least the boy would not remain confined within a fortress. She and Bebba exchanged a brief meaningful glance.

"The princess should rest. I too am weary from my journey," Bebba said, and they bowed to the king and left the hall together.

They did not speak until they were well outside and walking through the quiet herb garden towards the warmth of the queen's hall, when their steps slowed.

"So, he has somehow managed to separate us again," Bebba said at last, her expression impossible to read for the shadows. "Each time I assert my will... somehow he finds a way to thwart me."

They stood in silence for a moment.

"At least you will have Donal with you," Acha said. "You will be able to watch over him."

Bebba took her by the arm and steered her towards the doorway. "Come. We must not have you catching a chill so soon after childbirth. It seems I cannot have both you and Donal at my side, so you must take good care of yourself. I know you have given up your chamber to me and I'm grateful for that."

Back in the guest chamber, Megan got Acha settled in bed with a soothing drink, but just as she grew sleepy there came a demanding wail from Oswald's crib.

"Are you sure you don't want a wet nurse?" Clover asked.

"I do not," she insisted. "Bring him to me."

The following morning, a messenger from Bebbanburgh arrived to deliver gifts from Deira. Aelle had sent a slender, beautiful gold armband for the queen and for his daughter a carved wooden image of the goddess Freya, her round belly marked with fertility runes.

"Have you news of my brother?" Acha asked, as her hand strayed to the thread box that still hid the oath braid.

"Prince Edwin is betrothed to a princess from Rheged," the messenger told her."

Acha felt uneasy. "Rheged?" she murmured. "Why Rheged?"

Her father was clearly hedging his bets by making a new marriage kinship with the old British kingdom, while *she* was expected to keep their Anglian overlord content. Athelfrid would not be pleased to hear of Aelle's links with a kingdom that owed tribute to Bernicia.

"Deira has a new high priest of Woden," the man went on. "The old priest died in the bitter months and his son took his place."

"Coifi is high priest?" she murmured.

"Yes."

"And the harvest?"

"It promises well!"

She sighed. At least there should be grain this year, providing the rains held off. She frowned for she found these snippets of news somehow unsettling. Many changes had taken place since she'd left her home almost a year ago and the news made her long to be there.

When the messenger had left, Bebba came to join Acha at the fireside.

"Will you take Enfrid travelling with you?" Acha asked her.

"No," Bebba shook her head sadly. "He thrives and he will be safer in Bebbanburgh, where I know that Edith will care for him."

Acha couldn't imagine being parted from Oswald, now or ever, though she knew the time would come when she must be. Princes were never allowed to stay at their mother's side; but must join the company of men and be trained as warriors. For the present, she was grateful that she could stay quietly at Goats' Hill, taking care of her babe.

Tents were packed, cartwheels repaired, men equipped and weapons honed until once again the royal cavalcade was ready to leave. Bebba and her women added to the splendour. The king and queen sat upon their mounts ablaze with gold. The king's flame-bearer standard headed the procession, and the jewel colours of the women's veils floated in the breeze. Behind them rode the priest of Woden with his raven totem, backing their magnificence with a non-too subtle threat.

At first sight of this extraordinary cavalcade, the King of Rheged would order the slaughter of cattle and broach his best vats of wine and mead, though his heart must sink at the dearth they'd leave behind them.

"I hope Rheged can pay," Acha whispered to Megan. "For their own sake – and for fear of where Athelfrid might look next?"

Megan nodded grimly. "I hope so too," she said.

Acha took Oswald from Megan's arms and held him up to his father to be kissed. Athelfrid must leave with the reassuring image of his Deiran bride and child in mind. With the usual blowing of horns, fuss and confusion, the cavalcade moved off. Bebba turned to wave with a last sad look of farewell and Goats' Hill was left blissfully quiet, once again.

CHAPTER 20

SUMMONED

Acha and her women wandered back to the queen's hall in the company of the reeve and his wife; a trail of serving women followed them. There was a general sense of relief that duties would be a little lighter for a while. A sliding movement caught Acha's eye as she looked up towards the now almost empty stables, then she saw somebody peeping out at her from the shadowy doorway. It was Bree, left behind and clearly feeling uncertain as to where she might fit in. Acha smiled wryly, Bree's presence on this royal tour might have been considered insulting to the queen. She turned to Clover.

"Go over to the stables and tell Bree to stop spying on me and come to my chamber," she said. "Tell her I need my tunics and under-gowns altering, for I'm losing my belly fast."

Bree appeared in the women's hall, a little later.

"I feared you'd still be angry, lady," she admitted hesitantly.

Acha sighed and shook her head. "You have no more choice in these matters than I have," she said. "I want you to be my wardrobe mistress once again – for a while, at least."

Bree made no reply, but surveyed the discarded gowns and folded cloth that had been piled on top of a wooden chest. She picked up a length of newly-worked braid and regarded in critically. "I could trim the blue linen gown with this weld and madder tablet weave," she commented. "The blue of the weld will pick out the main dye well, and bring out the colour of your eyes."

"You see… this is what I need," Acha said with a smile. "I wish that you could *stay* forever in my service."

Bree dropped the cloth and smiled reluctantly. "I wish it too," she admitted with a sigh.

"And that reminds me," Acha said. "I have another happy duty to perform."

Acha walked over to the stables and found Duncan combing Sidhe's smooth coat with the meticulous care he lavished on all the beasts. He stopped his work and looked stunned when she offered him his freedom, but then quickly shook his head. Acha sighed and shrugged. "Just as the king predicted," she said. "But you are free to go at any time. No one would follow you – I would make sure of that."

His expression changed almost to one of pain and she began to regret her well-intentioned gesture, but the moment passed and he bowed deeply to her.

"You honour me, lady," he said, "but I cannot accept. This stable is my home, these mares are my family now. I mean no disrespect by my refusal."

She regarded him with some understanding, remembering that she too had felt unsettled when she received news from Deira.

"So you reject my offer, but I understand you better than you think," she said. "When the messenger arrived from Deira, I too felt that it was not my home anymore."

"We are exiles," he said, giving her a weary smile. "It is never a comfortable thing for an exile to return to his homeland."

She sighed. Had Bernicia too become her home?

"The offer will always be there," she said, as she moved to the stable door.

He resumed his work, gentling Sidhe with a firm but loving touch.

When Acha returned to her chamber she found Bree sewing seams at a fast, steady pace. As she sat down to nurse her son, she revelled in the warm, milky scent of him and a sense of tranquillity came to her, for despite Duncan's polite refusal and her sadness that Bebba had been so swiftly snatched away, she still came to feel that Bernicia held many that she counted as friends.

A few days after Athelfrid left, Acha dressed herself carefully and called for six strong slaves. She set out in her litter, Oswald in her arms, to be carried up the Sacred Hill to visit the carlin.

The old woman emerged from her hillside home and accepted gifts of honey, mead and grain without comment as was her due. "Did it not come to pass as I told you it would?" she asked

"Yes," Acha admitted. "He is my little prince and I cannot honour Goat-headed Freya enough for her generosity to me."

"Your sincere respect is all she requires," the carlin said; then she added meaningfully. "Your sincere respect and loyalty, for there are new gods nowadays. They do not have the bountiful nature of Goat-headed Freya."

Acha understood this reference to the god of Brother Finn, whose priests honoured him by standing waist-deep in cold water.

She smiled at the memory, but replied politely. "I will not forget Freya's blessing," she said.

Afterwards Acha sent the litter away and walked down the hill, with Clover at her side and Oswald in her arms, enjoying the warm spring sunlight, the bleating of the goats and the gentle clanging of their bells. Freya had truly blessed her.

The weeks that followed were blissful. The weather grew warm and Oswald thrived. Bree settled back into the old way of working, stitching, dyeing and embellishing Acha's clothing with enthusiasm. Sometimes the girl set her work aside to play with Oswald, laughing as he stretched out his small hands to catch the beads and feathers she waved above his head. As she watched them play, Acha wondered if Bree knew ways to avoid conception? Megan held such knowledge and sometimes shared it with desperate women. What status might a child of Bree have? There'd been a few young warriors around her father's hearth who were known to be his sons.

***

In the ancient town of Caer Lignalid, Elffin, King of Rheged watched anxiously as his daughter Morffin offered the drink-horn to Athelfrid.

She was sweet-faced and very young, dressed in the finest gown and tunic her father could provide. Her hands shook as she proffered the heavy vessel.

"So… Princess Morffin," Athelfrid said. He raised one eyebrow and surveyed her closely. "You are betrothed to Prince Edwin, I hear – I suppose you will expect to be making your bridal journey to Deira before the summer is over?"

"Yes, my lord." She modestly dropped a curtsey, but trembled so much that a few drops of golden mead splashed onto her embroidered sleeve.

Athelfrid looked past the courteous, smiling face of his queen to catch the eye of his priest of Woden. "I, too, may be making a visit to Deira," he said.

Bebba looked up at her husband surprised, for it was the first she'd heard of such a visit, but courtesy made her simply smile and nod as the feast continued.

The bard had a fine voice and great skill with the harp and also in flattery, he worked hard to entertain, but his diversions were not enough, the atmosphere remained tense. Since Catraeth, Rheged had struggled to pay the large tribute demanded each year by Athelfrid, their overlord and victor.

Bebba retired early to the comfortable guest chamber that had been provided for her and her husband, for she was feeling weary and on edge, with all the strained courtesy that covered the deep resentment felt by Rheged towards Bernicia.

She fell asleep, only to wake at the first touch of dawn to discover that her husband paced the room.

"Come to bed, husband," she murmured.

Athelfrid strode over to the shutter that had been left open to the warm spring air. "They will not get the better of me," he growled. "They think they can ride on both sides of the battlefield, but they are utter fools. They played into my hands when they sent me their sacrificial ewe and they think they are safe now that she has her little lambkin."

Bebba sat up, disturbed. "What has angered you, husband?" she asked. "Here in Rheged they have offered you the best they have – I feel sure of it."

"It's not Rheged that troubles me," he said. "But it's nothing for you to worry about," he added. He threw off his cloak at last and came to lie at her side, giving a dark chuckle. "Nothing for you to worry about – my queen!"

Athelfrid fell asleep, but Bebba lay wide awake, troubled at what he'd said.

***

As Gentle-month began, the herb garden at Goats' Hill blossomed with sharp, refreshing scents. Acha's son fed well and grew and in the absence of the king; a comfortable, homely atmosphere still prevailed.

The weather was warm and, by the beginning of Weed-month, the fields around the settlement stood high with barley, wheat and corn. Almost everyone went out into the fields to help gather it in. Acha and her women often carried Oswald out to watch the workers. She grew rosy-faced and brown-skinned, as did the child who was often there in her arms. The grain was threshed and stored in the barns and Acha felt reassured that Deira would not need to be asked to send more.

Horses and cattle that were sent as tribute also began to arrive from the surrounding area. They trundled into the curving compound where the king's horses had once trained for battle. The beasts were measured and counted by the reeve and, though the summer would soon be coming to an end, there was still no word of the king's return.

Acha began to ride again, gently at first. It was a delight for her to be on horseback once again, and she freely explored the pleasant countryside that surrounded Goats' Hill. More and more she took Bree to attend her and they both enjoyed the ride and the freedom of the hills.

One fine afternoon towards the end of Weed-month, when they were out riding, they breasted a gently rolling summit, to discover a great company travelling along a lower track in the valley below. A trail of men, women and horses headed steadily towards the north-east, in the direction of Bebbanburgh.

Acha stared down at them. Why had such a large group passed so close to Goats' Hill, but not stopped to enjoy the hospitality offered to any honourably intentioned traveller who came to the gates?

She urged Sidhe forward a few paces, then reined her mare in, stunned, when she saw the standard. It bore a bright representation of Bebbanburgh upon it.

Bree brought her mare up close behind her and Acha turned to the girl, distressed and angry. "That is Bebba's standard," she said. "Why does the queen pass this way and not stop at Goats' Hill? She *must* know that I am still here."

Bree sidled her mare forward, frowning. "Yes, it's Bebba sure enough," she agreed.

"Why?" Acha asked, deeply hurt by this avoidance.

Bree shrugged and spoke frankly. "Maybe the queen feels less friendship for you than she pretends – there are many that would say she has every right to resent you."

Bree spoke with honest common sense, and Acha's heart sank. Had she so badly misread the queen's overtures? Was she being snubbed? Just one night's stop at Goats' Hill would have eased the queen's journey and given them the chance to exchange news and it would not have delayed them unduly. She stared down the hillside and suddenly anger blazed.

"I will *not* allow her to ignore me!" she said.

She kicked her heels and urged Sidhe forward, setting off to canter down the slope towards the head of the queen's caravan.

Bree spurred her mount to follow her mistress. Bebba's outriders looked up startled by the fast thud of their horses' hooves. They slowed their beasts and glanced back to see what orders might be given. Bebba held up her hand for a halt.

Acha rode past the outriders and headed straight for the queen, whom she addressed breathlessly as she reined Sidhe in. "Dear lady," she said, "will you not come and join us at Goats' Hill? The kitchens are stocked with game and mead and you might rest for a few nights before you go on your way to Bebbanburgh."

Bebba didn't answer straight away, but looked down between her horse's ears. Acha felt most uneasy. "Dear lady… dear friend," she began again, speaking more softly – almost pleading.

Bebba raised her head and spoke sharply. "And is it up to *you* to invite the Queen of Bernicia to one of her own palaces?"

Acha was stunned, mortified by this sharp response. It seemed Bree must have been right.

"I meant no disrespect, lady," was all she managed in reply, blushing furiously.

The queen, at last, looked Acha properly in the face and seemed to have a change of heart, having seen how much she'd hurt her. She sighed heavily. "Forgive me, Princess," she said wearily. "Of course we shall come with you to Goats' Hill."

"I'm glad," Acha replied, more startled than ever by the sudden reversal.

Bebba nodded to the captain of her escort and the outriders began to retrace their path. Acha turned Sidhe's head and the two wives of Athelfrid rode side by side towards Goats' Hill, Bree following close behind.

"I see you are recovered from the birth and can ride again," Bebba said.

"I'm taking good care," Acha said, defensively.

"You did not look very careful when you came careering down that slope towards me," Bebba said.

Acha looked up sharply, but to her relief, the queen was smiling. "I couldn't bear for you to pass me by without even..." she began.

Bebba glanced towards her attendants. "We will talk in the queen's hall," she said.

They rode on in silence. Acha's spirits floundered, for she sensed that there might be something coming that she didn't want to hear.

Another thought occurred. Having glanced back down the train of horses and carts, she caught no glimpse of Donal or the monk. She hoped very much that the queen's strange mood didn't signify that something had happened to the boy.

CHAPTER 21

REMEMBER LOKI

By silent consent, as soon as they arrived at Goats' Hill, they went straight to the queen's hall and ordered food and wine to be brought. Megan had kept the fire burning even though the day was warm, and they settled beside its comforting glow.

When at last they were alone, they still sat on in silence for a while and Acha feared more than ever what Bebba might reveal.

"Lady," she began at last. "I think you have something difficult to tell me… I'd do all I could to help, if it were in my power to do so. Have things gone badly in Rheged?"

Bebba smiled sadly. "We were entertained royally, though I think it was a struggle for him, King Elffin managed to gather together the tribute that was asked. We met your brother's bride… a pretty girl. Prince Edwin will be pleased with her, but I'm afraid Athelfrid was angered to hear of the alliance."

Acha sighed. "I feared it might be so. Will this bring trouble – do you think?"

Bebba shook her head. "I hope not," she said. "We parted cordially at Caer Lignalid."

There was a moment of silence again and then Acha felt she must ask more. "What of Prince Donal?"

Bebba shrugged. "He rides with the king's companions – they make kindly jest of him, while Finn watches closely. I had no choice but to leave him in their care. I cannot mother the boy for ever."

Acha could think of nothing to say that might offer comfort.

Bebba sighed heavily and spoke again.

"You were right to stop me in my tracks and drag me back here to Goats' Hill," she said. "None of it is your doing. Much of what I have to tell you will please you and I must try to be generous about it, but I feel that I am overlooked as queen and disregarded in this.

Athelfrid and his companions have left Rheged, to ride south to Deira."

Acha's eyes widened with surprise, for this was obviously not good news.

"Yes," Bebba said. "They go to meet your father at Catraeth, and you need not look so worried. It is just what the king calls a friendly visit with no demands for tribute to be paid. But I am dismissed. The king does not want an older Pictish wife at his side, not when he's meeting with Deirans. I am discarded and sent home, not honoured as his queen."

Acha was still puzzled. "You haven't quarrelled with the king?" she asked.

Bebba shook her head. "Quarrelled? No. *Can* one quarrel with Athelfrid? He simply tells me what to do, and I am left struggling to discover what is really behind his words and actions. Were you not still fresh from childbed, I think he'd have sent for *you* to accompany him. Next year I suspect he'll ride south and take you with him to visit your homeland, and of course I can see that such a thing would make you happy."

"But you say he was unhappy about my brother's betrothal?"

"Yes," Bebba agreed. "He does not like that alliance at all and it may be that he goes to make that plain to them."

"My father will not take kindly to that," Acha said, though she could not deny that her heart beat a little faster at the possibility of riding home to Deira at Athelfrid's side – almost as though she were his queen.

"All Deira knows that Bernicia has a Pictish Queen," she hastened to say, hoping to soothe Bebba's hurt pride. "My father made it very clear to me that I was to show you every respect."

"And you have done so," Bebba said softly. "You did so… even when I was cruel to you. Well… you need not fret over it. I grow weary of riding with the men, and if Athelfrid wishes you to accompany him to Deira next year, I shall not object. I have Bebbanburgh, and I am assured that Enfrid is his heir. But once again I advise you to be wary."

"Next year... next year," Acha murmured, her hopes swinging back and forth at the thought of a visit to Deira.

They sat in comfortable silence until Bebba spoke wearily. "I'm tired, and now I want to be back in Bebbanburgh with Enfrid and Edith at my side. I'm glad that you stopped me in my tracks, but I'll travel on tomorrow. Whatever happens – we two understand each other once again."

She got up to go to bed and kissed her.

"Stay true to me," she said. "That's all I ask!"

"Always," Acha agreed.

Acha mulled it over as she prepared for her bed. She couldn't quite suppress the excitement that bubbled up at the thought of a visit to Deira. Could there be any truth in what Bebba had said? Might she be offered the chance to accompany her husband next spring? To see Edwin, Lilla and Coifi!

Bebba left the following morning and Acha promised to visit her soon. The weather turned cool, and on the Night of the Dead they carried soul cakes and mead up the Sacred Hill to dance and drink and celebrate. Acha and Megan left before the fires burned down, anxious to see Oswald fed and settled.

More tribute continued to arrive, but there was still no word from Athelfrid. Finally, halfway through Blood-month, outriders brought forewarning of the king's return. Acha set about ordering a lavish feast and she was glad that she'd made good preparation, for the king arrived with Prince Donal at his side, and Brother Finn and what appeared to be an army at his back.

Acha went out to offer the mead-horn, and Megan followed with Oswald in her arms. Athelfrid greeted his secondary wife with a hearty kiss and a squeeze of the buttocks. He took Oswald from Megan's arms and swung him around, delighted at the sturdiness of his limbs.

"Good stock this whelp!" he said as he threw him into the air. "I hope his mother does not feed him like a slave girl still."

"He's almost weaned and eating sops," she said.

"Then he'd better not keep me from your bed," the king said heartily. "I want more sons, like him."

His companions made crude comments and laughed, while Acha blushed.

While he went on to speak to the reeve, Acha turned to welcome Donal. "You are grown a full head," she said. "The Queen will be so pleased to see you safely back and I am delighted too."

The feast went on late into the night, but as soon as Acha rose to leave the mead-hall, the king got up to follow her to her bed. He made love enthusiastically and she protested teasingly, laughing at his eagerness.

In the morning he woke her early and began again, so that her women found her weary but contented when they arrived to help her dress.

Athelfrid stayed at Goats' Hill for two more weeks, while preparations for Yule began. One frosty morning Acha woke to find him sitting up in bed looking thoughtful. He spoke of moving on to Bebbanburgh. "I must see my other little prince and greet my queen. Will you and Oswald come too?"

Acha nodded, pleased to be asked rather than told.

"Our nights together must cease for a while," he announced, "for the queen rules in Bebbanburgh and I would not offend her."

"Nor would I wish to offend the queen," Acha agreed.

Athelfrid lay back in bed, grinning wolfishly and stretching luxuriously. "I am a lucky man," he said. "But I make my own luck… me and my god Loki! In the spring, sweetheart, there will be time to be together. In the spring!"

It seemed the army had been boosted with many Rheged men – part of King Elffin's payment of tribute. The Rheged warriors were left to spend the winter at Goats' Hill, but a busy procession of hearth companions, women, children and servants moved on to Bebbanburgh in time for Yule. A train of wagons packed with grain, smoked meats, washed fleeces and gifts, followed them. Bebba greeted them all graciously, saving her warmest welcome for Prince Donal.

"Look at this lad!" Athelfrid cried, as he swung Enfrid above his head. "Look at the strength in these kicking legs!"

The queen led Acha to the old guest chamber, refurbished now with newly-stitched wall hangings and intricately carved wooden stools and chairs, still redolent with polishing oils.

"Oh you have done this for me?" Acha cried, touching all the new furnishings with pleasure.

An elaborately carved cot for Oswald had been set in a small alcove and fitted with a soft down-stuffed mattress.

Acha was deeply touched to see how much care had been given to her comfort; the two wives of Athelfrid embraced each other with sisterly warmth.

The feasting and celebrations on Mother's Night were wilder and louder than ever. Many babies would be conceived that night, but once again Acha sat with Bebba in the queen's hall, excluded from such wild dancing and excesses. The Yuletide Feast that followed went on all day. Courses of wild boar, venison, roast goose and swan, were carried in one after the other. Honeyed fruits and sweetmeats followed – treats that had been prepared days before and served to finish off the meal. Full of food and drink, the company listened to the bard's exciting tale of a monster, a hero and an honourable and beautiful hostess.

The king and his growing number of companions settled to live in rather cramped quarters through the bitter months, drinking, gaming and telling wild tales. Mud-month passed and Athelfrid announced a return to Goats' Hill to gather his followers together. Acha felt she must tell him that she was pregnant once again, though she feared that this news might take away her chance of travelling south with him. He hugged her in delight and ordered a special feast in celebration of this news. It was as they sat replete after the most splendid meal that he made an announcement that surprised his two wives.

"As you seem so cosy in each other's company," he said. "You may stay together in Bebbanburgh until the warmer weather comes."

Both women were glad, but Bree, who had accompanied Acha to Bebbanburgh came to her distressed. As soon as she saw the girl's face she guessed that she would have to lose her once again.

"He says I'm to ride with him," Bree said.

Acha sighed and kissed her, helpless to intervene. "Take good care," she said. "And when I can…"

Bree nodded, her expression resigned. "I can come back to you?"

"Of course you can come back. I shall be missing your help… and I shall be missing your company."

Bebba and Acha stood side by side to see them leave, Prince Donal was once again at Athelfrid's side. Bebba hated to lose him, but made no protest.

As the vast caravan disappeared into the distance, they wandered back to the queen's hall together.

"Peace for a while," Acha said.

Bebba nodded. "I'm glad to have your company," she said, but then frowned a little. "It's just not what I expected – and it leaves me wondering what he is planning now."

Acha and Bebba lived contentedly together through Easter-month, taking great pleasure in watching their healthy boys develop and thrive. The weather grew warmer and Acha waited impatiently, hoping that maybe orders would come for her to ride south to meet Athelfrid, but no such orders came. As her pregnancy advanced, her hopes of seeing Deira faded. Such a journey by litter would be very slow and arduous. But, one afternoon, early in Gentle-month, Duncan rode into Bebbanburgh from Goats' Hill asking to speak to the queen alone.

Acha was slightly offended. "Duncan is *my* servant," she complained to Megan. "He was part of my morning-gift and should be looking after my breeding mares, not riding to Bebbanburgh with messages for the queen."

"I thought you made him a free man," Megan remarked drily.

"And so I did! But he is still *my* servant."

"We are all of us Athelfrid's servants, even the queen herself."

Duncan and Bebba were closeted in the queen's chamber while Acha paced restlessly outside. At last she was invited to join them, and didn't have long to wait for an explanation.

"It is as I thought," Bebba said. "You *are* to go to join the king. He has left Catraeth to travel south to Deira."

Acha's spirits leapt.

"Athelfrid will meet you near your father's summer palace at a place called Lond… Londe…"

"Londesburgh!" Acha cried.

The very name brought a rush of happy memories. "But I did not think he'd allow me to ride, because of the child. And it is such a long way to travel by litter," she faltered.

Bebba shook her head and smiled. "You are to go by sea. *Flamebearer* will carry you to meet your father at Londesburgh, and then you'll all go on to Eforwic. Your mare and your litter are to travel in the boat with you. And," she added with a sigh, "you are to take Oswald."

Acha's heart filled with joy – she'd be able to show her precious son to Edwin, Coifi and Lilla. Her mind began to spin at the thought of it.

"To travel in the royal barge?" she murmured. "All down the coast of Bernicia and then the coast of Deira too. How long will it take?"

"The tide washes southwards and speeds the journey," Duncan told her. "Two nights, maybe more, depending on favourable winds."

"And of course, you must go in the barge," Bebba said. "You take a royal prince with you. Oswald is to be presented to his grandfather, and Duncan is here to act as escort and see that you and your mare are transported safely."

Acha stared, bewildered. "But… to take Sidhe, you say? And yet the king forbade me ride…"

Duncan shook his head. "These are the king's orders, Princess," he said. "I am to escort you to Londesburgh, and there I will inspect horses sent as tribute from the kingdoms of Elmet and Rheged."

He bowed and left the two women alone.

Despite her joy, a worm of doubt twisted its way into Acha's mind.

Why was Athelfrid demanding more horses as tribute? Had he not got enough horses already?

"Is tribute to be demanded of my father, do you think?" she whispered anxiously.

Bebba looked uncertain. "It sounds as though Athelfrid means to put on a show, for you are to take your richest gowns and jewels. The mare could be led behind you in procession. Such a beautiful beast, she'll make an impression, whether you ride her or not. This is his way – if not threatening war, he dazzles with wealth and power, so that others will feel compelled to comply with his wishes. Whatever he intends, if you are there to act as peaceweaver, you may manage to soothe away signs of trouble."

Acha's expression softened and a slow smile lit her face.

"Londesburgh and Eforwic..." she murmured, unable to keep the joy from her voice. She longed for home.

Bebba nodded, understanding well. "I hope you will be safe," she said.

"How could I not be safe, in my own father's kingdom?" she replied. "When do we go?"

"At once," Bebba said. "*Flame-bearer* is ready at the quayside. Her captain says the tide will turn tomorrow at noon. Can you be ready by then?"

Bebbanburgh was thrown into uproar. The queen put her own women at Acha's disposal in an effort to prepare her goods in time. Megan and Emma were to travel with her, their own joy undisguised. Clover was included and was perhaps more excited even than anyone, for she had never been in a boat before.

Despite the short time allowed, all was ready by the following noon. Acha and her women walked down to the quayside to find Sidhe settled aboard in a specially prepared stall that was filled with straw and had been padded at the sides according to Duncan's instructions. Acha's cumbersome litter had been stowed. The moment of departure arrived.

Bebba threw her arms around Acha and kissed her warmly. "Do not stay away too long," she begged. "And always remember Loki."

Acha nodded. Eager to be off, she strode up the gangplank and stepped aboard. The plank was drawn up, hawsers released, the anchor lifted. Forty strong men took their places at the oars and *Flame-bearer* was quickly rowed out to sea; as soon as her sail was released, it bellied out with a northerly wind behind it. The men hauled in the oars and the barge set off southwards at a good speed.

Good progress was made, helped not only by the wind, but also by the steady pull of the tide that rolled southwards down the coast. Before the light faded, they had passed the mouth of the River Weir and a tiny island off the settlement of Amble. It was almost growing dark when the captain swung the steering oar to avoid the mouth of the River Tyne.

Acha staggered wobbly-legged to the forward prow to watch the distant shoreline as it passed, and stood there determined to enjoy every moment of this longed-for journey home. Megan hid in the shelter feeling sick, while Emma patiently soothed Oswald.

Clover left the other women and struggled down to stand by Acha. "Oh lady," she cried, her voice shrill with excitement. "I never thought to go sailing far-away like this."

Acha smiled. "It is not so very far," she said, but then she clapped her hand to her mouth as a strong lift and dip made her stomach lurch. They stood watching until darkness closed in around them, and at last returned to the shelter.

"Give me the babe," Acha demanded. "He will keep me warm."

With Oswald in her arms, contentment washed over her as she settled for the night.

Propped on comfortable cushions and well wrapped in rugs, the women slept fitfully and woke at first light to the sound of a steady drumbeat. Though the wind had turned against them, the oarsmen rowed onwards as they passed the mouth of the River Tees.

"The land you now see is Deira," the captain announced.

Acha smiled, despite the cool breeze in their faces. "I am home," she murmured.

They ate and sipped mead, and as the vessel neared the shoreline once again, Acha stumbled back to see Sidhe in her straw-strewn box, being watched over by Duncan. The mare tossed her silver mane fretfully, but snaffled a handful of oats.

Acha smiled at Duncan. "The exile returns," she said.

He nodded. "I'm pleased for you lady and I pray that you will find happiness in your return."

The sun grew sharp and bright and they raised the sail, carried south-west once again by wind and tide, the oarsmen dozing on their benches.

"What river is that?" she asked, seeing a sharp indent in the coast.

The captain passed the steering oar into the capable hands of his helmsman and came to her side. "It's the Usk," he said. "That settlement is the Bay of the Beacon."

"I've been there," she said. "My father travelled this way checking all the beacons, each one placed in sight of the next so that a warning might fly down the coast, should we be invaded."

"No need for beacons now," he said with a smile. "Now there's peace between the kingdoms; those beacons were built when the Romans ruled these lands."

Clover overheard and got up to join them. "I cannot wait to see your father's palace at Eforwic," she said. "They say it too was built by the Romans."

Acha shook her head. "The old fortress walls were the work of Romans, but my father built his wooden hall inside their sheltering shell. We are never safe from flooding there. I left my father's hall in ruins and can't say what we'll find at Eforwic, nor at my father's summer palace."

Clover smiled determinedly. "It will all be a wonder to me," she said.

CHAPTER 22

DEIRA

The following wind continued throughout the morning. *Flamebearer* sailed close to the thin spit of land that stretched out into the sea and marked the entrance to the River Humber. Once there, the steady northerly wind hindered them, for the oarsmen had to row across the turning tide, but by the time the light faded, they had rounded the tip and rode smoothly at anchor in the lee of the northern headland.

"We rest over night," the captain declared. "And pray Thor sends us an easterly wind in the morning."

The boat rocked gently as Acha took Oswald in her arms and carried him to the forward prow. "You will see where your grandfather first set up camp," she whispered, "and where he built his most southerly beacon. Once I danced on these sands with my brother and feasted here with our good friends Lilla and dear Coifi."

Oswald smiled and imitated her words with charming baby babble as though he understood every word.

"Coifi's an important man now," she whispered.

Megan managed to get up and stagger across the deck towards them. "What nonsense is she telling you, little one? Coifi will be pleased to see your mother – but there'd best be no sheep's eyes between them."

Acha nodded. "I know how a princess should behave," she protested.

Oswald slept in her arms again that night, wrapped well in woollen rugs. Acha inhaled the warm scent that rose from his silky head with pleasure, but found that she couldn't settle to sleep herself due to the excitement that bubbled inside her. With good winds and a fast tide, they might reach the ancient river crossing at Brough the following evening and get ashore before it was dark. At last, exhausted, she dozed briefly and woke to the sound of the drum, the pull of the oars and Clover's excited voice.

"Lady, we are moving again! This wide river stretches out before us like another sea!"

Acha knuckled the sleep from her eyes and sat up, to find that Emma had taken Oswald from her arms. She struggled to her feet and went once again to stand in the prow, while *Flame-bearer* moved swiftly onwards up the Humber.

Megan struggled to her feet a determined expression on her face.

"Home at last," Acha said.

"Yes – home at last my girl," her nurse said, with satisfaction.

***

Athelfrid paced restlessly outside his tent, his stomach tight with tension, his fist clasping and unclasping the pommel of his sword. He hated waiting about – anything was better than waiting. Ulric would return as soon as he'd caught the first glimpse of the royal barge approaching and then unbeknown to them it would all begin – he'd set his subtle plan in motion. He'd left Rheged with an army at his back, having asked for a tribute of warriors rather than gold or grain, but he knew that he'd left a trail of suspicion behind him. Had knowledge of this approaching force reached Aelle, or even more damaging that young milk-sop of a boy who was brother to his secondary wife? He'd put paid to any marriage plans the lad might have had by forbidding Elffin to make the alliance under threat of war. That would teach Aelle to go crawling to Rheged behind his back, seeking to make links with the old defeated kingdoms of the British.

He lifted his head at the sound of hooves fast approaching.

Ulric rode into the camp. "They're here, my lord! The vessel has been sighted in the mouth of the Humber!"

Athelfrid flashed a fierce grin at the man as a flame of excitement leapt through his body. He was The Trickster, and with Loki's help, he'd show the world that there were more ways than one to win a kingdom!

***

All morning the wind blew in their favour, but by noon the tide had turned and the wind dropped. The oarsmen rowed on, but made slow progress with the wind against them and the water choppy. Acha began to fear they'd have to spend another night aboard, but the captain was determined to get there. He wrested the last scraps of strength from his men and they managed to come close to the river crossing just as the light began to fade.

Acha had to blink back tears as she stepped from the gangplank onto the sandy soil of Deira.

"Now we are really home," she whispered.

"But for how long?" her nurse asked sourly. "We must not allow ourselves to get too comfortable here. He'll want this new child to be born in Bernicia?"

With a joyful snort, Sidhe allowed Duncan to lead her down the gangplank. Six oarsmen lifted the litter from the boat and almost at once they heard hooves in the distance – they'd been spotted.

A rider emerged from the shadows carrying Athelfrid's flame-bearer standard, followed by foot-slaves with torches. It seemed the king himself had come to greet his secondary wife. As he rode into view, Acha went forward to meet him, smiling happily with Oswald in her arms. Freckled Donal rode at the king's side, and the monk was just behind them.

Athelfrid leapt down from his stallion to embrace her.

"Praise Freya! You have arrived safely," he said as his eyes swept over her person and gently swelling belly. "Come… we have tents set up in the flat land where the Romans once made their camp; there's food and drink and comfortable bedding ready for you. Tomorrow we will meet your father at his summer palace. Bring forward the princess's litter," he ordered.

Still carrying Oswald, Acha willingly climbed inside.

It was dark by the time they arrived at the Bernician camp, but torches lit the ground and trestles had already been set out. They sat down at once to a meal of roast venison, smoked fish and freshly baked bread. After they'd eaten and drunk, seeing her grow weary, Athelfrid led Acha to a tent that he'd had especially prepared for her.

"I will leave you to rest," he said.

And giving his men a sharp wink, he gently pushed her towards the tent flaps. Acha lifted the skins and stepped inside to find that candle lanterns lit the space. A light wooden bedstead was all set up with a comfortable down-stuffed mattress and pillows, and standing by the bed was Bree, looking scrubbed and neat, if a little anxious.

Acha hesitated at the sight of her. "What are you doing here?" she murmured.

Bree folded her arm defensively across her chest. "Well, lady, *he* says I can act as your maid while you are here… but I wouldn't blame you if you didn't want me."

Acha smiled at the girl's straight talk. "I'm glad you're here," she said. "Come – give me a hug and help me off with this travel-stained gown – I am exhausted. Emma is busy with Oswald and Megan can't deal with my clothes as you can. I'll need to look my best tomorrow."

"Huh! I heard that," Megan said, as she ducked her head to come in through the flaps. Emma and Clover both grinned at Bree; for once it seemed Athelfrid had managed to please them all.

Acha lay in the bed feeling warm and cosy, full of pleasant anticipation as to what the morrow might bring – especially the old friends she'd meet again. It was sheer joy to be back in her father's kingdom and at last she drifted off to contented sleep .

She rose at daybreak and woke her women to help both her and Oswald dress, for she wanted her father to be impressed by her new matronly dignity. She fussed over her appearance, but at last felt satisfied. As she emerged from her tent in sunlight, she was shocked to see the full extent of Athelfrid's army, for when she arrived the previous night, darkness had disguised their vast numbers. Warriors from Elmet, Rheged and Dalriada had joined the ranks. The sprawl of tents and corals stretched as far as the eye could see.

Athelfrid joined her as she stood looking at them in consternation.

"This army will not march with us to your father's summer palace," he said. "I would not expect Aelle to entertain them. They have brought their own supplies – all part of the tribute."

"But they look like... a war-host," she whispered and a shiver ran down her back.

Athelfrid shook his head, annoyed. "I would not approach your father with an army at my back... you should know me better than that. I look to the west for more land, perhaps Gwynedd, that is why I am gathering these forces." She bit back a protest, that he'd surely got enough land to rule already, because she feared provoking his anger just as she was about to see her home once again. Quashing the flash of unease, she nodded her acceptance and climbed into her litter. As the journey got underway, her spirits lifted, for she was so hungry to see Londesbrough again.

As they came within sight of the summer palace, Athelfrid came to help her from her litter. They spied a party in the distance advancing to meet them. As they came closer, Acha looked anxiously for Edwin and Coifi, but could see no sign of them. It was Aelle who rode out to meet them, surrounded by his thanes. The sight of Godric cheered Acha.

As the party arrived and came to a halt, she saw that her father had difficulty dismounting. He looked smaller than she ever remembered him to be. She felt a touch of pity at the fragile old man he had become.

But Aelle hauled himself upright and assumed that aspect of fiery dignity, which she'd sometimes feared throughout her girlhood.

She curtsied and her father greeted her warmly. "Welcome, daughter," Aelle said as he kissed her on both cheeks. Then he stood back to look at her and as his gaze travelled down her body he saw that she was with child again. He laughed and slapped her thigh.

"Hah! See what good breeding stock I sent you," he said as he turned to Athelfrid.

"Hail to you, Aelle, kin by marriage," Athelfrid replied formally, but then he too laughed. “I am well pleased with my Deiran wife. Meet your grandson.”

Emma strode forward at his gesture, with Oswald in her arms.

“He has passed his first birthday, and he stands strongly and even tries to walk,” Acha said with pride.

Aelle chucked the child under the chin, but almost at once his expression turned distant and Acha knew that the sight of her son had set him mourning the loss of Aelric yet again.

She sighed inwardly. The joy of her homecoming waned a little at the thought that this beautiful boy, of whom she was so proud, meant little to her father compared to his lost son. Oswald had been a useful bargaining tool for fending off the payment of tribute, but little more than that.

She searched once again through the ranks of familiar faces, and saw Coifi. He stood very tall, behind Aelle, dressed in the regalia of the priest of Woden. She resisted the urge to run to him and gave only a distant nod of recognition

“Is my brother here?” she asked.

“Your brother is in Eforwic,” came her father’s rather gruff reply. “You can meet him there later, but for now I bid you welcome to my summer palace. Come – food and drink is prepared in the mead-hall.”

Godric came forward to welcome her with a warm kiss. They mounted their steeds and Acha climbed back inside her litter, hugely disappointed not to see Edwin. She hoped Athelfrid would not see her brother’s absence as a discourtesy. With her spirits low and her back aching, she suddenly wanted to be alone in her old chamber more than anything. There was little chance of it, for as peaceweaver, she must strive to keep harmony between her husband and her father.

Her spirits soared again as they entered the main gateway to Londesbrough, and she saw that the old crumbling palisade had recently been repaired. The hall and stables were also freshly thatched. She stepped from her litter to discover that her father was already leading her husband up the steps to the mead-hall. Someone touched her gently on the arm and she turned to find that she was looking into the lean, solemn face of Coifi.

She smiled and then glanced behind him to discover an even happier sight. Edwin strode forward looking tall and strong for his sixteen years, and with a sparse, golden beard. He was mud-stained, clearly fresh from the saddle, with Lilla behind him leading steaming horses.

"You're here, after all!" Acha cried, and she threw herself into Edwin's arms.

He laughed and hugged her tightly. "We've ridden since dawn to get here," he said. "I set off from Eforwic as soon as I heard that you were coming."

"You didn't know that I was coming?"

"Father didn't think to send a message," he said.

The touch of hesitation told Acha much. He looked like a man, but she saw that there was still something of the vulnerable boy in him. Why had her father not made sure that he would be here?

"Ah, sister," he said, looking at her swelling belly. "You have become so much a woman."

"Come… you must meet my husband," she said imperiously, taking his arm.

"Not yet! I will clean myself and present myself properly," he insisted. "Then I will join you in the mead-hall. Let Coifi lead you inside."

She nodded and turned to take the hand that Coifi offered. "It's good to see you too," she whispered.

"As priest of Woden I may escort you lady," he said, with a quiet smile.

They followed the two kings as Edwin slipped away to his chamber. "Do Father and Edwin not see eye to eye?" she murmured. "I know Edwin is still young, but…"

"I fear they disagree," Coifi said seriously. "Edwin spends time in Eforwic, while Aelle holds court here. They see Deira's future differently, Edwin wants to make Eforwic the thriving trading centre it once was, under the Romans, while your father conserves his resources and does not travel so much these days. He criticises your brother's plans, and Edwin is of an age to resent it. I try to make peace between them, but I do not succeed."

She sighed.

Coifi spoke again on a lighter note. "Your father hopes that you will carry the drink-horn round to our guests as you used to do."

"Of course I will," she said. "And you… you look most impressive," she added, with a quick sideways glance.

He smiled.

The interior of the Londesbrough mead-hall had been refurbished with seasoned timbers and richly coloured wall hangings to keep the draughts out. Freshly-painted shields decorated the walls, along with many ancient swords.

Trestles were laid and a smiling servant brought the drink-horn to Acha. It took her a moment to recognise the girl and as she glanced around she began to see many more familiar faces, though the boys had broadened and grown thick beards, while the girls had filled out into womanhood.

Acha offered the mead to her husband first and her father next, and they both sat down to eat together. She forgot her aching back as she moved on from thane to thane to offer the cup and greet old friends.

CHAPTER 23

BLOOD-FEAST

When at last Edwin arrived in the hall, he looked much more like a prince. He wore a warrior jacket of dark blue wool with red tablet weave trimmings, brocaded in gold thread. Aelle glowered for a moment and then gruffly presented him to Athelfrid. "My son!"

Edwin bowed respectfully and Athelfrid nodded curtly.

"You are very like your sister," he said. "It is strange to see a face so familiar on a man."

Edwin straightened quickly looking somewhat offended. Had his sister's husband seen him as womanly then? Acha feared her brother hadn't made a good impression on her husband, but Athelfrid courteously made space beside him for the young man to sit.

Acha offered the mead-horn to Edwin, who received it with a rather sullen glance. She moved on, carrying the vessel to other guests. As the feast went on, she noted that Godric never left the king's side, performing many personal services for him. He made sure his food was to hand and that it consisted of small tender cuts of meat. Aelle's sight was failing fast, and it seemed that his limbs would not always obey him as they once did.

When at last the men gathered around the hearth and settled to drink steadily through the afternoon, Acha felt that she could politely withdraw to rest for a while. She would have liked to take Edwin aside and find a quiet place to talk properly, but that would have to wait. She found Megan and Emma in her chamber, talking animatedly with old friends, and was amused to see that for once it was Clover and Bree who looked wide-eyed and lost.

"You two can help me get undressed," she said. "Leave that lot to cackle together. I must lie down. There's to be another feast tonight and I daresay they'll expect me to act as hostess again. My husband wishes Oswald to be presented, so he must be dressed in his new smock and he must not be tired or hungry."

"Bless him!" Emma tore herself away from the chattering group, going at once to the chests of clothing they'd brought with them.

"You are a great lady," Clover said, "I hadn't realised that you were 'first lady' in this land."

"And to think you once wore my gowns," Bree added with a smile.

"My father's palace was deep in flood water and most of my own clothing ruined when I went to Bernicia," Acha explained. "I was grateful for the clothes you gave me."

"But here you are now, "Clover said. "Just like a queen, in your own father's palace."

They helped her undress and she lay down on her own old bed, as they set the smoothing stones to warm. She felt that it was bliss.

The feast that night was worthy of any great king. Aelle proudly displayed his recovering wealth. Acha worried a little that Athelfrid, alert to any opportunity that might bring him more wealth and power, might see her father's lavish display and demand tribute once again. Surely her success in her role as heir-provider must now make her husband waive any claim on her father, whether it be grain or gold. Six oxen had been slaughtered and roasted outside in the courtyard, along with four hogs and many lambs. The dishes were presented with rich embellishments of cream and honey. She carried her father's gold-trimmed mead-horn to the guests, anxious to please everyone and smooth out potential misunderstandings before they even arose. The two kings appeared to be in jovial mood as they sat together at table. Godric eventually got up from his place at Aelle's side and insisted that Acha take his seat. As she sat down, she caught Edwin's eye and he smiled, his hand straying to a plain leather thong about his neck. She understood at once that the oath-braid hung from it, hidden from sight. She lifted the thread box that still hung from her girdle and smiled too.

Musicians played and sang, tactfully recalling the heroic fight at Catraeth when both Bernicians and Deirans had fought side by side to establish their right to the northern lands.

Acha blushed at the verses that followed, which expressed warm appreciation of her, the peaceweaver princess who brought kinship to the two kingdoms. She bowed to the musicians as their performance drew to a close.

A ballad in praise of Edwin, future hope of Deira, followed, but before it had finished Athelfrid rose to his feet, flushed and bright-eyed. He held up his hand for silence and the song came to an awkward and ragged conclusion, as gradually a hush fell over the hall.

"I honour you Deirans!" Athelfrid began and everyone clapped. "I honour your wise king who has ruled so long and I thank you for your warm hospitality. But this is the moment to announce to you, my friends, that Deira, of all my subject kingdoms, is to receive the greatest honour."

He paused for effect and the whole hall held their breath.

"No further tribute shall be required from Deira." he announced, "Not now... not ever!"

He paused again to give time for his announcement to sink in – and then the hall erupted with applause. The feasters rose to their feet, they banged the trestle tops, they stamped and clapped and cheered with wild abandon.

"And now Deirans," he said, holding up his hand for quiet again, "I wish to present to you my son!"

Emma came forward carrying Oswald, freshly scrubbed and wide-eyed. He blinked with surprise to find himself in such noisy and excited company. Athelfrid took the boy and held him up to be greeted by more avid applause and many smiles of amusement as the expression on his little face changed to one of anxiety.

"Behold a Prince of Bernicia!" the proud father cried. "But he is a Prince of Deira too – and I name him heir to his grandfather's throne!"

Those last words brought a sudden hush, followed by confused whispers.

"What was that? What did he say?"

"His grandfather's heir? What does that mean?"

Murmurs of consternation spread fast through the gathering. Acha sat at her father's side, stunned. She thought she must have misheard what her husband had said. Surely Athelfrid would not have said that.

Whispers flew all around her.

"What did he say?"

Aelle too stared blankly, uncertain that he'd hear aright.

But then the whisper was voiced clearly from the lower hall.

"He names his child as heir to Deira! We shall have none of that!"

"No, we have our own heir!"

"Edwin is our heir!"

Acha stared aghast at Athelfrid, as Aelle turned too. She caught Edwin's eye and the shock and anger that she saw there turned her heart to ice.

The old king sprang to his feet, all frailty vanished.

"What did you say?" Aelle's voice roared above the murmurs of dissent.

Athelfrid's expression was flint-hard. "This child," he said, raising Oswald up again, "shall be the acknowledged heir to Deira. And in return, no tribute shall be required. Not now... not ever!"

"Deira already has an heir!" Aelle bellowed. He pointed at Edwin, whose cheeks had turned ashen. "He may not be the warrior his brother was, but he is *my* heir and *he* shall inherit. Our council of elders has agreed upon it!"

Shocked silence fell. Fear spread among the crowd!

"Edwin was not the firstborn," Athelfrid said with a shrug, his expression now showed amusement, as Oswald unsettled in his father's arms, began to struggle. "And Acha is your eldest living child, so *her* son may take the kingdom, just as the Pictish kingdoms allow."

"As the Picts... as the Picts!" Aelle's voice rose in fury.

Acha turned to Edwin, distraught at the accusation in his eyes. His resentment and anger bore into her belly like a physical pain, like a knife cutting deep. "No," she cried, rising to her feet. "I do not agree to this! My brother must be king in Deira."

"Edwin for Deira! Edwin for Deira!"

The low, angry chant rose as chairs crashed to the floor, benches scraped and the whole gathering rose to its feet.

Aelle, with a burst of astonishing strength, overturned the high table, so that drink, food and plates shot in all directions. He reached up towards the wall behind him and snatched down an ancient sword, which he swung in both hands as he advanced on Athelfrid. "Fight me for my kingdom!" he growled. "Edwin was right all along! You are a usurper and a dog! I should never have trusted you, or given my daughter to you!"

Acha could only stare in horror as her father levelled his blade at her husband, her son still in his arms. The sword swung clumsily and caught Athelfrid on the side of his neck. A stream of blood flowed from the wound.

"Give the dog a sword!" Aelle roared. "Stand and fight like a man, great warrior that you claim to be! Usurper I say! Come out into the courtyard and fight me!"

Bernician and Deiran thanes snatched up meat knives, while others rushed outside to claim the weapons they'd discarded – honour-bound to bear arms with their lords. Once more, Aelle lunged at Athelfrid, the sword swinging dangerously close to Oswald's head.

"No! No!" Acha screamed.

"Wicked daughter!" Aelle turned towards her. "Better that I slaughter that brat of yours now and put paid to this dog's claims! W*e* are not barbarians like the Picts."

"Kill my child?" she gasped. "Then you must kill *me* first!" Acha cried.

She knew that Athelfrid was terribly wrong to make this claim for Deira in Oswald's name, but she'd give her own life to defend her child.

Edwin, shaken at last from the shock that had gripped him lifted his clenched fist. "I challenge you! I challenge you, Athelfrid of Bernicia! Fight *me* for this kingdom, not an old man."

Athelfrid shifted the child's weight awkwardly to his side, looking for someone to take him, but warriors surrounded him. He held him with one arm, and Acha saw him reach smoothly behind his back. She knew at once the danger hidden there – he always carried a dagger concealed beneath his cloak.

Sounds faded as she gasped for breath, helpless to prevent him. Her father paused in his tirade, his mouth gaping wide in shock. Only she knew what it must mean – a deadly dagger had been thrust with precision between Aelle's ribs. .

Aelle stared at his son-in-law for one astonished moment, and then he sank downwards.

Edwin lunged forward, drawing the meat knife that he carried, but Lilla hauled him back, shaking his head. "Too many of them," he cried.

Acha wanted to scream, she wanted to howl, but no sound would come from her throat. Then a desperate wail rose from her child. She knew with a sudden, dreadful clarity that this moment had changed their world for ever.

She thrust aside a stunned servant girl who stood in front of her, and shoved and butted her way past burly warriors, who stared unbelieving. She saw her father on the floor, blood spurting from his chest, but Acha did not go to his aid, she stood before her husband, eyes blazing.

"Give me the child!" she roared at him.

Obediently he handed over the babe. Then chaos burst forth. Unarmed servants, both men and women ran, from the hall screaming. Many of Athelfrid's companions returned with weapons ready in their hands, but found the doorway blocked by those who fled. In the madness and confusion that followed, weapons swung savagely, blood spurted, wounds gaped – and many lost their lives.

Acha staggered down from the dais, still clutching Oswald in her arms. The child howled terrified, and she felt as though her knees would give way beneath her. Almost at once she felt strong arms about her.

"Come, Princess," a voice spoke low and urgent in her ear. "You must get out of here!"

It was Duncan. He'd seen her plight and fought his way to her side. He hauled her to her feet, protecting her with his own body. When they turned, they saw that enraged men, arms and legs flailing wildly, fighting with whatever came to hand blocked the way to the main door.

Suddenly Godric was there on her other side. "Behind the dais!" he shouted. "There's a way out there!"

Between them they half carried Acha and her child round to the back of the dais, but there they found Lilla and Coifi struggling to get her brother away from the fighting. Acha fell heavily, still clutching Oswald to her breast, to find that Edwin lay beside her, restrained by his friends – his eyes dark and murderous.

"Let me fight!" he bellowed. "I will kill him!"

"By Woden's ravens!" Lilla cried. "Have you seen the men and weapons that they have? No – we get you out of here, to fight another day!"

"Brother," Acha pleaded, distraught to see such hatred in his glance. "I would *never* betray you, *never*! I knew nothing of this!"

But his friends dragged him away behind the wall hangings at the back of the dais, where there was a small doorway that led outside.

Acha struggled once more to her feet, with Oswald howling and terrified in her arms. "Come away," Duncan urged.

Suddenly, Coifi was there beside her with Woden's ritual horn in his hand. He blew one sharp blast. "Cease!" he cried. "Deirans put down your arms. Our king is dead! It is futile to fight on – we must bow to an overlord."

Even Athelfrid looked across at him astonished. Those who fought staggered crazily together, wondering how this could be happening. But Coifi dropped down on one knee before Acha and both Deirans and Bernicians watched, astounded, as he took Oswald's small bare feet between his hands and bowed to kiss them.

"Let this babe be our heir and his mother our queen. Our king is dead! This is Woden's will!"

His pronouncement flew round the hall, from mouth to mouth. Even Oswald ceased his howling, soothed a little by the warm touch of Coifi's hands. Godric too bent sadly to kiss the babe's feet. Oswald gasped and hiccupped at the touch of his beard.

Some seized the moment to slip away, but others followed their priest and chief thane's example. These were the two most powerful men in the kingdom, bar the king and his heir. One by one all around the hall men sheathed their swords and bent their knees before the babe. Bernician thanes and warriors watched in amazement, but they too lowered their weapons.

Never slow to seize the moment, Athelfrid strode to Acha's side. Nausea rose in her throat at the sight of her father's blood-soaked body and the proximity of the man who had killed him. Her husband had slaughtered her father in his own hall, without a thought, like a worn-out Blood-month bull. Athelfrid's ornate, embroidered sleeves bore the marks of spattered blood – even her child was spattered – her vision turned dim.

"The child," she murmured.

Athelfrid swooped to catch Oswald as darkness closed around her. As Acha fell to the floor, he raised the child above his head.

"Deirans… here is your king!" he cried.

Acha opened her eyes and shut them quickly again. She didn't wish to leave the comforting black darkness that had surrounded her; she did not even want to find herself in her old chamber, where she'd longed to be.

The wrinkled face of the carlin floated above her and she thought she caught the scent of goats. The price is blood. Not her blood, and not her child's blood, the carlin had assured her of that and the carlin always spoke true. It was her father's blood.

Acha kept her eyes tight shut, wanting only black oblivion to return, but instead she felt herself lifted and pulled by strong arms into a sitting position, propped on pillows.

"Drink!" Megan ordered. "You must drink!"

Megan was there at her side, though her voice sounded strange and flat and distant.

"No," Acha whispered; then a brief moment of hope came to her. Her eyes flew open. "Did I dream?" she asked.

The silence that followed told all. She closed her eyes again, having glimpsed her women, standing about her bed, their faces grim and grey.

"You must drink," Megan insisted again.

The rim of a cup was forced between Acha's lips and tipped. A strong-tasting, warm liquid filled her mouth and ran down her chin and Bree's voice told her firmly. "Drink this and it will make you sleep again."

Obediently she swallowed, wanting to sleep and never wake.

CHAPTER 24

LOKI

Athelfrid paced outside his tent. He would not step inside the palace for fear of revenge. It had not gone as planned, but maybe it had worked to his advantage. He'd got rid of the stubborn, doddering old fool with a dagger's stroke. Aelle had brought it on himself. His own thanes had seen him snatch up a sword, while Athelfrid, the visiting guest, had offered conciliation. No one, not even these hapless Deirans, could gainsay that he'd acted in self-defence. But it was not what he'd planned – no, no, – and now he'd need the woman more than ever. He could see no way to console her, so he must force her to see sense if she wanted to avoid more bloodshed.

He was The Trickster, not a lady's fop – not a man of peace. Gentle words did not drip from his mouth, like they did from the monk's.

He glanced up at Ulric, who'd faithfully warded off any approach to his master in this mood. They had the men to march on Eforwic – and they'd follow him still, even if in fear rather than love! He'd give the girl one chance and if she failed, like a fool, to see the need, she'd have to go. The brat was his – he could tackle it his way and win – so long as he had the brat.

***

Acha didn't know how long she slept, or how many times she woke before falling into a fitful sleep again. Her body was hot, and her head thundered when she surfaced briefly from the sweeter dark oblivion. Now and then she glimpsed anxious faces bending over her, and once she thought she saw Athelfrid. She screamed in horror at the sight of him and he vanished like a nightmare demon. When at last she woke properly to bright morning sun, she begged for more poppy juice. This time it was refused.

"Two days you have slept," Megan told her. "And now it's time to wake and face what must be faced. You are needed here. The king forbade me drug you again, and indeed it would not be good for the child."

"Oswald… where is Oswald?" she cried, opening her eyes. How could she have slept like this when her *child* needed her? "Bring him to me!" she cried, as she struggled to sit up.

Megan nodded to Emma, who went to fetch him from the outer chamber.

"It was the other child that I was thinking of," said Megan. "The one you carry."

Acha looked down at her rounded belly. "Best let it be lost," she said, "for I can never look its father in the face again."

Oswald appeared in Emma's arms. Acha snatched him from her roughly, and he began to cry. "Sorry… oh I am so sorry," she cried. She covered his head with wild kisses, which made him howl again and hold out his arms to go back to Emma.

"Take him!" Acha sobbed, distressed.

"You are going to have to calm yourself," Megan told her gruffly. "The fever has settled and the king wants to speak to you."

"No!" she said at once. "Never again! I will not set eyes on him."

A soft sigh seemed to pass around the chamber. Clover and Bree were unusually silent and Acha saw then how exhausted they looked. And of course they must be in fear of their lives. As Bernicians they'd be suspected of treachery. They'd come here pretending friendship, when their king had another motive altogether.

They stood around her in silence and then Megan spoke.

"What's done is done," she said bluntly. "It cannot be undone. You've slept two days and nights, and we have slept hardly at all. All is quiet now out there. Athelfrid has taken charge, with Coifi at his side. The whole Bernician army is camped around this palace and Edwin has fled – we don't know where. You are Deira's only hope for a peaceful settlement. Your father's body lies unburied in the temple of Woden and Athelfrid will not have it moved until he has spoken with you. I think you must see him now; he won't be patient for much longer."

"No," she howled. "He is my father's murderer."

The others backed away, deeply distressed, but Megan stood her ground.

"You would not be the first wife who has had to deal with her father's killer," she said. "Athelfrid is the only man strong enough to hold this kingdom now. You know I am Deiran through and through, but I say this to you! You must deal with him."

Then Megan followed the others out of the chamber and they left her alone.

She lay on her bed in silence, trying desperately to seek oblivion again – but sleep wouldn't come. She heard a commotion in the outer chamber, followed by the sound of men's voices and women protesting.

"What is happening out there?" she demanded.

She struggled out of bed, but her legs refused to hold her steady. Staggering forward, she managed to pull aside the curtain at last, only to find the outer chamber empty – even Oswald's cot had vanished. As she stared at the space trying to understand what had happened, the outer door opened and Athelfrid stepped inside.

Acha turned away at once, refusing to look at him. She stumbled back to her bed and Athelfrid followed, saying nothing. He was prepared to wait it seemed and at last when she could bear the silence no longer Acha spoke. "Where is my child?" she asked, her voice hollow and shaky.

"He is my son."

"Please..." she pleaded. "Give him back to me."

"You are my wife!" he said. "Oswald is safe and your women too – but if you want them back you must listen well to what I have to say."

He had all the power while she had none. With a slight inclination of her head, she miserably acknowledged this and he spoke to her a little more gently. "Get back into your bed; I would not have you swoon again."

He reached out to help her, but she pulled away from him. "Do not touch me," she growled.

He waited until she sat down, and then chose his words carefully. "I did not mean it to fall out this way," he said. "I bore your father no ill-will."

"But you meant to take his kingdom from him," she protested.

"Your father's death was brought about by his own foul temper," he said harshly. "It could all have been done without bloodshed, by peaceful agreement; that is what I intended."

"But my brother," she cried, anger seizing her. "What of Edwin?"

"Your brother might have ruled as sub-king of Deira after your father's death while Oswald grew to manhood, if only he'd had the sense to consider his nephew's claim before his own. Now *your* Edwin has chosen to bolt like a coward, leaving only his sister to speak for him."

"Sub-king! A puppet king, you mean," she said, her eyes blazing, "a puppet king, who must bow to your every command."

There was a moment of heavy silence. Acha tried to calm her breathing and when she spoke again it was more in sorrow than anger. "You have started a blood-feud here, a nightmare of a blood-feud, for my brother is now honour bound to kill my husband and my son in revenge. Many a youth his age has done such a thing."

A sneer twisted Athelfrid's face. "I don't see that your Edwin will have the guts to return. I cannot see him gathering an army."

"There are those in Deira who will fight for him," she warned. "And he will not always be young. Edwin is the heir, not Oswald, and though I love my son dearly I say it is my brother's right to rule here."

Suddenly Athelfrid lunged forwards and grabbed her. He forced her to look up at him, crushing her cheeks. "Do you say that you love your brother more than your son? You stupid woman! Don't you see what I offer you? Queenship! No longer a secondary wife! You will be Queen of Deira, and your son will be king."

"No!" she cried vehemently, as she twisted away from his grasp. "Not at this price… never at this price!"

"I shall do it, whether you wish it or not," he said, his voice now measured and firm. "It can be done without more bloodshed if you,

Aelle's daughter, are at my side as we march on Eforwic. *You* must be seen and Oswald must be seen, and then maybe your fool of a brother will have the courage to come out of hiding and play his part."

She shook her head. "Edwin hates me now," she whispered miserably. "I saw it in his eyes."

Athelfrid took her by the arm and dragged her to the wooden shutter. He flung it open. "Look out there," he said. "What do you see?"

Unwillingly she looked and saw that beyond the palisade, where the rolling hills of Londesburgh should have been, there were tents, standards, horses and men, rank on rank of armed warriors.

He released her then and spoke without emotion, almost as though he gave orders to his grooms. "We will enter Eforwic together, you and I to claim Deira for Oswald. Or else I let loose upon this land the vilest bloody slaughter it has ever known. You see I have the warriors to do it."

Acha began to tremble uncontrollably.

Athelfrid swooped to pick her up and carried her back to the bed. He knelt before her and gripped her arms tightly, his face pushed close to hers.

He spoke through gritted teeth. "You came to me as a peaceweaver bride! Think well on this. I *will* take this kingdom with or without you. *Now* if you truly act as peaceweaver, I will send your son back to you. Otherwise…"

He released her, got up and left without another word.

Acha sat for a long while, before she got up and went to the outer chamber, to discover that two armed guards had quietly taken position by the doorway. She was a prisoner in the childhood home that she had once loved so much.

Trembling, she returned to her bed, lay down and tried to sleep.

Later that evening a frightened-looking maid came to her. The girl bobbed a curtsey and left food and drink, but spoke not a word. Acha tried to eat for the sake of the growing babe, but lay awake all night struggling to control both her misery and her fury.

He'd planned it all along, she realised that now, as she picked distractedly at the fine linen of her bed-gown. He'd schemed, not to kill her father perhaps, but he'd schemed and planned to take Deira. What a fool she'd been not to realise it.

When he called Oswald his little king, it wasn't just fond words – he'd been making plans to claim Deira in his name. Athelfrid would double his lands overnight. His ambition took her breath away.

And Bebba had sensed it, and warned her that there was something afoot. "His god is Loki"- she had said – the malevolent trickster god. How right she'd been.

Acha picked over every detail, every hint of trouble. She saw that she should have questioned what her husband was about, when she'd seen the vast stretch of tents, the weapons, the ranks of men. Her longing for her home had made her blind. She'd looked away.

Athelfrid had taken his pick of warriors from both Dalriada and Rheged; he must be invincible. She wondered which of his men had known of the plan. Who could she trust?

What were Coifi and Godric about? Coifi had helped haul Edwin away from the fight – she'd seen him do it. Then he'd quickly accepted Oswald as Deira's heir and Athelfrid as overlord. He'd stopped the fight and somehow made them listen to him.

She wandered over to the window and pushed open the wooden shutter, vaguely wondering if she could climb out. To do so might risk the child in her belly. She rested her hand on her stomach and felt a faint answering movement inside and small rush of protective love warmed her a little. None of this was the child's fault.

As she stood there looking out, she saw Prince Donal and Brother Finn arrive. They dismounted and led their horses towards the stables, their faces grim. What would they think of her now? They at least would surely understand that she'd had no part in this treachery? She struggled back to her bed. Darkness fell and more food was brought to her and again she tried to eat a little. All through the night she lay awake, agonising over what had happened, and it was only when dawn came that she dozed for a while, having come to some sort of acceptance of her situation.

As the sun came over the horizon, she set about dressing herself and arranging her hair. It was a long time since she'd done these things for herself and in her weakened state it seemed surprisingly difficult, but she told herself harshly that she must no longer play the fool.

She searched for what she needed in her chests and boxes of jewels and at last took up her mother's mirror to examine her reflection. She must look like a queen.

When the maid brought her food, she called to the guards and ordered them to take a message to Athelfrid. "Tell him Acha of Deira wishes to speak to him," she said.

One of the men bowed and hurried away at once, and it seemed he'd been given instructions to act quickly should such a summons come. She made herself eat, and was just finishing her meal when Athelfrid appeared.

He stepped lightly into the chamber, waited for a moment to assess her state of mind, then bowed over her hand and kissed it. He was so clever, this trickster; she must be clever too.

"You are right, husband," she said at last, struggling to keep her voice clear and steady. "What's done is done and we must make the best we can of it. I will do what you ask of me, but I must have my son returned to me immediately, and all my women too. That means Bree as well; there will be no more riding with the men for her."

Athelfrid opened his mouth to speak but she hurried on, not allowing him time to reply, not daring to pause for fear her courage fled.

"I will see my father buried as befits a great king – and all Deira must see his funeral rites performed with honour. Only then is there a chance that they'll accept our son as his heir."

Athelfrid looked as though he'd make a dismissive reply, but she went on. "And I need Godric and Coifi here. They are old friends, men that I trust, and I can only do what you ask of me, if they are at my side."

Athelfrid raised an eyebrow, stared for a moment, and then nodded. "It shall be done," he said and turned to go.

One more condition flashed through her mind and she knew she must speak while she had the anger and the courage to demand it.

"And Prince Donal," she said. "He has been here with us long enough. If I ride into Eforwic at your side then Prince Donal must be allowed to travel north to Dalriada; his time as a hostage has come to an end."

His jaw dropped slightly as he frowned, and then bowed in assent. He said nothing more, but turned swiftly, barking orders as he went.

CHAPTER 25

A SMALL VICTORY

Acha collapsed onto her bed, drained of strength, shocked that she'd managed to make her demands so calmly while her father's corpse still lay in Woden's temple and her brother hid in fear of his life.

She didn't have long to wait before her women arrived in a noisy huddle with a mixture of relief and fear there on their faces. Megan carried Oswald in her arms and the babe looked no worse for his brief abduction.

"Thank you Freya!" Acha breathed. She took him gently into her arms and rocked him, comforted somewhat by the soft warmth of his little cheek against hers.

Two Deiran women carried Oswald's crib back into the chamber. Acha knew them well from long ago, but she could see from their blank, surly, faces that it would be no easy task to win such as them over. All Deira might think her a traitor now.

She put Oswald carefully back into his cot and then flung her arms about each of her women in turn.

Clover's face crumpled in shame. "I never thought this of him, lady," she whispered. "He was a strong king, but always honourable…"

"I don't think he planned it this way," Acha allowed.

Bree shrugged and looked away; perhaps more than any of them, she knew the extent of Athelfrid's ruthless nature.

Acha took Megan aside. "I have agreed to what he wants," she said, shame-faced. "I have agreed, though I am sick to my boots at the thought of it. My father's killer takes his throne – and in the name of my own innocent babe."

Megan's eyes were red and swollen, but her voice was as firm as ever. "No choice," she said. "You have no choice."

"But how can I make myself do it?"

Megan shrugged. "You can and you will, for the sake of your child and the one who is to come; a mother can do anything to keep her children safe. Do what you have to do and don't question it."

The women set about their usual tasks, but an atmosphere of fear and uncertainty hung over them all. True to his word, Athelfrid sent Godric and Coifi to her. There was a moment of awkwardness when they arrived; they bowed but hesitated to speak. Acha sent her women to wait in the next room, and as soon as they'd gone she went to Godric and buried her head in his bony shoulder. A sorrowful smile touched Coifi's lips as he watched them and she stretched out her hand to clasp his.

"I'm so glad *you* are both alive and here with me," she whispered.

Godric was more of a father to her, than the peevish, unloving father that she had feared for so long, and Coifi, she knew, had always loved her.

When at last she pulled back, she felt Godric tremble a little; he was an old man.

"Come, sit down," she said. "You supported me, when you could have made other choices. It must have cost you dearly."

"There was little choice in it, Sword-queen," he said with a rueful smile.

"You should have gone with Edwin," she said, turning to Coifi.

"Edwin needs someone to stay here," he said quietly.

She understood and dropped her voice. "Do you know what has happened to my brother?"

"He is safe," Coifi told her.

"Is he close by?"

He shook his head. "He is safe – that is all I will tell you. Lilla is with him and there are others who left when they saw the way things went."

"He'll never forgive me," Acha murmured. She struggled to keep her chin from trembling. "I saw it in his eyes."

"I doubt he will forgive me either," Coifi admitted with a shrug.

"Did he see you bow to Athelfrid?"

"I didn't bow to Athelfrid," he said. "I bowed to Oswald and to you, Princess. There was no choice but to accept what Athelfrid demanded. If Edwin had not been dragged away – I doubt he'd be alive today."

She nodded, awed that he'd been able to think so fast, while she'd stumbled around in a nightmare daze, unable to do anything but fearfully clutch her child.

"What you did saved lives," she admitted. "But I saw Edwin's face and it was full of hatred. Will he rally his supporters in Eforwic?"

Godric shook his head. "Edwin cannot match the forces your husband has out there," he said nodding towards the open shutter. "He has an army of battle-hardened warriors at his back; Edwin wouldn't stand a chance, however full of rage he might be."

"Lilla knows the truth of the situation," Coifi said. "Your father was growing old. After you left he became… difficult, especially with Edwin!"

"I saw my father's frailty," she agreed. "But frailty did not dampen his pride or his anger," she added, remembering how he'd flown at Athelfrid.

Godric shrugged. "Edwin suspected that Athelfrid wished him ill ever since he heard that he'd forbidden the alliance with Rheged and persuaded King Elffin to refuse to give him his daughter in marriage."

"Athelfrid prevented Edwin's marriage?"

"He ordered the King of Rheged to withdraw the offer of his daughter's hand and threatened war if it was not done."

Acha nodded, she'd feared something of the sort.

"Edwin will want revenge," Godric admitted, "but for now we must trust Lilla to keep him safe. Though," he added with a sigh, "we know that Athelfrid's vanguard-men are searching for him even now."

Acha shuddered at the thought of what would be sure to happen if they found him. "I wish I could speak to Edwin," she said. "But I see that I cannot. I pray that you are right about Lilla. Where will they go?"

Neither of them wished to answer.

"You are quite right," she said. "Tell me nothing! My husband is eaten up with ambition, and nothing will stand in his way." She whispered, knowing that such words would be considered treason by any of Athelfrid's followers.

"You must never speak so to another living soul," Godric said.

There was a moment of quiet between them; then Coifi spoke again. "Eforwic is not the place it was, Princess. The floods ripped the heart from the settlement and, for a while, it was deserted. Now traders are moving back, but there is still much ruin and struggle. "

"What of my father's hall?" she asked.

"It had to be abandoned, but Edwin has been re-building further to the east in a more open space, this was part of their quarrel. Aelle has turned his back on the town and put his resources into re-building Londesborough. He hadn't the heart for starting in Eforwic again, I think."

"There's much for me to learn," she admitted, with a weary sigh.

Godric got to his feet. "You need rest," he said. "We will leave you now, but be assured that we will endeavour to keep the peace here in Deira. Maybe a time will come when it will be possible for your brother to return."

"I have rested too long," she said. "I need to act!"

Godric kissed her forehead and Coifi her hand, then they left her.

When they'd gone she sat down quickly, her mind still struggling against the mist that was left by the poppy juice that had protected her from pain. She saw that Edwin could return only on her husband's death – or even worse to contemplate – the death of Oswald or any other child of hers.

At noon Athelfrid sent for her to attend him in the mead-hall.

"I dare not go into that place again," she said when she received the message, for she seemed to see her father's body fall and crumple at Athelfrid's feet again and again.

"But I think you must," Megan said. "It's been cleaned and made decent," she added with sharp practicality.

"Will you come with me, then?" Acha begged.

"Of course I will."

Megan had been right – an army of slaves had been set to wash and scrub and now the hall smelled of fresh rushes and strewing herbs. A fire burned in the hearth, while hunting dogs and house cats lolled together in the warmth once more. It was hard to believe it had so recently been the scene of brutal slaughter.

Athelfrid sat by the hearth with Coifi and Godric in attendance, along with his Bernician thanes. As Acha walked in, all the men rose to bow to her, even Athelfrid.

"Come, sit down, lady," he said, indicating Aelle's carved gift-stool. She took her father's chair, knowing that she must not betray a scrap of weakness, under the gaze of her husband's followers.

"We will travel on to Eforwic and camp one night upon the way," Athelfrid began. "When we enter the town, we will put on a show of power and strength that won't have been seen in Eforwic since the Romans. Deira will know that resistance is useless and *you,* my queen, must head our procession and be seen by all."

She wanted to scream in protest that she was no queen, Bebba was his queen – but she glanced at Godric's anxious brow and breathed in deeply. "We shall stop at Pockleton," she said; Godric's hall there would feel familiar and safe.

Godric bowed his agreement. "You are welcome, as ever, Princess," he said. "It's just a morning's march from there to Eforwic."

She turned back to Athelfrid. "Have you food and supplies enough to feed your army?" she asked. "There must be no scavenging from the land if you are to win my people over."

He looked taken aback to be questioned by her on such practical matters, but recovered quickly. "We have provisions to last until the harvest," he replied. "Once I have Eforwic secured, I will send both Dalriads and Rheged-men, home."

She leaned back for a moment, thinking fast, for his courteous words implied a subtle threat. The kingdom must be settled fast and the army disbanded, or Deira would be sure to pay a high price at harvest time.

And yet there was another important matter; her father's body lay neglected in Woden's temple. The bonds between Aelle and his children were weak, but still he should be given the funeral rites a warrior-king deserved. It was a matter of honour. The ceremonies might also allow her brother time to escape to safety.

She pulled herself up to sit as straight as she could, lifted her chin and turned to speak to Athelfrid. "However urgent our progress to Eforwic," she said, as she struggled to keep her voice firm and strong. "One vital thing remains to be done. My father deserves a warrior king's death rites. He died with a sword in his hand and must be sent to Woden's Hall with all honour due – and Deira must see it done."

Her husband's thanes stared aghast to hear her plainly challenge their king's decision to ride for Eforwic at once. Even Godric looked concerned and for a moment she feared she'd gone too far, but Megan gave a sharp nod of approval. The silence in the hall was so intense that for a few moments, only the soft yelping of the dogs and the crackle and spit of the fire could be heard, but at last Athelfrid gave a brief nod and turned to Coifi.

"Can you do what needs to be done quickly and let it be seen to be done? As high priest of Woden here, you must conduct these rites."

"Yes lord," Coifi bowed. "A Deiran king's death rites should be held at Goodmanham, where the temple of Woden stands. It isn't far from here. It should take two days to build a pyre and send messengers out. The food and drink required must be prepared."

Acha held her breath and there was another moment of silence.

"Very well. See to it at once," Athelfrid brusquely replied.

Coifi bowed and left the hall.

Frustrated by this brief delay, Athelfrid clenched and unclenched his fist, but his wife's argument was sound enough, and maybe Eforwic would prove easier to tackle if he'd already appeased Aelle's followers by allowing his funeral rites to take priority. Suddenly, drained of strength and energy, Acha rose to her feet.

"I must prepare for my father's death rites," she said and left the hall quickly, followed by Megan, before Athelfrid changed his mind.

Once outside, all her courage ebbed away and she clutched her old nurse's arm, feeling suddenly breathless.

The old woman rubbed her back. “Don’t fret,” she said. “You did well – a small victory, I think.”

“A small victory,” Acha agreed.

It was true that Athelfrid had almost treated her with the sort of respect he usually gave to his comrades. There’d been an unspoken acknowledgement of her power, but would she find the strength to continue in this manner?

***

Athelfrid stared after her, uncertain as to why he felt disturbed. She seemed to be doing all he’d asked of her – all he’d asked and more. Perhaps that was what unsettled him. He frowned as uncertainty flitted through his mind – who was the trickster now?

CHAPTER 26

CONSPIRACY

The days of preparation for Aelle's rites seemed to pass slowly and the hall was full of tension throughout. Every raised voice, every angry response, every dropped platter or beaker, brought fears that the palace might erupt into violence once again. Everyone from the waiting women to the servants and slaves was touchy and easily offended. Hardest of all to bear for Acha, was the way that so many former allies from her childhood, now looked away from her, distrust written on their faces.

"They hate me here, where once I was loved," she confided when Coifi came to report on the preparations he'd made.

"They watch me too with suspicion," he said. "They have no knowledge of the narrow path we tread, but they are alive and living much as they did before – and in time I hope they will come to see that neither you nor I have had any choice in this matter."

"Blessed Freya… I pray that you are right," she said. "I cannot tell you how much I have missed my home and longed to be with people who knew me since I was a child. Now I am here, it is bitter as poison."

"Hold fast!" he said. "Things will change. They will see, in time, that you've saved lives."

"I pray they will," she murmured.

"Your father's death rites may be difficult for you to bear," he warned. "There will be moments that may shock you, when you stand in front of your father's pyre."

She looked at him curiously, feeling that there was perhaps more to his words than he felt he could openly say.

"I will hold fast," she said.

The day of the funeral dawned and Athelfrid tactfully remained behind at Londesbrough while Acha was carried to Goodmanham in her litter. Megan and Oswald rode with her, the child smiling and waving cheerfully at the horses and dogs that trotted along beside them. Godric escorted them and provided a Deiran warrior band, though Athelfrid had insisted that his vanguard-men ride close behind them.

The pyre, though built in haste, could be seen from a distance. It was built with a low central platform and steps and was the work of skilled carpenters, even though it would go up in flames before the day was out.

Many of the local thanes and freemen had already arrived, their arms bright with gold rings carrying gifts of drink and offerings of sheep and goats. They milled around the ancient terraces that had been cut into the hillside long ago, just a short distance from Woden's temple. These terraces offered seating and a view of the important ceremony that would take place on Woden's holy spot.

Godric led Acha to the front. She followed him, her head held high, only too aware of tensions in amongst the gathering. Both she and Oswald must be vulnerable, but Athelfrid had insisted that the child be present and in full view of the crowd. It would only take a dagger's flash or a bold swordsman and they could both be slaughtered.

She let her guard slip for a moment and glanced fearfully back at Megan, who followed behind.

"Stay strong," her old nurse whispered. "If you can face Athelfrid and his thanes as you did the other day, you can deal with this lot."

Acha nodded and smiled sadly as an oddly comforting thought came to her. "You are right. What could happen? What could be worse than what has already happened?"

Megan nodded. "That's it, my lass."

They took their places, aware of resentful stares and angry whispers. Horns blared, making Oswald jump, and then an expectant stillness settled over the crowd. All heads turned at the sound of a beating drum. A long procession, accompanied by the sounding of more horns, set off from the temple in the distance.

Coifi led the priests of Woden in full regalia, with his raven-winged headdress and totem carried in front. As the procession moved closer, the watching crowd saw that Aelle's corpse was carried on an open litter, draped in a rich purple cloak, and a gold fillet had been placed on his head. The dead king's arms gleamed with gold bands and his sword had been placed in his right hand and set across his chest. There was now no sign of the ghastly death wound, but Acha found, after the first glance, that she could not look at her father's corpse again.

He was lifted from the litter by the priests of Woden and carried respectfully up the steps to be laid on the top of the pyre, which was hung about with shields. Three oxen were swiftly slaughtered by Coifi and carried off towards the roasting spits, where the butchers set about their work. None who attended the rites would go home hungry, and soon the scent of roasting meat began to drift across the terraces. Two of the king's oldest hunting dogs were slaughtered and laid on either side of their master. At last Coifi turned to Acha to invite her to take the torch and set it to the pyre, as she knew he would.

If Deira was to turn against her, surely it must be now. Would they allow her to stand up and take the role of queen? Would they allow her to light her father's funeral pyre? She handed Oswald to Megan and rose to her feet, stony-faced, as Coifi calmly held out his hand to lead her forward. Where now was the shy boy she'd feared could never take on the role of Woden's high priest? His quiet courage and warm squeeze of her hand, gave her strength as she walked towards the pyre.

Then, as she approached, a hooded man strode forwards, bearing the flaming torch that would light the pyre. Acha hesitated at something familiar in the way he moved. The dark cloak he wore and the torch he carried marked him out as a priest of Woden, but the slight flick of his head and the way he momentarily shuffled his right foot before taking a solid stance, were unmistakable. It was

Edwin who strode forward to meet her, in front of their father's pyre.

Another hooded figure moved close behind him – Lilla of course! She glanced at Coifi and understood that this was what he'd been trying to warn her about. What a dangerous game they played!

Her heart thundered as she moved again, afraid to give her brother away by the slightest quiver, the smallest sign of surprise or awkwardness. Her heart swelled with love for him – and fear. He seemed so brave and foolhardy, standing together with her in front of their father's pyre. She knew that Athelfrid's vanguard-men watched from the edges of the crowd and it took all her strength and courage to keep calm and still.

Edwin stared grim-faced at her for what seemed like a very long time. "You risk much," she said.

"Now is your chance, sister," he said. "Call forward your husband's men to take me!"

She smiled then, for she saw this was a reckless test of her loyalty. "I'd rather die than betray you," she said. "And I see that you are no longer the boy I left behind."

"I have aged many years, these last few days," he said bitterly. "But I see that this was no doing of yours."

"What can I do to help you?" she asked.

"Nothing" he said. "Stay here. Be queen, you have the right. Hold Deira for me. I will return."

"But… my son?"

Edwin's hand went up to catch the leather thong that still circled his neck. "By this oath that we once made… by Woden, by my father's blood… I swear that I will never harm you or your children."

"I thank you for that," she whispered.

"Take my hand, sister," he said, "and together we will light our father's pyre. Then I shall be gone."

Acha reached out to place her hand on his and the drumming and the chanting of the crowd grew louder. "Aelle! Aelle!" they cried.

Tears blurred her vision, but somehow they moved together along the pyre, thrusting the torch into the stacked green wood. A sudden rush of smoke caught at her throat and made her eyes water, but it was a good omen. Plenty of smoke that curled and twisted high into the sky would carry Aelle's spirit with it to the feasting hall of Woden. At last the wood sparked and caught fire; flames roared into life. A blaze of sudden heat blasted her face and forced her to let go of the torch and step backwards.

Coifi caught her by the arm and guided her back towards the terraces. When she looked again, Edwin had vanished.

"It was well done!" Coifi said. "It was very well done!"

"It was cleverly done," she whispered.

She went back to her place and Megan handed Oswald over with a brief, knowing smile.

"You knew," Acha whispered.

Megan shook her head. "Not until I saw him."

The fire burned fiercely, so that even the priests of Woden were forced to edge away. Acha glanced about her, to find that the Deirans watched the blaze solemnly, their faces shimmering with reflected flame and shadow. They gave no sign that their hunted prince was present, but they knew, she felt sure of it – all of them knew. She had become part of a dark conspiracy and her heart was filled with joy at the thought of it. She resolutely lowered her gaze to drop a kiss on Oswald's soft head. Even he was still and quiet, watching wide-eyed as the flames leapt higher.

"Freya, preserve my brother and my children," she murmured.

At last the fierce intensity of the blaze eased a little, and smuts flew through the air, to mark the onlookers' cheeks. Then suddenly the peace was broken as warriors took up their swords and began beating on their shields.

Oswald gave a small cry at the thudding of hooves in the distance. The sound grew louder and everyone turned their heads in eager anticipation. Glimmers of flame on metal heralded the approach of the riders they knew would come. Ten of Aelle's thanes appeared on horseback; they burst into view to gallop around the pyre. Acha closed her eyes in fear, for she saw that Edwin was leading them, still hooded in priest's garb, but mounted on a black mare. She froze and held her breath, while the crowd began chanting wildly once more.

"Ride on ravens, wings great warrior

Fast to the feasting hall of Woden

Sleep sweet on the breast of the battle maidens

Fearless, fighter… Aelle! Aelle! Aelle!"

Clutching Oswald, Acha turned frantically to Megan. Her nurse put her arms round them both and held them tightly. Would the people rally to him now and turn on Athelfrid? Edwin rode around his father's funeral pyre, carrying the banner of the spreading oak tree of Deira. The thunder of horses' hooves beat in time with the booming roar of the crowd.

"Blessed Freya," Acha whispered.

The noise became deafening, but then all at once the horsemen circling the pyre turned south and headed fast away. The drumming and shouting faded and Coifi strode forward to blow one long blast on his horn – the signal for the feast to begin.

"I thought for a moment… I feared they might…" Acha gasped with relief.

Megan shook her head. "They are not such fools!"

"He has gone now, hasn't he?" She felt bereft, wondering if she'd ever see Edwin again. Would he ride to Eforwic to mount rebellion against her husband, or leave quietly under Lilla's protection?

But she was glad he'd been there. Aelle – loved or not – was their father. Edwin had more right to ride around the funeral pyre than any other. As the flames died down a little, the nature of the ceremony changed. The succulent, cheering scent of roasted oxen drifted around the gathering and melded with the honeyed aroma of mead. Quiet greetings were exchanged, as food and drink was passed amongst the crowd.

Acha felt she could not eat, but Megan bullied her to take a sip or two of mead and nibble some fresh bread. "Think of the child," she said.

"I'll have no more children," Acha said.

Megan rounded on her quick as a whip. "Will you have the choice?"

Coifi bowed distantly in their direction, and she sensed that he was avoiding her now. Perhaps he was right to do so, for so many reasons – she could not have refrained from asking questions that he could only refuse to answer. Godric saw her pallor and suggested that they return to Londesbrough. "You have done all you possibly can," he said.

"Did you see…?" she began.

"I saw nothing," he cut in quickly.

She nodded, falling obediently quiet, as she allowed him to guide her towards her litter.

"Blessings, lady," a soft voice murmured beside her.

"Blessings, Aelle's daughter," someone behind her said.

As she passed through the crowds, she received more bows, curtsies and softly-spoken greetings. Her heart lifted at the kind words, for it seemed the bitter resentment she'd been aware of might in time ebb away. Perhaps Deira was beginning to understand that she had done her best in an impossible situation and still stood firmly with them. She'd stood shoulder to shoulder with her brother to light Aelle's pyre and neither by word, nor deed, had she given him away.

Athelfrid hurried out to meet her when she arrived back at Londesbrough. He saw at once, as she stepped down red-eyed and pale-faced from her litter, that she was exhausted. "One day of rest," he pronounced, "and then we travel on to Pockleton."

Acha nodded. That would allow another day and night for Edwin to ride away, or to slip onto a boat that might carry him downriver and along the coast to some safe haven.

Just as she was settling to sleep, Megan came to disturb her.

"I know you are bone weary," she said. "But there are two friends out in the hall who are asking for you, and I thought you'd want to see them."

She struggled up from her bed and allowed Megan to wrap a cloak about her sleeping shift. Out in the hall, sitting by the hearth, she discovered Prince Donal and Brother Finn. She greeted them with a cry of joy, but they rose to their feet and Donal sank down on one knee before her, bowing formally.

"Lady, the king has released us," he said. "Athelfrid has set us free, but we know who we have to thank for this. We will never forget you – or your kindness to us."

Acha pulled him to his feet and hugged him tightly.

"Oh, but I will miss you both," she said, looking sadly past him to Brother Finn. Then she pulled away, feeling agitated. "And you must go at once. Slip quietly away now, while Athelfrid needs my support and there are other things to distract him."

"Princess, from this day on Dalriada will be in your debt. You and yours will always be welcome there – and if ever you need friendship or aid, look to us."

Acha smiled, deeply touched by Donal's words. She remembered the lost and frightened boy, the young hostage brought to Bebbanburgh. "Well, you could help me now," she said. "There is one true friend that I have left behind in Bernicia. I'd be so grateful if you could break your journey northwards to speak to her on my behalf, to explain a little of what has happened here."

Brother Finn nodded, smiling sadly. "Of course we will ride to Bebbanburgh and speak to Queen Bebba on your behalf."

CHAPTER 27

SWORD-QUEEN

After the one day of rest allowed to her, Acha felt better in her body and more certain in her mind. She climbed into her litter, dressed comfortably for the journey, while Athelfrid's army waited with Godric and Coifi. As soon as she was settled, they set off towards Pockleton, Sidhe following behind her, led by Duncan. There were moments when Acha thought wryly that she'd be more comfortable on horseback than in the swaying litter. They arrived at dusk and Acha slept that night in the familiar hall, comforted by memories of happier times. When Godric appeared at her chamber door the following morning, looking embarrassed, she braced herself for more bad news.

"The king has sent me to ask… no, to beg, that you dress in your richest gown and jewels," he told her. "He wishes you to enter Eforwic as its queen."

"I will dress with care, of course," she agreed, puzzled that Athelfrid should send such a message.

Godric coughed uneasily. "He says that you are to ride your white mare in through the gates and into the old centre of the town, so that everyone can see you and your fine steed. New clothing is also provided for your little prince."

Acha and her women stared, astounded. No wonder Godric was uneasy… for he was asking a pregnant woman to ride, when most would think she were much safer in a litter.

Acha smiled wryly. "So… after all his warnings for my safety and that of the babe, it seems this second child means less to him," she murmured. “Now I see why he sends you to me, dear friend. He dare not face me and say it himself.”

“Our princess cannot ride!” Emma protested.

Godric shook his head sadly, unable to hide his distress.

Acha turned uncertainly to Megan and the old woman shrugged. “Can you trust your mare to carry you amongst a busy crowd?” she asked.

“Yes,” Acha nodded, with a smile. “I'd trust her anywhere.”

“Then I think you must obey,” she said.

Godric nodded too. “Sword-queen, you were always an excellent horse-woman, none better,” he acknowledged.

“Then we'd best get on with it,” Acha said. “There's many a farmer's wife rides safely to market when she's pregnant. I don't see why I cannot do it.”

“There will be nowhere in Eforwic fit for you to stay tonight,” he warned. “Even the elders and thanes now build new halls outside the walls. This taking of the ancient capital must be symbolic, as things stand. Only Edwin struggled to renew the centre.”

“Then I shall return here to your hall, if you are willing,” she said.

“You are always welcome here.”

So quietly they set about preparing her. They dressed her in a loose gown of finest linen, weld-dyed to a soft green with the sleeves trimmed heavily with gold thread and braiding. Tiny flowers had been stitched all over the gown and against the deep red of her under-gown the gold and green gave an impression of opulence and ripe fertility.

Acha watched Bree as she helped her dress, with solemn concentration on her face. “You know what we are about,” she said. “You know what he wants.”

“Yes,” the girl acknowledged. “You are to be his queen in Deira.”

Bree braided her hair and fixed it high on her head, then set a gold and garnet diadem in place. Acha fingered her girdle with all its useful implements and reluctantly set it aside, but not before she'd removed a small dagger that she usually carried in a sheath there. “I won't go without it,” she said quietly.

Her women saw what she'd done and looked alarmed, but Bree took the dagger and sheath and fastened it with a leather thong onto Acha's left forearm, so that it lay there, easily accessible, but hidden by the wide sleeves.

"Thank you," Acha whispered. "You understand me well."

As a finishing touch they set a red cloak about her shoulders.

"You are a queen," Bree said.

Clover nodded sombrely. There was no joy in any of this.

"It's what we wanted for you long ago," Emma said. "Aelle's daughter *should* have been a queen, but not like this."

Athelfrid hurried forward when she appeared in the courtyard with her women, and she saw relief on his face. Bree had chosen her robes faultlessly yet again. Her husband bowed low over her hand and kissed it, she received his salute without comment or response.

Duncan led Sidhe forward; she was fitted with a roomy, soft-leather saddle and rigged with an unfamiliar, sumptuous gilded halter and bridle, decorated with tassels of gold thread. None of this was Duncan's doing. He'd never caparison a mare in such fancy gear. Bronze bells tinkled as she tossed her head, and Acha guessed that Athelfrid must have had these trappings specially made, at great expense, some time ago.

How long had he been planning to take her father's kingdom, she wondered? Was it since she gave birth to Oswald? Did the idea go even further back – had he intended it since he accepted her as payment of tribute? A memory came back to her from that day, when he'd whispered the words – "sons of royal Deiran blood"!

Sidhe turned her head and blew softly in greeting as she caught her mistress's scent. A wooden mounting block was carried forward and both Godric and Duncan helped Acha mount. Despite the slight awkwardness of her growing belly, she managed to settle herself in the saddle, and once there the familiar feel of the sturdy beast beneath her was calming. She leant forward and stroked the muscular withers, wishing more than anything that she could turn the mare's head and ride off instead towards the heather moors.

"Whenever you wish to stop, just hold up your hand," Athelfrid told her, then he turned and mounted his black stallion. "To Eforwic!" he cried.

They moved forward without saddle-mead or speeches, the vast army slowly falling in behind. Acha prayed silently that Edwin was already far away.

As they travelled on through the familiar landscape, the swinging motion of the horse beneath her brought some comfort. Bree rode beside her, dressed modestly, and Acha was reassured to see the strongly-built wagon that followed, bearing Oswald and her other women. It was only then that she saw that the wagon itself was draped in fine leather hangings, decorated with repeated motifs of Deiran oak leaves that circled the torch-flame of Bernicia. Those hangings must have been months in the making… all stitched and painted with care – the work of Goats' Hill craftsmen, she'd swear.

The linked symbols fluttered everywhere on flags – they decorated shields, and the standard that led the procession. Even Oswald's little tunic, made of spun gold thread, carried the symbol embroidered on the front. What a fool she'd been!

Athelfrid rode ahead, the sun catching the golden flame on the crest of his war helmet. He'd been planning this all though the bitter months, while his wives had sat cosily together, listening to the waves and the singing of the seals at Bebbanburgh! He had her trapped by her love for her child and her fear of seeing Deira run with blood. He was a clever man and she hated him.

She glanced back to Coifi and Godric, who rode behind the wagon, Woden's raven totem carried in front of them, and knew that she must submit for the sake of peace. The child she carried would be born in her homeland. She need not return to Bernicia – not now, perhaps not ever. She should have listened more carefully to the queen's warnings – Bebba had sensed Athelfrid's duplicity – and against her own interests, tried to alert her sister wife to danger.

As they came in sight of the walls of Eforwic, every tree, every bush and rolling hill became familiar. Since the devastation of the floods, it seemed that Freya had blessed this land, though famine could still come quickly upon them if this army stayed for long.

They passed the lake where, as a child, she'd once stripped naked to swim with Edwin and his companions, and the old shepherd's shack where they'd built a fire and sat late into the night, until Megan came searching for them.

Now they rode through hamlets fallen into ruin on the outskirts of the town, and she remembered what Godric and Coifi had said about the quarrel between her father and Edwin. How frustrated her brother must have been by her father's refusal to set Eforwic to rights. Its situation at the joining of two rivers made it the perfect trading spot and the walls of the old Roman fort were a strong protective shell within which to build again, though the old site Aelle had chosen must be avoided in future. The town needed embankments and ditches perhaps. Had resources been put into strengthening Eforwic sooner, Edwin might have been able to gather an army to garrison the town as King Peredur was once said to have done and thrown off this invasion – for that was what this was, an invasion.

The seed of an idea began to grow in Acha's mind, an idea that somehow gave her hope. Could she build up the strength of Eforwic herself, in preparation for her brother's return?

Bree glanced at her and smiled. "This was your home," she said.

"And it shall be again," Acha replied. "A poor home at the moment, but if Athelfrid wants a queen he shall get one – a queen who builds towers and river defences."

Bree nodded and narrowed her eyes in glee. "More than he bargained for!"

Acha smiled to herself and made a private promise: I *will* build in readiness so that Edwin may one day return to the Eforwic he wished for.

As they advanced on the south-eastern gateway they were spotted by lookouts, who sounded warning notes on their horns. Without hesitation, Athelfrid rode on, but when he reached the gates of the old fortress they were swiftly shut against him. There was a flurry of activity above, as armed warriors appeared on the walls to stare down at them.

Let this not turn to bloodshed, Acha prayed! Let them not resist!

Athelfrid's followers beat their swords on their shields and sounded their horns, creating a deafening cacophony, which howled and thundered all around the ancient walls and announced the presence of a vast army at the gates. From their elevated position, the defenders stared in terror as rank on rank of warriors marched into their sights.

Acha's hand moved to check her dagger; this must be the moment of decision. Which way would it fall? But she need not have feared, for as more and more of Athelfrid's fighting men marched into sight, and Godric and Coifi were recognised, a decision was quickly made and the gates were opened again to reveal a hesitant deputation of her father's thanes. They fell to their knees and humbly laid their weapons down in the dust.

Acha closed her eyes for one brief moment, not wanting to see; these were men she'd known and respected throughout her childhood, and it was deeply humiliating for them to capitulate so swiftly. When she forced herself to look again she saw that none of them were Edwin's men. Those who offered their swords in submission were the older warriors, elderly thanes, the reeve and some of the merchants. Where were their sons? With a small leap of hope, she saw that all the younger warriors were missing. If Edwin had escaped into exile, he had not gone alone.

Athelfrid accepted the swords graciously enough and returned them to their owners. He made them form an advance guard, so that those who'd surrendered were now forced to lead the usurper into Eforwic. Then suddenly every face turned Acha's way. She quailed at the attention, and searched helplessly for approval, but saw that the capitulating elders regarded her blankly, their faces tight as masks.

"What now?" she murmured.

Athelfrid rode back to the wagon and spoke to Emma, who held Oswald out to him. Acha was not pleased. Surely he couldn't intend to ride into Eforwic with Oswald on his saddle. How vulnerable would the child be to any glancing blow or dart? But Athelfrid brought his horse to a halt beside her own, and it was then that she understood what he intended.

"Take the boy in front of you," he ordered. "Take our son and lead us into Eforwic. You are to be Queen here. I promised you that."

Oswald smiled and held out his arms to her. "Maa… ma," he cried.

She had no choice, but maybe she could buy some small concession. Ignoring her child's eager face, she spoke to her husband.

"I will do what you ask," she said. "But in return, *you* will not bring your army within these walls."

Anger flashed in his eyes, but it was swiftly followed by a rueful lift of the eyebrow.

"You cannot ride in there alone," he objected.

"No. I will ride with Coifi and Godric at my side and the Eforwic elders. Bring your hearth-companions to escort us, but send your army back to set up camp."

"Maa…ma!" Oswald glanced worriedly back at his father and reached out again to Acha.

This time she took him and settled him in front of her, where he proceeded to click his tongue as though eagerly urging Sidhe to walk on. At the sight of his hopeful little face the atmosphere around them lightened a little and Acha dropped a kiss on the soft golden head.

Athelfrid shrugged. "Maybe there is some sense in this," he admitted.

He turned to his captains to give orders, and then gathered his household thanes around him.

"Go ahead!" Athelfrid said. "Take your kingdom… take the queenship I have promised you! Go with Woden's priest at your side." Holding his stallion back, he ushered her forward with a sweep of his hand.

Coifi urged his horse on too, so that he rode at her side, while Oswald flapped his hands, excited to see so many faces ahead of them.

Their first glimpse through the archway told them that the streets of Eforwic were crammed with hastily-armed men and curious women. There was a moment of shocked silence as Acha and her child rode through, followed by an audible gasp. She tightened her grip on Oswald, stretching her fingers across his belly to touch the hilt of her dagger. She would kill them both rather than be taken as a traitor. But it seemed she need not have feared such a thing.

"Welcome your queen, Acha of Deira," Coifi cried.

"It is Acha… Acha and her bairn," they murmured.

"And look… is she not with child again?"

Cheers rose around them and she recognised a few familiar faces in the crowd. So, with the standard of Woden behind her and Coifi at her side, Acha entered the town of Eforwic. Athelfrid followed a few paces behind, an expression of quiet satisfaction on his face.

Far away towards the north, kittiwakes cried, sea eagles soared on the soft breeze and seals raised their mournful song as they emerged from the water to bask upon the wide stretch of golden sand. A young boy and a man rode in through the gates of Bebbanburgh with important pledges of love to deliver, from one sister queen to another, before they could set out on the long journey westwards to their home in Dalriada.

CHAPTER 28

A QUEEN IN EFORWIC

Acha moved on into Eforwic. At first the jostling, cheering throng was overwhelming, but as she moved on through the familiar streets, she noticed that several thatches needed repair and many buildings were uninhabitable. Gradually the welcome became more subdued and the eager crowds moved back a little, giving her space. She crossed the River Foss at the ford and people flocked after her to splash through the shallow water. Instinctively she had guided her mare towards the site of her father's old palace, but what she discovered there brought a lump to her throat. There was little left, just piles of dank, rotting timber that was so useless that nobody had even bothered to steal it.

Those who'd gathered about her broke up into hushed groups. The dismal sight brought back the shame she'd felt that terrible night when she rode away, turning a deaf ear to the screams, the cries for help, the desperate mothers' pleas.

Now she'd returned to Eforwic in triumph, with a powerful warrior at her side. But what they'd taken was a struggling town. The magnificent columns of the ancient Roman meeting place stood amongst piles of filth and rubbish.

Athelfrid stared about him, amazed at the sight of the ruined palace and the neglected Roman splendour. Something deep within her wanted to laugh – if she were not so close to tears. Did he think it worth it, she wondered? Was this what he'd killed her father for? Godric was right – there was nowhere fit for them to stay. Even

Oswald had grown still and silent, perched on her saddle, sensing the tense atmosphere.

But then a little way towards the north-eastern gate, beyond the desolation, she glimpsed a sturdy timber frame in the process of being built. She stopped to survey the work and then urged Sidhe towards it. The people followed her, whispering and curious as to what her reaction might be.

This new building had been well thought out, and was set on a low mound, not too close to the Roman walls to form a flood trap. The post holes that supported the timber frame were deep and packed around with heavy stonework. Small but sturdy huts and workshops had developed around the edges of the structure, with stalls selling bread, pottage and oatcakes to the hungry workers. Women with clean, well-fed, warmly clothed children in their arms appeared from doorways. This developing area of the devastated town still appeared to thrive and held some hope for the future. It was Edwin's project, the one that he'd been so keen to promote, against his father's will.

She glanced around to catch Godric's eye, grateful that he had warned her of the situation. She reined her mare close to Athelfrid.

"This work must be finished," she said. "I shall live here."

Applause broke out around her, and her husband had little choice but to agree. "It is positioned well," he acknowledged.

"And the debris from the old palace must be cleared," she added.

He ground his teeth. "I will bring in men to do it," he said.

"No," she shook her head. "We need grain and goods, not men. The carpenters, thatchers, and builders who started the work must finish it. They are Eforwic men – see, they live close by, they have all on hand. But they must be well paid for their labour."

A roar of approval rose around her. Athelfrid's sharp intake of breath filled her with dread – had she gone too far? She urged Sidhe closer so that the two of them could speak more privately. "This is how we will win them over," she said.

He shook his head, whistled softly and smiled. "You should have been my queen," he said.

But she shook her head. "No – it was always agreed. You have a true and honourable queen in Bebba."

Then, feeling suddenly very weary, she turned back to Godric. "Please lead us back to your hall for tonight, dear friend."

Godric led her out through the gates again and Athelfrid and his men followed. Seeing them leave, the murmuring crowd began to disperse.

In the days that followed, Athelfrid kept his word and the carpenters and tree-smiths were soon at work again. The word went out for thatchers, metal-workers, hurdle-makers, spinners, weavers and potters. They too were paid well and supplied with good food, so that work progressed fast. Acha persuaded her husband to disband his vast army of followers, so that the men could go to their homes to help with the harvest. Even Athelfrid seemed satisfied for the moment with this new kingdom that he'd gained. By the time Harvest-month had ended, the hall was finished. Within days of moving into the building Acha went into labour rather earlier than Megan had expected her to.

Her nurse made soothing drinks and spoke calmly to her as ever, but Acha sensed something hesitant in her old nurse's attitude.

"Is there something wrong?" she gasped in the brief space of relief that came between her pains. After all that had happened during her pregnancy it would not be surprising if the child had been harmed.

Megan sighed. "There is nothing wrong as far as I can feel," she said, "but my fingers grow stiff and I cannot see as well as I used to, and when the head starts to crown..."

"You should have told me," Acha said sharply.

"You had enough to trouble you and I thought there'd be time..."

"Ah – here it comes again!" Acha cried.

Megan fell quiet and reached up to rub her back as another wave of pain washed over her. When at last it eased Acha looked hurriedly around her at the troubled faces of the Deiran women who now served her. Who could she trust wholeheartedly? She knew that Emma was at Londesbrough looking after Oswald while a new nursery chamber was prepared for him, and she'd put Clover in charge of ordering the evening feast.

"Bree – fetch Bree," she demanded.

Bree was called from the hearthside where she sat embroidering the hem of a new gown.

"Roll up your sleeves," Acha commanded. "You will have to act as midwife under Megan's instructions."

Bree glanced at Megan and chuckled, though she rolled up her sleeves at once.

"This you never foresaw," she said.

"No I did not," Megan agreed, "but needs must. You will have to be my eyes and listen well, I can feel that the child is almost ready to appear and you must be ready to clear the nose and mouth, to tie the string and cut the cord."

Despite the difficulties, they worked well together and it was Bree who handed Acha her second son. Despite his early arrival and the hardships that his mother had suffered during her pregnancy, he appeared to be strong. They named him Osgood, hoping that the gods would make him as beautiful as his brother.

Acha smiled up at Megan and Bree, with the new babe in her arms. "You've both done well," she said.

"I'd best teach this one a few of my remedies," Megan said.

Acha nodded, noticing sadly the weary stoop of Megan's shoulders and the awkward stiffness in her old nurse's movements. She should have seen it herself, but she'd been too wrapped up in her own troubles. How would she ever manage without her loving care?

Athelfrid waited a few days to see that the child thrived, and then prepared to head northwards. It was time to oversee the gathering of tribute at Goats' Hill, and harry those late payers from the immense stretch of tributary lands that he now claimed.

It was with relief that Acha, newly-risen from childbed, carried the farewell mead-horn round to his hearth-companions – and when they'd gone it was almost as though the whole of Eforwic heaved a sigh. She was queen of lands that she felt she had every right to hold, but she quietly reminded herself and her trusted friends that she held them only until the rightful king returned.

***

Over the next few years a pattern developed through the seasons. Athelfrid returned each harvest time, anxious to reinforce his rights over Deira, even though each year the lands he ruled as overlord grew wider still. Acha acknowledged to herself, with secret guilt, that the more land her husband ruled, and the wider the borders he maintained – the fewer and more infrequent, became the burden of her wifely duties towards him.

For eight summers he held true to his promise to demand no tribute from the kingdom of Deira, not of grain, nor gold, nor men. Throughout that time Acha ruled Eforwic and the lands around with the steadfast support of Coifi and Godric.

Outside the walls to the south of the town a busy trading area steadily developed, close to where the great River Ouse and the Foss came together. Tanners, leatherworkers, and furriers set up workshops, bringing sea-traders up the river to buy and sell in the marketplace within the walls. Acha ordered pottery, wall hangings, furs, rugs, cauldrons and cooking pots. Metalwork hearths flared with sparks, kilns were fired daily and the whole place thronged with the bustle of work and trade. The tapping of hammers was heard everywhere. The debris from Aelle's hall was cleared or covered with river sand, and as Edwin's hall was completed, spirits soared. The building was both strong and lofty, a symbol of hope and enterprise, so that many Deiran thanes built smaller halls around it, both inside and outside the walls. The renewed trade brought wealth and business to the town; all this work and activity also brought a sense of thriving and warm approval towards Acha from the populace.

Athelfrid's regular visits were anticipated with a mixture of pride in the bustling town's achievements, and dread that their new found wealth should be dispersed and sent elsewhere. Acha welcomed her husband with feasts and the best entertainment that could be provided. Their coupling was polite and distant. She did not trust her husband and could not dredge up much warmth for him. Even the old excitement that his lean, muscular, warrior's body had once inspired in her had fled. Athelfrid grew leaner still as the years passed and at times she sensed a strange, unsettling, distant fire in his eyes –

as though he saw not her, the woman, but only what she represented – the kingdom of Deira – the land.

Their dutiful mating brought her another son, the following spring and she named him Oslac, then two years later came Oswy. All her sons she loved wholeheartedly. Each time she gave birth she privately nurtured hopes that she might produce a girl, just one child that would not be taken from her to be trained in warrior skills, but no daughter was born. Oswald adored his father, though he saw so little of him, and Acha did nothing to undermine his adulation of the warrior lord who rode into the town at summer's end, an ever-growing army at his back. She dreaded the moment she knew must come when Oswald would ride away from her at Athelfrid's side.

In the winter following Oswy's birth, Godric fell from his horse and gashed his head. He lay ill for a few days before he died, leaving her bereft of the wisdom and the true fatherly kindness that he'd always given her. More devastating still, Megan caught a lung fever after nursing those much younger than herself who'd gone down with the sickness. Acha felt as though she'd lost a mother rather than a nurse. Those two deaths brought a great feeling of loss and sorrow, for she had relied utterly on them both. How would she ever have managed to face Athelfrid as a young tribute bride, without Godric's stalwart support at Goats' Hill? Without Megan's wisdom she might still be fighting with Bebba, rather than knowing that Bebbanburgh still held for her, a true and loyal friend.

More and more she came to rely on Coifi and Bree for support and advice. Even Athelfrid came to treat his former concubine with more respect. She bustled about the new palace, keys clinking at her girdle. Now more a reeve than a lady's maid, she also took on much of Megan's nursing care.

Acha's sadness at the loss of her two old friends was relieved a little by her pleasure in watching her two youngest sons grow. Some deep instinct told her that Oswy, with his sweet round face and golden mop of curls, might be her last child. Whenever she could steal time from her responsibilities, she fled to the nursery, where

Emma took charge, to play games and sing the old Deiran rhymes that Megan had once taught her.

One Easter-month, when Oswy was three years old, Athelfrid arrived unexpectedly early in the year. He brushed aside Acha's apologies that a feast was not prepared for him, but made clear the purpose of his visit: he wanted Deiran warriors to further swell the ranks of his followers.

"But you promised no tribute from us," Acha answered, fearful that Deira's period of peace was over.

"I do not ask for tribute," he growled, "but for your loyalty, wife. I travel to the south-west and I need men at my back. The King of Gwynedd has offended me and I shall have his lands!"

"But surely my lord has enough land," she protested.

"A great king can never have land enough," he replied and he seemed to look beyond her to some vision of glory that only he could see. She sensed with dismay that he could never be satisfied and would always hunger for more land and power.

She guessed that gentleness might be more use to her than strong words. "You are so great a king, you rule so many lands," she said. "Surely you do not need more."

Then suddenly anger flashed and his eyes grew flinty and hard. "I am your husband and lord? I leave you to rule Deira as you please, and I expect loyalty from my wife? Shall I take my oldest son instead?"

A cruel hand gripped her heart as he threatened the thing she feared most and she hurriedly agreed to his demands.

Athelfrid went south with a good contingent of Deiran warriors at his back, young men who rode under the leadership of a few of her father's old thanes.

Coifi stood at her side as they watched them disappear.

"It feels like failure," she admitted. "There are moments when I fear my husband may be slipping in and out of madness that he feels he needs more land – and yet more."

He nodded. "But you must not be heard to say such things," he said quietly. "Not to any other than myself and the trusted few. I believe he leaves a network of spies behind him – stable lads, who know little of horse-care – your man Duncan knows of them."

"I will be careful," she promised, but she was heavy of heart to see so many familiar faces ride away. "How has the King of Gwynedd offended him?" she asked.

Coifi simply shook his head.

***

The battle lines were drawn up close to the old Roman settlement of Chester and Athelfrid saw at once that he was outnumbered, though some of those facing him appeared to be unarmed. The King of Gwynedd had called up every man of fighting age and they had answered the summons to defend their lands, whereas as harvest month drew close, Athelfrid had strayed far from his own borders and many of his men had slipped away. He turned to Woden's high priest, whose blood-stained robes betrayed the sacrifices that had been made the night before in the hopes of victory.

"Desperate measures!" he said softly. "What kind of warriors are these? Are they slaves?"

"They line up their holy men against you," the priest said, shaking his raven-headed staff. A large gathering of men stood with their shaved heads bowed and their arms stretched out before them, palms upturned to the sky.

"I have seen this before," Athelfrid said, as the memory of one silent priest rose up before him. A man who'd stood still while freezing water crept to his waist.

"They are Christians – shaved like slaves," Woden's man agreed.

"And they have a hundred priests, while I have only one," Athelfrid said. Anger burned in his heart against this king who, his spies told him, had given refuge to Aelle's son, the young man who still laid claim to the throne of Deira. He caught the eye of his cavalry captain and raised his hand in the direction of the shaven heads. "Cut them down!" he cried.

The mounted riders looked astonished – they hesitated and looked askance at each other – even Woden's priest gaped at his lord.

"But they are unarmed!"

"They join battle against me with their prayers," Athelfrid growled. "That is enough!"

He raised his sword towards the Christian holymen and charged, bellowing the war-cry as he gathered speed. His cavalry drew their swords, raised them high and followed him, their horses' hooves sounding like thunder.

***

Acha cantered over low grassy hills to the south of Eforwic. She'd had an exhilarating ride in sharp sunshine, with just enough of a breeze to lift the silky hairs on Sidhe's mane. Attended only by Bree, she had snatched a precious escape from duty, a brief period of freedom. Bree loved to ride almost as much as her mistress did, and both were aware that this might be the last ride that they would manage this year, for Blood-month had just begun and with it came the first winter frosts. Acha's pleasure was marred only by the recent news that had come from Bebbanburgh: Bebba had given birth to a girl and was very weak, though the child lived – thanks be to Freya. She longed to visit her and missed Megan bitterly, for if her old nurse had been alive she'd have sent her to Bebbanburgh to nurse the queen. Though they had not seen each other for eight years, they had regularly exchanged small gifts and messages.

As they headed back through Eforwic's busy market area, Acha saw many faces turned to her with an expression of shock and disbelief. She urged Sidhe into a steady trot, sensing that something was amiss. Since he'd ridden south towards Powys they'd heard no news of Athelfrid and she feared that this sense of unease in the marketplace might herald his return. Her four boys were all well and strong and she'd give anything to keep them safe and happy, but four sons must surely be enough – even for Aelthefrid.

As she rode in through the gate she was further disturbed to find it unattended and saw at once that the streets ahead were filled with people who clamoured and shouted in excitement.

The crowd made way for her and she dismounted hastily, to find a blood-stained, mud-splashed messenger at the centre of the gathering. As soon as he saw her, the man went down on one knee.

"What is it?" she asked.

"Victory, lady," he announced. "Your husband has won a great battle at Chester against the King of Gwynedd. That land is now in his control and the king and his army will overwinter in Bangor, where the settlements are stocked with grain."

"I thank you for this news," she said. "Come to our hall for food and drink."

She led the way. Though she was well practised at hiding her emotions, this time she struggled to disguise the relief she felt at the messenger's news. It seemed that Athelfrid would not be coming back to Eforwic again before the spring, and that thought brought solace.

Though the arrival of the messenger caused a stir, the news that Athelfrid had gained victory in Gwynedd meant little to the inhabitants of Eforwic. She suspected that most Deirans would share her relief. Her private pleasure at the news was short-lived however, for she began to overhear uneasy, shocked mutterings from the palace servants as the details that followed the news of battle began to creep out.

"They slew Christian monks – a thousand of them. It was punishment!"

She heard those words whispered in the courtyard and again in the stables – and on the morning she sent for Coifi to come to her chamber. He came, grim-faced, and she sent her women away.

"Have you heard what they are saying?" she asked. "That my husband has slaughtered many Christian monks? Unarmed men! Surely not?"

A small muscle flickered at the corner of his mouth. "I've heard it too," he said. "It seems that it is true, for seven of our own men returned last night and they repeat the same story."

"Eforwic men? They have returned against Athelfrid's orders?"

"Yes – bitterly ashamed of what happened and desperate to be away from his war."

"They risk his wrath," she said. "They risk death. But I think I cannot blame them."

The image of unarmed men with shaven heads falling before swords returned to her, and somehow she found that each slaughtered victim bore the face of Brother Finn.

"They say Athelfrid claimed that the monks joined battle against him," Coifi explained reluctantly. "That they fought against him with their prayers."

"And what do you say to that?" she asked. "Does not every king order his holy man to pray for victory when he goes into battle?"

He nodded.

"And as Woden's priest, would you support his action?" she insisted.

Coifi looked up at her and she saw that he struggled to disguise his repugnance at this news. He spoke through gritted teeth. "I have *never* seen Woden's honour served by the slaughter of unarmed men. They say your husband has gone to Bangor now to destroy the monasteries there."

"This really is madness," she whispered. And a memory came to her of Athelfrid's sudden fury when he watched Finn pray as he stood in freezing water. "I think he always envied the quiet strength of Prince Donal's tutor, the Christian monk," she said. "At the bottom of his heart, he fears the power of this Christian God!"

Coifi shook his head. "I think there is more to it," he said. "I heard that Edwin has spent some time under the protection of the King of Gwynedd. It seems this is their punishment for harbouring your brother."

Acha closed her eyes. She shivered with fear, and tried to push away the bloody images that came to her. Athelfrid's ambition had surely driven him far beyond reason and his rage against her brother would never cease.

"And what of Edwin?" she begged. "You must tell me that he is safe!"

"I too have spies," Coifi said with a nod. "He is safe. Edwin has married the daughter of the Mercian king and had a son with her, but fearing Athelfrid's army moving towards those lands he has fled further south and taken refuge at King Redwald's Court in the Kingdom of the East Angles."

Acha could only pray that her brother would stay safely there, away from Athelfrid's growing fury.

"When I heard that Athelfrid was staying away all winter I was… relieved," she admitted guiltily. Her hands trembled as she rubbed them anxiously together. "Little did I know the price those men had paid for *my* peace of mind!"

A tear trickled down her cheek.

Coifi put his arms about her and she crumpled against him. She wanted to bury herself in his embrace and howl out all the sorrow and frustration of her life – but it would not do. She quickly recovered and pulled away from him. "You had better go, dear Coifi – for I fear that Athelfrid's spies might take more news to him. You and I may be his next victims."

He kissed her tenderly on the forehead and left.

More warriors straggled back to Eforwic and those that had followed Athelfrid into battle feared terrible retribution, from both gods and men. Most of the Dalriad warriors were Christians themselves, but the slaughter of the monks had been so deeply dishonourable an act that even the followers of Woden could not countenance it. It seemed that the number of Athelfrid's warriors who obediently stayed in Bangor with him diminished by the day.

Acha tried to push away disturbing thoughts as preparations for the festival of Yule began. Hunting parties returned from the woodland to the north of the settlement with wild boar and deer, and a good summer's harvest meant that there was plentiful grain. The halls were decorated with holly, ivy and mistletoe and Yule feasts were held, so that the townsfolk filled their bellies with roast game, roast beef, mutton pies and rich, creamy, puddings washed down with mead – but despite the luxury of the feasts, and the cheer of mead and ale, the atmosphere remained tense. Might Gwynedd find allies and come north to seek revenge for Athelfrid's attack? Blood must be avenged – and who could say how terrible the punishment might be for the deaths of so many monks.

Bitter-month and Mud-month were always harsh, but with good stocks, Eforwic fared better than most. As Easter-month approached and the weather grew warmer, there developed a sense of restlessness in the town. Surely now they could expect the retaliation to take place – and where was Athelfrid? Acha too became restless, fearful that she might have to organise defence of the town. Every day she dreaded hearing news of the king's return.

***

Athelfrid rode northwards along the ancient road towards the old Roman town of Danum. The road was still in reasonable repair, but the going was slow and the journey tedious. Hunched in the saddle, he rode at the head of his most loyal hearth-companions – battle-hardened men who were experienced in warfare. The army that straggled behind him was a different matter; many had been forced into the role of warrior unwillingly, and were bone-weary of fighting and still so far from their homes. Athelfrid himself was struggling to tolerate this long march back to Deira. News of Bebba's illness had reached him, and he didn't much want to witness his long-suffering queen's death. It was becoming hard to find the energy to rally his troops and somehow, since the battle against the Welsh, the fire had drained out of him. He knew what was said of him: the gods were angry, Woden had deserted him. But what of Loki? Did the trickster god disapprove of slaughtering unarmed men? As they approached the ford that would take them across the River Idle, Athelfrid wearily held up his hand to call a halt.

"We'll camp here for the night, close to the river crossing," he said. "Water the horses!"

Wearily, they began to set up tents and build fires, when the sound of fast hooves could be heard on the road. One of their scouts who'd gone ahead suddenly appeared, galloping back at a killing pace.

"Beware – beware!" he shouted. "To arms – to arms!"

Athelfrid and his tired warriors blinked and stared at him. They were in Mercian territory here, on the borderlands of Deira – almost into their own country. Who could possibly be threatening them here?

But behind the galloping scout, over the breast of the hill, appeared the battle standard of King Redwald alongside the banner that Athelfrid dreaded to see most of all – the symbol of the spreading oak tree. Was this some ghastly dream? Was he losing touch with reality in his exhaustion?

As Athelfrid stared, a man on a white warhorse appeared – and for a moment he thought he glimpsed Acha on Sidhe. It was her face, but stronger, harder, and yet with that same courageous lift of the chin that had once touched him, though of late her expression towards him was distant and cool. Behind the figure rows of heads appeared, helmeted, carrying spears, and he saw that this was not Acha – this was a man full grown with a close cropped beard, leading an army; a tall, upright warrior, just coming into the fullness of his strength. This was the nightmare face he'd seen in dreams. It was Edwin of Deira, with a huge army at his back!

As more and more men advanced against Athelfrid's makeshift camp, the young warrior steadied his horse, and drew his sword with a practised hand. Raising it above his head, he bellowed out a war cry. "Edwin for Deira!"

Athelfrid scrambled for his own sword and raised it in response, all his dread, fear, and fury unleashed. To his utmost horror, before he could rally his troops, some from his own ranks rushed forward to join the enemy ranks, their faces alight with joy.

"Edwin! Edwin for Deira!" they cried.

Athelfrid shut his eyes for one brief moment and turned to Ulric. "The time has come," he said.

"No master – no!"

"The time has come," he insisted. "Ride now or I shall kill you where you stand! Do not mourn – I am weary of life! This night I shall feast in Woden's Hall!"

Ulric hesitated, but as more and more warriors breasted the hill he too saw that there was no chance of victory. The time was now, they'd known it must come in the end and it had been discussed many times. He made no more protests, but gripped his master's arm briefly, then mounted his horse and set off upstream, away from the coming battle. Athelfrid's companions drew their swords, their faces grim, as they gathered about their leader, and prepared to take as many of the turncoats with them as they could. There would be good cheer for them that night in Woden's feasting hall.

***

Easter-month arrived in Eforwic with the first signs of spring and a message from Bebba via the captain of *Flame-bearer.* He'd berthed the royal barge in the River Humber.

"The queen is dying," he admitted sadly. "Lady Edith fears she will not last the summer. All our queen asks is that *you* will come to her."

Acha was distraught. "I wish with all my heart to go with you, but I cannot. If I leave Deira wide open while Athelfrid is away, I fear what might happen here."

The man nodded. "Lady, I understand, but Queen Bebba needs you too. I will wait one month close to the old Roman Camp at Brough, in the Humber, in hope that you may change your mind."

He returned to his ship, leaving her thoughtful and miserable.

CHAPTER 29

FLAME-BEARER

The news that Bebba had begged her to travel north to Bebbanburgh gave Acha no peace. The strong friendship that had developed between the two wives had been deeply threatened by their separation and by Athelfrid's appointment of Acha as ruler in Deira in his absence. But Bebba had consistently sent friendly messages and gifts, making it clear that she felt only sympathy towards her sister wife and understanding about the position she found herself in.

After a few days of restless thought, Acha came to a decision and sent for Coifi.

"I must see Bebba," she said. "Could you hold Eforwic while I am away?"

"Yes – I could do as you ask," he agreed. But he gave her a dark look. "I'd advise you to wait here a while though," he added.

"But Bebba..." she began, and then she stopped. She sensed something hidden behind his words – something that he would not, or could not, tell.

"Why should I wait?" she insisted, frowning at him. "Do you know something I do not? Is it news of Edwin?"

"There are things I cannot tell, for I would never endanger you. I told you that I have a few of my own loyal spies."

"But you endanger yourself with this knowledge, I think," she said.

"That is a different matter, Lady."

There was a moment of awkward silence. Acha's head spun with confusion, but before they had chance to say more, there came the sound of shouting from outside the queen's hall, and Bree rushed into the chamber.

"Lady you must come quickly! Ulric has arrived with just his armour-bearer. He is in a terrible state and will speak to nobody but you!"

Acha stood as Ulric strode straight into her presence. He was covered in road dust and sweating heavily and remembered only at the last minute to pull his helmet from his head.

"What has happened now?" she cried.

"There is no easy way to say it, lady – your husband is dead, and his companions have gone down in battle! Only myself and my man bear the shame of living."

Acha stared at the grizzled old warrior, stunned at his news. "No shame that you live," she murmured weakly. "You were always his most faithful companion and captain."

"No – it is deep dishonour," Ulric insisted, his face betraying the utter misery of his position. "Athelfrid made me promise, that when the moment came – I would leave the field and ride to you. You must take your sons at once and flee to Bebbanburgh. I will escort you there!"

Acha could find no way to speak or think clearly; she struggled merely to draw breath. Coifi strode to her side.

"Princess – stay here – you will be safe," he said. "Your brother reclaims his kingdom and he will want to find you here."

Ulric turned pale beneath the grime that spattered his face. He drew his sword to threaten Coifi. "You knew of this!" he accused.

Woden's priest did not flinch and Acha instinctively stepped between them, knowing only that she must protect her friend.

"Ulric, put your sword away!" she cried. "Or you will kill the mother of Aethefrid's sons. This man has kept peace in Deira since my father's death – his loyalty is to me not Athelfrid. He was always true to Deira."

Ulric flushed angrily. "But he has conspired against your husband – how else could he know that your brother returns? What he says is true. It *is* Edwin who has killed your husband."

Acha's head spun. "Edwin?" she gasped.

Coifi held out weaponless hands to Ulric. "You speak truth. I *am* traitor to Athelfrid and have longed for this day – but even *you* must see that I'm no traitor to Deira. Aelle's son returns, as we always knew he would. This attack was not unprovoked. I told you lady, that I too have spies. Athelfrid has offered gold to Redwald in return for Edwin's death. Three times he has offered it and on the last refusal he threatened war. King Redwald had no choice but to kill your brother or march north to settle this dispute. Athelfrid has brought it on himself."

Ulric looked stunned.

"You did not know of this?" Acha asked.

Ulric shook his head and lowered his sword. "No, I did not, but it was King Redwald that marched with Edwin."

There was silence for a moment between them as Acha and Ulric struggled to take in this news, but then Coifi spoke again in a conciliatory manner. "Ulric – despite our differences you and I must now share one aim – and that is that Acha and her sons be safe."

"You are right," Ulric admitted. "Athelfrid's sons are my concern. Redwald and Edwin will be following us here soon."

Acha put her hand to her heart; she saw Athelfrid in her mind, falling – slashed and wounded, bleeding out his lifeblood as her father had done – and she felt nothing, only a dreadful, empty numbness.

"Exile again," she whispered.

"No Princess, you will be safe here in Deira if you remain," Coifi began. "Your brother will greet you with affection. He'll understand how difficult it has been for you and I will tell him how hard you have worked to ensure the kingdom's prosperity in readiness for his return. Athelfrid would have bled these lands dry, were it not for you."

But the mist that had filled her mind now lifted, and it felt as though a harsh, brilliant sun had come out from behind a cloud allowing her to see clearly. "No, my dear Coifi," she whispered. "This is a blood-feud."

"But he knows you had no part in Aelle's death."

Acha looked lovingly into his face, but shook her head. "Edwin might find it in his heart to make peace with *me*, but every code of honour says he must slaughter my sons."

"She's right," Ulric intervened. "Whatever Edwin wants, Redwald will make sure that none of Athelfrid's sons are left alive! The princes must flee with me! Do you think Redwald would march his army so far north and risk his men, his sons, only to allow his enemy's kin to live? What kind of Woden's priest are you, man?"

"A strange one, I admit," Coifi acknowledged. "For I find I cannot approve these rules of war that require a victor to slaughter innocent children."

"You are my dearest friend," Acha said. "But you must see that I have to go. For my sons' sakes – I must go!"

"But *where* will you go?" Coifi asked.

She smiled fiercely, for her moment of clarity had brought to mind a plan – a plan that filled her with energy and confidence.

"First I must return with Ulric to Bebbanburgh," she said. "For more than ever now I need to speak with Bebba. The royal barge *Flame-bearer* is ready moored in the Humber, close to Brough and if Hella spares the queen we'll flee together with our children either to her brother's court or to Dalriada, where Donal Brecc will give us sanctuary."

Coifi looked defeated.

Acha took his hand, heedless of Ulric watching. "This is the moment you and I have longed for," she whispered. "Edwin will reclaim his kingdom and I rejoice for him. But Deira is no longer safe for my sons, or me, nor will Bernicia be safe for long. Athelfrid's lands must be left wide open for Edwin to take; I leave them willingly to him."

She kissed Coifi tenderly on the cheek and Ulric looked away, strangely moved.

"Come with us, Coifi," she whispered. "You and I could make another life together in a far off place. I have been a good wife to Athelfrid, I have done my duty as a peaceweaver bride – but now I am free. Do you remember how Brother Finn once told us of an island in the western sea? Iona – a place of refuge. You know that Finn would welcome *you* there too!"

Ulric intervened impatiently. "If your priest must come with you, let him come," he said. "But we must waste no time. The boat is a blessing, but King Redwald keeps a fleet of ships. He may have already sent them north to block the Humber estuary."

Coifi nodded his acceptance. "Where are the princes?" he demanded with sudden urgency.

"Oswald is hunting with his companions," Acha said. "The others were playing close by just a while ago. I will send a messenger to warn *Flame-bearer's* captain of our plans."

They all hurried off in different directions to prepare for the journey.

When Acha announced what must be done, Bree threw open the lids of coffers and began frantically stuffing clothing into bags, scooping up handfuls of jewellery to hide amongst the clothing. Clover hurried to the kitchens to pack food for the journey, and the news flew around the palace. Acha found her younger boys in the courtyard playing with little wooden boats in a tub of water, while Emma washed their clothes. Water scattered everywhere, as the maid rushed to prepare for travelling north.

Acha strode over to the stables to speak to Duncan. Reluctantly she begged him to stay with her mares and foals, and found herself trembling as she tried to explain.

"When my brother comes here," she spoke breathlessly. "Please give Sidhe to him and say: this was your sister's morning-gift, along with the house of mares and foals at Goats' Hill. They are all that I truly own for myself and I give them to him as a token of my love and good will."

Duncan listened sadly and began to protest, but seeing her distress and determination he bowed his head and agreed. "I will do as you say, lady, and I will care for your mares as long as I live."

Suddenly, despite her desperation, she glimpsed beyond her own pain, to see his. "No! I cannot ask this of you," she said. "Why should you stay as a slave in yet another foreign land, when you could flee with us?"

He shook his head. "I am no slave. You set me free, lady – I will always be free in my heart, whatever happens. Go now – never fear for your mares, I choose to stay here to care for them."

"This is true friendship," she murmured.

But as she turned to go back to the great hall, ten-year-old Oswald rode into the stable with his grooms. He was tall for his age and growing fast, eager to acquire the warrior skills of a full-grown man. He saw at once from the stricken looks about him that something was wrong. Acha required all her courage to tell him that his father was dead, for despite the rarity of their meetings, Oswald still hero-worshipped the man. He was shocked to hear of his death and devastated to be told that he must flee.

"No, I stay here," he announced. "My father named *me* Deira's heir. The people love me and cheer me when I ride through the streets. I remain here with Duncan!"

Acha hated to break his innocent courage, but she had no time for gentleness. "You will come with me for your own safety – you owe it to your father to survive!"

"But it is my uncle who comes to Eforwic," Oswald protested. "He will support my claim; I am his sister-son."

"No," she said, through gritted teeth. "Your father killed his father, and by the laws of blood-feud Edwin must kill you in vengeance. My brother is honour-bound to make his own son heir to these lands." She paused for breath, hating the terror that her words must bring to the boy. "If you do not come willingly, I'll order Duncan to bind you hands and feet!" she cried in desperation.

"Mother!" he whispered, aghast.

But her message had hit home and he perceived the danger they were in.

"Please come willingly," she begged. "I need your help. Your brothers are too young to understand the peril we are in, but they will follow *you* and copy all *you* do. Ulric is here – come speak to him."

"I will," he agreed at last.

As soon as baggage could be gathered and horses saddled, they set out to ride through the night. Ulric and Coifi lead the way towards the south-east and the emerging dawn, past Pockleton and memories of Godric, and down to the Humber, where they were able to board *Flame-bearer*. The oarsmen took their places as soon as they arrived and the captain shouted orders. Coifi carried Oswy aboard and set the boy gently down before his mother. She saw that Woden's priest had brought no baggage with him.

"Where are your goods Coifi? You haven't even brought a cloak!"

His face was marked with sorrow. She remembered the painful parting, long ago. "I hold Deira for your brother," he said quietly. "In Woden's name, I must be here to greet him with the raven's welcome. I cannot come with you."

Her heart sank. She took his hands and they stood together in silence looking sadly into each other's eyes. At last she nodded. "Deira," she murmured. "We have both of us given up our freedom and our happiness for this land. Do you not fear that Edwin might claim *your* life too? How will he understand what has happened here?"

Coifi shrugged. "I will do my best to explain to him, and even though he orders my death – still, I must stay."

She saw that she could do nothing to move him.

"Tell him… tell him…" she begged, fingering the small pouch that still swung from her girdle, "that I refuse to be his enemy. And pray that he will never hate me."

"I will," Coifi promised.

There was so much more she wished to say, but there was no time – for they were casting off the mooring ropes.

"Kiss me again," she whispered.

He bent his head so that their lips touched in a long sweet kiss that made all those who watched glance away.

A steady drum beat sent the oarsmen reaching forward and Coifi pulled away from her at last and leapt ashore. Acha struggled along to the stern as the oarsmen bent to their oars and the boat began to move. She watched the lonely figure until it disappeared. Here was yet another heart-breaking loss, another leave-taking. Again she'd forfeited the only man she'd ever really wanted to be with, but this time she left behind with him a royal town of sturdy halls and huts, with a thriving market and a trading port. She left a kingdom spread with fertile fields and well-stacked granaries.

The sun rose over fields that were already springing with green shoots and buds ready to burst with blossom on the trees.

Flame-bearer moved out into the wide river as the sun rose in the sky. "Blessed Freya… I am more sorrowful at this parting than I am at my husband's death," she murmured.

Bree came to throw a woollen cloak about her shoulders as the wind got up. "Come inside the shelter," she said. "Oswy is fretting and needs his mother, and I have prepared a drink for you."

Acha nodded and joined her sons.

Once out in the wider river, the wind and tide worked in their favour. They made good pace with the sail belling out and the oarsmen were able to rest awhile, but before they reached the estuary the tide had turned against them. Fearful of losing time and becoming trapped, the captain made his oarsmen battle onwards against incoming waves. *Flame-bearer* dipped wildly up and down and thunderclouds clapped in the distance, promising rain. Acha's women sat stoically huddled together, and young Oswy clung to his mother. The older boys gathered around Ulric, wrapped in their cloaks, trying hard to emulate the older man's grim-faced dignity.

As the boat struggled northwards, Acha managed to dredge up some small flicker of regret for Athelfrid's passing. His ambition and his anger had turned to madness – but still his men had followed him. He'd been the greatest warrior of them all and he'd died a warrior's death. Remembering how he'd forced Ulric to flee for the sake of their sons, she dropped a kiss on Oswy's thick, golden curls, and then reached out to gently touch Ulric's shoulder.

"No king could have asked for truer loyalty from his closest companion," she whispered.

The man nodded grateful for her acknowledgement.

The storm broke as the oarsmen hauled *Flame-bearer* around the thin, curled spit at the mouth of the Humber. Still they battled northwards against the flow of the tide. Darkness fell and the oarsmen rowed on without rest. Acha watched them, dry-eyed and full of gratitude.

As the first light of dawn spread across the sky, the wind swung round to blow from the south. The captain raised the sail and the oarsmen collapsed where they sat, exhausted, their skin marked with salt and their knuckles raw.

"Are we safe, do you think?" she asked Ulric.

"I think we are safe from Redwald's fleet," he said.

All through the next day they sailed northwest following the line of the coast, rowing hard when the tide turned against them. Just as the sun was setting, *Flame-bearer* pulled alongside the staithe at Bebbanburgh. Everyone aboard was exhausted and bedraggled, but their spirits soared with relief that they'd safely reached harbour. Ulric helped Acha along the gangplank where Bebba's litter was already waiting for her, the boat having been spied in the distance as it neared the shore.

Acha stepped straight into it, leaving Ulric and the women to follow more slowly with the boys. She was carried quickly up the slope and into the courtyard of Bebbanburgh.

CHAPTER 30

YOU WILL RECEIVE WHAT YOU GIVE!

Acha emerged from the litter to find herself enveloped in a fierce bony embrace.

"Blessed Freya, thank you!" Edith cried as she clung to her. "My lady is desperate to speak with you."

Edith's husband, Bron, hovered anxiously behind, with a long-legged lad beside him, his cheekbones decorated like the queen's with Pictish scrolling.

"Enfrid... you must be Enfrid!" Acha exclaimed.

He came forward and bowed with formal courtesy. "Welcome to Bebbanburgh, lady," he said. "My mother has told me how you helped at my birth. She has related it many times."

Acha curtsied to him respectfully. Though he was still very young, Enfrid might feel that he'd have the right to claim at least Bernicia in a few years time, once he knew that Athelfrid was dead.

"I'm so sorry – I bring terrible news for you," she said gently. "The king, your father, has been killed in battle, fighting bravely." Bron gasped and Enfrid turned pale, but Edith did not seem at all surprised. "Then... the priestess of Hella spoke true," she said. "She warned of his death. Now it is all the more important that you hear what Bebba has to say."

"Is she really so sick?" Acha asked.

Edith nodded. "She is naught but skin and bones – and she clings to life only to see you, I swear it is all that has kept her going. Come quickly!"

Acha was reluctant to leave the boy, but Bron quickly recovered his composure and took Enfrid firmly by the arm. "Princess, you must go to the queen," he said. "The prince and I will take a mug of mead while you speak. We men will think what should be done."

Reassured by his kind gesture, Acha hurried along with Edith towards the queen's hall. As they went, she noticed that the older woman looked ill herself, with dark shadows beneath her eyes as though she hadn't slept for days. They hurried up the familiar steps and strode past empty weaving frames. When they entered the queen's chamber, Bebba lay quite still, propped on cushions her eyes open but unfocused. Acha feared she'd come too late. Bebba's body made little impression amongst the luxurious furs that covered her bed.

"Dear lady!" Acha cried, dropping down on her knees beside the queen's bed, as Edith quietly took up her station at its foot.

A slight tremor touched Bebba's face at the sound of Acha's voice. She was very frail, and each breath came as a shallow gasp. She turned her head with painful effort; suddenly her eyes focussed and she closed them briefly, in an expression of relief.

"Thank you, Freya," she whispered, her voice as faint as the rustle of dried leaves. "No time for welcome now… no time for joy."

Acha wanted to weep. She took the fragile, trembling hand that reached out to her; it felt like the hand of a starving child, the Pictish patterns had faded on cheeks the colour of parchment. She remembered the vigorous, astonishing woman that she'd first met – and grown to love.

"Lady, our husband is dead," she said gently.

Bebba's gaze turned dim for a moment, but then flickered alive again. "So soon," was all she said. "He… died in battle?"

"Yes – he died with his sword in his hand."

"Your brother…?"

"Yes."

Again Bebba closed her eyes. "We always knew it would be so."

She lay still for a moment. When she spoke again her voice was stronger. "Please… you must take my daughter… my little Aebba with you… and you must be a mother to her. This is all I want. Promise me this… promise me this!" She grew agitated.

Acha's eyes brimmed with tears and she struggled to speak. "I… I promise you," she managed at last.

Bebba lay back and smiled gently. "It is all as it should be," she gasped, struggling again for breath.

Acha stroked the queen's white hand, looking down at the faint grey whorls that still patterned it. "Rest, dear one," she said.

But Bebba would not rest. "Where… will you go?"

"I had in mind to go to Dalriada," Acha told her, with a smile.

And Bebba too smiled faintly. "You cannot trust your brother then?"

Acha swallowed hard. "I love him dearly, but he rides with Redwald of the East Angles. His allies would demand that he take revenge, were my boys anywhere near to them. You know their code of honour… no kin left alive so *all* our children must be taken to a place of safety."

"Your poor heart must break," Bebba whispered and her words crackled with sympathy. "I know how you loved your homeland."

"The safety of our children is everything to me," she replied. "Donal and Finn once offered me refuge. I think maybe Finn sensed this coming, when he spoke to me of the place they called Iona. What do you wish for Enfrid?"

"Enfrid must go to my brother, Nechtan," she said. "But not Aebba… please take her to Dalriada with you… she needs a mother's love and you are the only one that I can trust to give it to her."

The tears that had been welling spilled over and ran down Acha's cheeks.

"You gave me my son," Bebba said. "Now I give you my daughter."

"Megan… she once spoke of something like this," Acha said, remembering the terrible moment of decision. "The runes spoke through her and they said that what I gave, I would receive – and I have so longed for a daughter."

Bebba lay back, smiling, she looked a little better. Relieved from the necessity of speaking, she lay peacefully for a moment and then gradually slipped into unconsciousness.

Edith looked up at Acha, a gentle smile on her face. "You have brought her the peace of mind she craved," she said quietly. "Should I bring the prince to see his mother, do you think?"

"Yes," Acha agreed. "That might be best."

Edith went away and left Acha quietly holding Bebba's hand. Strangely, she too felt a sense of peace flow through her. It wasn't long before Enfrid appeared hesitantly in the doorway. Acha beckoned him to the bedside. "She is content," she told him. "Don't be afraid, she seems comfortable. Sit there and take her other hand."

The boy sat down obediently.

"Has she gone?" he asked in a little while.

"Yes, my dear," Acha said. "I think she has."

"I'm glad you came in time." His voice broke with emotion. "She wanted to see you so much."

"I'm glad too," she whispered.

Edith carried a lighted candle to the bedside and set it there.

"You must both go to rest," she said firmly. "Bron and Ulric are preparing horses, for you must ride at daybreak; there's no time to wait. I shall sit here and watch with her."

"But will you not come with us?" Acha asked.

The old woman shook her head and smiled. "No," she said firmly, "I stay here to conduct my lady's funeral rites and see her ashes laid on the Island, beside her little ones. My Bron will not leave his post; he'll keep this stronghold, until… until your brother arrives."

Acha turned to Enfrid. "Will you ride north with us to Dun Eidyn?" she asked. "It is what Bebba wanted."

"Yes," he said sadly. He let go of his mother's hand and rose to his feet. "I hate to leave her," he said, glancing back, "but I know what I'm to do. I'm to go to my Uncle Nechtan in the Pictish lands. We spoke of it often."

"Then we must all ride at dawn," Acha agreed. "We will head north west to Dun Eidyn first, and I will see you into your uncle's care. Then I must travel westwards on to Dalriada."

He bowed and left the chamber. Acha turned to Edith. "Take me to the babe."

A young nursemaid sat in the nursery chamber, where a lighted candle was set on a small chest beside a cot. Acha put her finger to their lips, to indicate that she had no wish to wake the little one.

She looked down on a beautiful year-old girl; her softly curling red hair made her want to weep afresh.

"Get her ready to travel as soon as she wakes," Edith quietly explained to the nurse. "The queen is dead and Princess Acha will take the children north to safety. Pack warm clothes for yourself, and rugs, and all she needs for you must go with them to help with the babe."

But the girl looked terrified. She rose to her feet and backed into a corner of the chamber. "I cannot go!" she cried, clasping her hands together. "I've never been north of Berwick Town. My mother is sick and she has no other child to care for her… I have my own little one at home… and besides, the little princess is all but weaned… she can eat sops. I cannot go."

The sleeping child woke, troubled by the sound of raised voices, and set up a frightened wail. Acha scooped her into her arms and began to rock her gently, finding comfort herself in the touch of the tender cheek.

"Aebba, my little Aebbe," she whispered. "It is all going to be alright. You will be safe with me!"

Edith looked back at Acha, for guidance. They could order the girl to go, but who could trust a reluctant nursemaid?

Aebbe's wails quickly subsided to soft murmuring sounds as she felt herself held warm and firmly. Acha looked at Edith with a smile. "Let the girl go home," she said. "I will look after the little one myself, and I shall take pleasure in the task. She shall ride with me, wrapped in my cloak and Emma will be there to help me, should I grow weary. We need fresh milk, napkins, a few soft tunics and a hooded cloak to keep her warm as we ride. Can you get those for us, nurse?"

"Oh yes, lady!" The girl hastened to obey, her face pink with relief.

Acha turned to Edith, smiling softly. "Return to your mistress," she said. "Have no more fears about the child."

As Edith hurried away, Acha carried her new daughter down to the hearthside, to find her sons were already there, eating hungrily alongside Enfrid and six of his companions. The other lads were all pale-faced and frightened and she realised they were sons of thanes who'd gone down fighting at Athelfrid's side. They understood that their fathers had died in battle and knew that they, too, must fear the coming of Edwin.

"These lads should come with us," Ulric explained.

She nodded. Their party seemed to be growing by the moment.

"Will you take charge of them?" she asked.

Ulric nodded fiercely, almost eagerly, and she saw that the care of these lads, all sons of his fallen companions, might bring purpose and some sense of honour back to the old warrior.

The nursemaid brought bread and milk sops to the table and Aebba ate happily, turning now and again to gaze curiously at the strange woman who seemed to understand her needs. Hunger satisfied, she sat contentedly on Acha's knee.

"Have we enough horses?" Acha asked Bron, regretting the loss of Sidhe.

"Yes Lady, we will take the best."

Though nobody was hungry, they made themselves eat, knowing that they must ride as far and as fast as they could without stopping. The boys whispered together, growing both fearful and excited at the very real sense of danger that surrounded them. Their cheeks might be pale, but their eyes gleamed with anticipation at the thought of the unknown future that lay ahead.

The horses were saddled and brought round to the courtyard as soon as the first pink streaks of light cut through the darkness. Enfrith and Oswald brought their horses side by side, quiet but companionable. Oslac and Osgood moved in behind their older brothers, and the dead thanes' sons bravely formed a protective group around the princes. Just like their fathers, they were willing to give their lives for their lords. Acha bit her lips, touched to see them so young and vulnerable, and yet determined to be brave.

Acha mounted a strong mare and Emma passed Aebbe up to her. Wide-eyed, but not afraid, she was well bundled in a soft woollen cloak and hood. Clover, Emma and Bree mounted the horses that were brought for them, baggage piled behind their saddles. Oswy fussed a little to see his mother with the tiny girl in his place, but Ulric offered to take the young boy up in front of him.

"Go with Ulric," Acha suggested. "Then you will become a brave warrior, just like him."

Oswy, quickly distracted, accepted Ulric's offer with a charming smile.

They rode out through the main gates and Acha turned, with a heavy heart, to glance back. The flicker of a low light still burned in Bebba's Chamber. Aebba struggled as they set off, but as soon as the mare got into a steady canter she settled against her new mother, thumb in mouth. Acha herself was glad of the extra warmth that came from the child tucked securely inside her cloak.

They headed in a north-westerly direction and, as they passed the Isle of Metcalfe in the distance, the sun rose and began to warm their backs. As she rode on, Acha glanced down and smiled at the sight of the few auburn curls that escaped from the wrapping of her cloak.

"Pictish whorls," she murmured. "When you are old enough to bear it, you must have Pictish whorls to decorate these lovely cheeks."

She smiled as the image of the younger Queen Bebba rose up in her mind again – the terrifying, beautiful, woman who had watched the upstart Deiran bride with such suppressed anger, and filled her with fear and dread.

Acha had lost much when she went into exile for the sake of Deira – but she'd found friendship and understanding where she'd least expected it. Megan had always spoken wisely, but the night she bade Acha try to save the queen's child, she'd delivered the best advice she'd ever given. Bebba had repaid her fully for the small act of kindness, and she'd come to treat her truly as a sister wife. Acha sighed at another thought – Bebba had warned her that something was amiss; she'd sensed trouble when Athelfrid had plotted against Deira, but Acha had been too eager to return to her homeland to heed her.

"Sisters," she murmured to the child. "We were sisters and friends to the end… it has not been all sorrow."

The tide rushed in to cover the sand, and, once again, Acha caught the wistful, melancholy music of the seals. A skein of turnstones swooped and skittered along in the same direction; screeching gulls and sea eagles soared overhead.

She looked down to find the little one staring intently up at her and then suddenly the child smiled. Acha tightened her arm around this soft burden as the sun grew warmer still on her back and shoulders. She tossed back her hood, for it was sheer joy on such a morning to be riding northwards to freedom, her precious sons safe at her side and a new little daughter in her arms.

EPILOGUE

TWO YEARS LATER

Edwin rode warily into Nechtan's kingdom. He was acknowledged as overlord of all the lands from the Pictish border to the Humber, known as the kingdom of Northumbria, but Nechtan's kingdom was unknown territory.

He waited for two days, camped by the crumbling ruins of the ancient stronghold known as Camelon, with only his household thanes in attendance. The greater part of his substantial army had been left behind, some of them at Goats' Hill and others at Bebbanburgh.

Some said the fortress at Camelon had been built by the Romans, and others said that it had become the northernmost outpost of Artos the Bear, the Romano-British leader, stories of whom still made exciting listening for children at their mother's knee.

Edwin harboured secret respect for the old Roman overlords, and he took great pride in his mother's claim to have Roman blood – but he knew that his companions were uneasy at camping so far from the safety of Northumbria's borders.

Even though Nechtan of the Picts had given permission for this strange meeting to take place on his land, still they felt vulnerable, fearing ambush or some subtle plot to bring back The Trickster's brood.

At last Edwin could bear the restless waiting no longer, and angrily gave orders for them to pack and go. Chaos followed as goods were gathered, tents lowered and horses prepared for the journey back.

But Lilla, alert as ever to their surroundings, gave a warning cry as a roan mare broke cover and emerged from a copse on the far hillside. The rider was at first glance a slightly built youth, hooded and cloaked.

Edwin's companions had unsheathed their swords, but quickly lowered them as they perceived the threat to be small, and even though a second and third rider appeared from beneath the trees they could see that this was no war-band. One of the newcomers was dressed in the garb of a Christian monk, his forehead shaved like a slave, while the third person was a young man with a mane of auburn hair, mounted on a black stallion and dressed in fine leather. There appeared to be just three of them – none of them heavily armed.

"Halt!" Edwin ordered.

He shaded his eyes to see better, wondering if this motley threesome could be the party he'd been waiting for.

"Sheath your swords – stay back, unless I call for you."

The three riders moved steadily forward and Edwin walked to meet them. Only Lilla followed, leading a startling silver mare, his right hand, as ever, resting on the hilt of his short sword.

The roan mare halted and its rider pulled back the hood, revealing long, braided, dark golden plaits. At the same time the silver mare lifted her nose and whickered softly, as though she recognised a familiar scent. Acha leapt down from her saddle and ran through the long grass towards her brother.

"Edwin!" she shouted joyfully. "You have brought me Sidhe!"

The monk caught the reins of her discarded mount. The red-haired young man dismounted, but kept a discreet distance from the brother and sister.

Acha slowed up, fearful lest the welcoming smile should falter and the hatred return to her brother's eyes. But as Edwin strode towards her, she saw that he was smiling. He'd become a mature, broad-chested man, who carried himself like a seasoned warrior – confident and generous.

"Sister… I see you still ride like a man!" he cried

She laughed and flung her arms around him. "And you have become so powerful, brother and… and so much a man."

They stood together embracing, while Sidhe snorted and stamped her hoof impatiently.

At last they moved back to look at each other properly and Lilla led the mare forward. He placed the reins in Acha's hands, bowing shyly, but Acha would have none of it. She caught hold of him and kissed him too. "Dear Lilla," she said," how glad I am to see you."

"And I you, Princess," he said. "You are much missed in your homeland."

"Now, surely, you will return to Deira! Come back with us," Edwin begged.

But Acha turned away from him to stroke Sidhe's silky nose, as the mare blew a warm greeting around her face. She shook her head regretfully.

"You I trust," she said at last. "But I cannot trust those who helped you gain your kingdom. They will never feel your kingship is safe with my sons in their sight."

An expression of pain crossed Edwin's face. "And I am the man who killed their father."

Acha nodded. "Athelfrid was a great warrior-king," she acknowledged firmly. "And my sons' safety means everything to me. Can we somehow find a way to make this blood-feud cease, brother?"

Edwin gave a brief, sharp nod. "I will swear it on oath… swear that I will never harm my sister-sons."

"Another oath!" Acha agreed. She fumbled for a moment to open the thread box that swung from her girdle. "And we… we are good at making oaths, brother." She brought out the braid of plaited hair that she still carried everywhere.

Edwin pulled at the neck of his own brocade-trimmed warrior-jacket and produced the matching braid, attached to a leather thong about his neck.

"We have kept our vow, sister," he said. "Though the spinners of fate contrived against us at every turn, still we managed to keep faith. You have suffered great hardships in your loyal support of me and I am sorry for that."

She shook her head, smiling. "It hasn't all been misery," she insisted. "I found friendship with Queen Bebba and even with

Athelfrid's concubine. I have my sons whom I love dearly, and for a short while I was queen in Eforwic."

"I'm glad to hear you say so, sister," he said. "And the gift you left me of a stable of brood-mares cheered me greatly, for it told me that you were still the sister I once followed everywhere. Coifi has related much of your secret support of me."

An expression of sadness and longing crossed Acha's face. "Coifi," she whispered. "I miss him still. Will you tell him that I miss him, and if ever…" she stopped, unable to go on.

A slight cloud crossed Edwin's face too. "Since my young wife died – I'm to have a new wife from Kent – a Christian princess, named Ethelburga. She wishes *me* to consider adopting her faith. Coifi has been my most loyal supporter, but how will it be, when my bride discovers that my chief advisor is Woden's man?"

"You make powerful allies brother," Acha said.

"Yes," he admitted. "Her kin and her friends call the princess Tata, which they say means darling."

Acha saw the difficulty. "Put your trust in Coifi. He will cleverly find a way to please your Kentish queen and as for you becoming Christian… well… there are worse things you could do. A princess called *darlin*g – it bodes well," she added with a smile.

He smiled too. "As ever you give me wise advice."

Acha turned to beckon her companions forward. The young man with the red hair strode to her side.

"This is Prince Donal Mac Bude – Donal Brecc as he is known, heir to the throne of Dalriada," she said. "A most Christian prince, he has given me refuge and offered protection and education for my sons. The other who watches from the shadows is Brother Finn, a Christian monk and kin to the Royal house of Dalriada. You see brother – again I made friends, where I might have expected to find enemies."

Edwin held out his hand and Donal strode forward to clasp it.

"I thank you greatly for your care of my sister and my sister-sons," Edwin said.

"It is a pleasure – I simply repay an old debt," Donal said smiling. "I was once a frightened boy in need of care and your sister offered me friendship."

"Come, brother," Acha said. "Let us make a new oath, with Donal as our witness. I swear to you, brother: I will never allow my sons to set foot in Deira or Bernicia while you or your sons live."

Edwin nodded and thought for a moment. "And I swear too, sister, that I will never pursue my sister's sons in enmity. Let us exchange our braids again in token of our new oath."

They exchanged the fading plaits of hair and then clasped hands. Donal put his hand over both of theirs to bear witness to this new promise. "I too swear that I will not set foot on Northumbrian soil in enmity."

The brother and sister hugged each other one more time and then reluctantly drew apart. Edwin bent to help her mount as he'd once used to do, and as she swung herself up onto Sidhe's back, the mare gave a joyful whinny.

Acha cantered back towards the sheltering copse, not trusting herself to look back again and Donal Brecc followed. Edwin watched until they vanished beneath the canopy of the trees, and then walked back with Lilla to his waiting hearth-companions.

He mounted his stallion with a thoughtful smile. "Let us go," he announced. "I have a new wife waiting for me."

Acha rode fast towards the west, joyful to be back on Sidhe, the sun on her face and the wind in her hair. She smiled happily, leaving her two companions far behind her.

AUTHORS NOTE

'Oswald was nephew to King Edwin by his sister Acha; it is fitting that so great a predecessor should have had so worthy a man of his own blood to maintain his religion and his throne.'

From Bede's Ecclesiastical History of the English People - Penguin Edition - Translated by Leo Sherley-Price, revised by R. E. Latham

This is Bede's only reference to Acha, leaving her a shadowy figure, mentioned only briefly, but she is usually accepted to have been the mother of both King Oswald and King Oswy – the king who called the Synod of Whitby in 664.

As the sources and firm historical facts are sparse, I have felt free to use my imagination. Acha being sent as a secondary wife to Athelfrid, in place of tribute, is invented, but not, I think, implausible. Athelfrid, as a powerful pagan king, could well have had more than one wife or consort at the same time. Bebba is mentioned by Bede as a former queen of Bernicia, who gave her name to the fortress that we now call Bamburgh and is usually thought to have been Athelfrid's queen.

Athelfrid's victory over Dalriada is recorded by Bede, as is the death of his brother Theodebald. The taking hostage of Donal Brecc however, is imaginary, though again, I think it not implausible, as hostage-taking of this kind was common. At a slightly later date – Oswy's son Ecfrith, lived as a hostage at the court of King Penda of Mercia, and was only released at the age of ten or eleven, when his father had killed Penda in battle.

Athelfrid's sons fled to Dalriada after Edwin killed their father, but it has always been something of a mystery as to why they should have gone to a Christian kingdom that had been defeated in battle by their father. They fled as children and pagans, but received an education in the monastery of Iona. Oswald and Oswy returned to Northumbria at a later date and, in turn, became powerful Christian kings of those lands.

The *Anglo-Saxon Chronicle* says that the sons of Athelfrid were: Enfrid, Oswald, Oswy, Oslac, Osgood, Oslaf and Offa. Only Enfrid, Oswald and Oswy survived to play their part in history, so I have left out two sons for the purpose of simplifying the story. Aebbe was the only surviving daughter of Athelfrid and she eventually became Abbess of Coldingham. It is unclear who her mother was, but because of the similarity of the name, I have made her Bebba's daughter.

Bede records that Athelfrid of Bernicia took over Deira, killing their king, Aelle, and driving his son, Edwin, into exile. I was interested to try to imagine how such a thing could have happened and how Acha could not only survive amidst so much violence, but go on to have more children with the man who killed her father, as she appears to have done.

It is usually thought that the Anglo-Saxons did not use cavalry in battle, but Athelfrid clearly became a ferocious leader, with exceptional battle skills. I was heavily influenced by Rosemary Sutcliffe's wonderful story *The Shining Company* which tells the story of the ill fated *ride of the Goddodin* and I felt that Athelfrid, though the victor at Catraeth – could not have failed to be impressed by such courage and cavalry skills.

At the time of publication I am reading *The King in the North*, by Max Adams. It is a clear, well-researched and vivid study of the life and times of King Oswald of Northumbria. I'd recommend it to anyone who wishes to find out more about this fascinating period.

Theresa Tomlinson
Whitby, September 2013
www.theresatomlinson.com

REFERENCES

The following works have provided much information and inspiration:

The History of the English Church and People, Bede, Penguin Classics

Cloth and Clothing in Early Anglo-Saxon England, Penelope Walton Rogers, The Council for British Archaeology

A Handbook of Anglo-Saxon Food, Anne Hagen, Anglo-Saxon Books

Peace-Weavers and Shield-Maidens, Kathleen Herbert, Anglo-Saxon Books

Battles of the Dark Ages, Peter Marren, Pen and Sword Books

Northanhymbre Saga, John Marsden, Llanerch Press

The Mead Hall, Stephen Pollington, Anglo-Saxon Books

Northumbria in the days of Bede, Peter Hunter Blair, Llanerch Press

I have also drawn ideas from Carla Nayland's work. Her website is a great source of information and inspiration – www.carlanayland.blogspot.com

I would also like to thank Christiane Kroebel, Archivist at Whitby Literary and Philosophical Society Library, for her help and encouragement.

ABOUT THE AUTHOR

Theresa Tomlinson lives in Whitby, North Yorkshire. She has been writing historical novels for many years; her titles include *A Swarming of Bees, The Forestwife Trilogy, Moon Riders, The Voyage of the Snake Lady* and *Wolf Girl*.

In recent years she has become fascinated by stories from the Anglo-Saxon period, her interest fuelled by archaeological finds, particularly the Staffordshire Hoard, and the discovery of a royal grave near Loftus in Cleveland, containing gold and garnet jewels.

Theresa is the author of many books for young people; she has twice been shortlisted for the Carnegie Medal. Her previous titles have also been shortlisted for The Lancashire Book of the Year and Sheffield Children's Book Award.